MW00640109

*To Carole,
with enthusi...
and appre...*

THE DUEL
FOR CONSUELO

CLAUDIA H. LONG

booktrope
Booktrope Editions
Seattle, WA 2014

Cover Design by Greg Simanson

This is a work of fiction. Names, characters, places, brands, media, and incidents are either the product of the author's imagination or are used fictitiously. Any resemblance to similarly named places or to persons living or deceased is unintentional.

PRINT ISBN 978-1-62015-217-1

EPUB ISBN 978-1-62015-313-0

Library of Congress Control Number: 2014904735

To my mother

Maria Judita Hostyk Hagadus

1927-2014

PROLOGUE

ROSA, 1638

THE SUN BLEACHED THE YELLOW CITY WALLS as *Toledo baked in the heat of the long Spanish summer. In the shade of a cobbled alley a dray horse pulled up to a blue painted door, an open cart clattering behind it. The door to the villa opened and Rosa Carmela de Argenta emerged, carrying a carefully wrapped bundle. She placed it on the seat of the cart, not in the large, empty bed.*

Strong men followed, loading the bed of the cart with a traveler's trunk, wooden crates, and other wrapped bags, until it was filled. Last, a tall, black-haired man stepped down, pulled the blue villa door shut behind him, and with a sigh, climbed into the cart seat next to Rosa. He put his arm around her plump shoulder, stroked her dark curls pulled tightly into a bun. "Our voyage begins," he said with a smile. She rested her head on his shoulder, but her eyes soon strayed to the road ahead.

The cart rattled and swayed on the cobblestones. Rosa pulled the bundle close, carefully shielding the blue and gold enameled plates her grandfather had made and the silver candlesticks her mother had given her on her wedding day barely a month earlier. "Remember to say the prayer," her mother had whispered. Rosa had promised. But now, embarking with her new husband on a ship to the Colonies, to New Spain or Mejico as some called it, she wondered if she would remember every Friday.

The motion of the cart caused the small gold cross that hung on a fine chain between her breasts to bounce between them. The heat dampened her creamy skin to a dewy sheen. She wiped her brow and smiled at Emilio. He was a sixteen-year-old woman's dream: rich, trim, with bright dark eyes, and the favor of the king. He came from a family like hers, known to be tainted with a drop of ancient Jewish blood, but that taint was so old now, in 1638, that she no longer thought of it. In her mind it was almost forgiven.

Rosa knew that it hadn't always been so, though she cared more for the present and for her future than she did for the past. Her ancestors, the conversos, *had converted a hundred and fifty years ago at the point of the sword. For a century they had been hounded to prove their commitment to their new faith or die at the hands of their torturers. Her grandfather still screamed out at night in his sleep sometimes, or cried and muttered in* Ladino, *and her mother clung to the bits of ritual, in the dark, in hiding, that secretly preserved hints of the old days. But Emilio and Rosa attended the Catholic Mass regularly, worked openly on Saturdays, and even relished a dish of pork. The taint was overlooked all the more as Emilio's talent with accounting assured big profits for the spendthrift King's accounts. When the Marqués of Condera, master of an outrageously profitable corner of New Spain, had requested the loan of his services, the King, eager to increase his profits from that distant holding, was only too happy to oblige.*

Her brothers had delighted in terrifying her with horror stories of the sea crossing and her sister shed tears as she listened to tales of the barbaric lack of amenities and civilization in the Colonies, but Rosa was excited. Although she was already sixteen and completely a woman, she felt still the excitement of a child before a treat. She would miss her family, to be sure, but the adventure, the chance to be truly free, wiped any regret from her already voyaging heart. I'm leaving, *she thought.* Who cares who sees me now? *Carefully she laid the bundle at her feet. With both hands free, Rosa pulled Emilio's face to hers and kissed him passionately, there before God, the sun, and all of Toledo.*

CHAPTER 1

CONSUELO, 1711

"LIGHT THE CANDLES, CONSUELO! Light the candles!" Leila cried out to Consuelo from her bed, thrashing against the blankets Consuelo had tucked around her. "Close the curtains! Get away from the windows, they'll see us..."

"The candles are lit, Mother. The curtains are closed. Hush, it's all fine."

"Say the blessing," her mother said.

"*Baruch ata Adonai,*" Consuelo whispered in heavily Spanish-accented Hebrew. Her throat constricted over the beautiful, if incomprehensible, syllables. The flickering candles lit the elaborately decorated blue and gold plates brought seventy-five years before by Rosa, her grandmother, from Toledo when she and her husband left Spain for the new world. She had heard the story from her grandmother more times than she could count. The precious plates were the only remnants of that ancient life, unless Consuelo counted the lighting of the Sabbath candles in the dark.

"Don't let them hear you," her mother whispered back.

It wasn't Friday, but Consuelo had closed the heavy velvet drapes and lit the candles for the Sabbath anyway. It was Sabbath to Leila and Consuelo knew there would not be many more. Consuelo had tried every herb in her apothecary but she was helpless against the raging fever that tore through her mother's weakened body. Consuelo smoothed her mother's hot, dry brow. It was not for her to decide when Leila would be taken by the Lord, Consuelo knew, and she silently chastised her own inability to submit to the increasingly evident Divine will.

Somewhere in the large house a door slammed. Her father, the *Alcalde*, or mayor of Tulancingo, serving by the good will of the Archbishop of Mexico, Viceroy, Duke of Linares, and by appointment from the Marqués of Condera, was home. Consuelo squared her shoulders as his heavy footsteps approached.

"What a blessed day." His voice was heavy and exasperated. "Good heavens, Consuelo. It's like a tomb in here. Open the curtains!"

"Mother wants them closed, for the candles." Consuelo edged away from the bed to the window. "Please, Father, keep the curtains closed."

"It is bad enough that she keeps at it with those candles." Consuelo heard something raw in his tone and she frowned. At her intent look he turned away. "At least she should know better than to light her candles on a Thursday," he added.

Consuelo pressed her lips together.

"Leila," Isidro said to the woman in the bed. "It's Thursday. Why do you want the candles?"

"Quiet, they'll hear you," her mother hissed.

Isidro shrugged and turned back to Consuelo. "You shouldn't let her rave like this. I had a very trying day."

"I'm sorry to hear that, Father," Consuelo answered, barely audibly. Did he think hers had been pleasant, in this darkened room, with her mother drifting in and out of lucidity? She moistened a cloth with a bit of vinegar and put it on her mother's forehead.

"I abhor that smell," her father said. "It was very difficult in town today. My fool of a deputy wants to hold a festival in the town square in a fortnight. He thinks that simply because of his connections and money that he can decide what happens here in town. He has no understanding of the things that finer people know instinctively. I told him that with the very important people who will be out of town for Joaquin Castillo's wedding, there was no possibility, none whatsoever, of holding a festival on that day."

Consuelo closed her eyes briefly. The whole region knew that Joaquin Castillo, the handsome and virile oldest son of Manuel and Josefina Castillo, was marrying a woman from a vast landholding family, uniting the Castillos' own enormous landholdings with hers. But Consuelo could not think of the wealthy and powerful Castillo family without thinking of the youngest of their three sons, the outlier, white-blond, blue-eyed Juan Carlos--and she did not dare to think of him at all. She had managed to build a wall in her mind and make herself impermeable to his memory, but now, with this wedding and her father's endless prattle, the wall was showing signs of cracking.

"They know me, you know. They know how important I am. Most exceedingly kind of them to invite us to the wedding. But of course we're invited, that was not unexpected."

Consuelo gripped the vial in her hand. "Of course," she replied evenly.

"We're invited because of my connections, of course, but also because of your mother." He turned back to his wife. "You are still the most beautiful woman in Tulancingo."

"Nonsense," Leila muttered. "Who is that man?" she whispered to Consuelo.

"Father. Come close to Mother so she can see you," Consuelo said. It was worse each day. Some moments Leila was completely clear, others she lay there confused, lost in a world forty years gone.

"Leila, for heaven's sake! Consuelo, open the curtains so your mother can see." She opened them a crack and the bright winter sunlight illuminated the rich draperies on the wall, the gleaming wood floors, and reflected off the vials of tinctures and liniments that crowded Leila's bedside table, all glistening in their impotent glory. Leila flinched against the light.

"Why are the candles lit? It's the middle of the day," Leila said querulously.

Consuelo took a crystal vial and poured a couple of drops into a spoon.

"We will all be going to the wedding," Isidro continued. "It is in ten days. Leila, you will be the most beautiful woman there. Oh, it will be grand, I will wear my medals. And the Marqués and Marquesa will be there, of course. The Castillos have such a long association with the nobility. Surely they will arrive a day early since they will attend the Mass. And Joaquin's youngest brother is back from Spain, from the university at Salamanca, you know. The fair-haired one. He brought artists with him, and some exiled poet, too. Did you know that Juan Carlos Castillo is back, Consuelo?"

Leila's body shuddered with a sudden fever tremor. The aroma of anise engulfed the close air of the stifling room though Consuelo had only spilled a single drop. From the crystal vial the sunlight refracted into a hundred golden shards.

ISIDRO

Isidro Costa Argenta, Alcalde of Tulancingo, passed a shaking hand across his furrowed forehead. "Now, mayor," his interlocutor said, "one hundred and fifty *escudos* is not too much to ask. I am sure we can come to an arrangement."

"I am sure," Isidro whispered, his voice stuck in his throat. One hundred and fifty *escudos* was an astronomical sum. An arrangement with the thugs of the Holy Office, or its representatives, would be an agreement drawn in blood.

"As you can appreciate, we are as eager as you are to keep this little matter private. Neither the Grand Tribunal nor the Viceroy's accountants need to know the details. A little departure from our normal ways, to be sure, but well within our authority."

Isidro looked down at the black-garbed priest with the red cross of his order emblazoned upon his chest. A departure indeed from the meticulous efficiency of the Inquisition, with its detailed record-keeping, its textbook torture, its witnesses and oaths. Instead, a meeting in a darkened room, a candle flickering ominously in two corners, and a priest, if he truly was, and no other witnesses but one, a heavyweight thug with a vein throbbing in his neck-- these were not the Inquisition's reputed ways.

But the claim was pure Holy Office. "Your wife, she is quite ill, isn't she. No longer herself, not in her own mind any more," the priest said. Isidro could not find the words to reply. "And your daughter," he went on. Isidro started in his chair but had the sense to control himself. "Good," said the priest, "your priorities are still in the right order. It is not her fault that her mother is a Judaizer. Is it?"

The priest reached out his hand, palm up, to Isidro. "Come now, I am sure the Alcalde is not completely without words. You are known, you know, for your, shall we say, voluminous eloquence." The priest's smile made Isidro's skin crawl. "Alcalde, I would like an answer."

Isidro racked his brain for the question, at a loss for an answer. "Your Mercy, I have nothing to say of any worth," he muttered.

"Excellent humility, so rare in a man of your standing. Now, what shall the payments be? Monthly? Bi-weekly?"

The thug breathed hard in the silence.

"Monthly," Isidro croaked.

"For such forbearance, a small fee, but do-able. With a sizable down payment for the first installment. Shall we say, fifty *escudos* now, and forty monthly thereafter?"

"Fifty? But, Your Mercy, we were speaking earlier of ten, maybe fifteen! And I could not get that much now, or ever!"

"Pity, Alcalde. Do not the coffers of Tulancingo provide you with sufficient income? For the beautiful, ailing Leila's wellbeing? Or for the lovely, erudite Consuelo?"

Cold sweat trickled down inside Isidro's shirt. His normally starched collar wilted and stuck uncomfortably to his embroidered doublet. He longed to grab that priest and choke the words from his throat. And he could do it, he knew, as he towered over the pale, cassocked sodomite. But the priest held Isidro's testicles in his hand, at least for now, figuratively.

"Thirty at most, Your Mercy."

The priest laughed. "As our Lord was sold for thirty pieces of silver, so would you buy your Judaizing wife's life. I love the parallel, and so will accept it."

"But the Viceroy," Isidro pressed. "He must not know."

"Of course not, Alcalde. If he caught you lining your personal pocketbook with municipal funds your next home would be the Viceroy's prison. I understand completely, Alcalde. Rest assured we hold your information in our most complete confidence."

CONSUELO

Consuelo heated the dense metal iron on the hearth. The warmth of the blaze made a line of perspiration form on her upper lip and the stifling room seemed to close in on her. Outside the pale winter sunlight did nothing to palliate her sense of imprisonment within the four walls of the house. Certainly she could walk outside if she chose, but in reality, she could not leave.

When the iron was hot enough Consuelo applied it quickly to the skirts of the dress she would wear to the wedding tomorrow. She knew she didn't possess her mother's delicate beauty but Juan Carlos had called her handsome, and voluptuous too, when she had seen him last. She had cherished the words until they became a mockery of his years of silence.

As children they had sometimes played together while their mothers conversed. Leila's wit had warmed the air, combining with Doña Josefina's softly charming poetry, knowledge Doña Josefina had gained at the feet of the renowned Sor Juana Inés de la Cruz decades earlier. Consuelo unconsciously absorbed the mothers' intellectual engagement, taking for granted their right to speak of such high ideas, while she and Juan Carlos bantered and romped, heedless of conventions. She had towered over the fair-haired, slim boy, even though he was almost two years older than she was. He was different from other boys she knew, somehow more intense, talkative and trusting. He took her once to see his greatest treasure, a long shiny sword his father had given him on his twelfth birthday. Though she was only ten, and a girl, he let her hold it, showing her how to manage the grip.

She recalled when everything changed.

She had turned fifteen that winter and her breasts had filled her blouse; blood had stained her skirts that Christmas and Leila had gently guided her in the ways of womanhood. Her first dose of powders to pacify the cramps had awakened in her a new curiosity, a desire to learn what other plants and powders could do.

But an interest in apothecary arts was not all that was awakened. When she arrived with her mother at the Castillo hacienda that spring she found herself for the first time looking eye to eye at Juan Carlos. And Juan Carlos's eyes, she noticed, had strayed downwards, not in shyness, but with hunger, to her curving embroidered blouse. The games they had played for the next two years had been far more dangerous than a shiny, sharp sword.

Consuelo quickly lifted the iron from her dress, relieved that there were no scorch marks. The memory of Juan Carlos's eyes and the hands and mouth that had followed were burns enough.

ISIDRO

Isidro watched a dust mote dance in the pale sunlight that streamed in from the long windows of the luxuriously appointed study. The magnificent trappings failed to soften the nature of his visit to the Marqués de Condera. Being caught stealing from the city's treasury, being accused like a thief, was a humiliation Isidro had difficulty bearing. But the consequences of this meeting if he didn't persuade the Marqués to forbearance would be infinitely more devastating. "Your Excellency," he breathed, "you are too kind. I will, I will replace every *escudo*, every *centavo*. But six months, it's not enough."

"It is more than enough time, Señor Alcalde. I understand the duress, the pain, but I cannot permit an exception to my goal. Ridding the Colony of corruption is our Viceroy's mission and while my heart grieves for your suffering others will have equally dramatic tales of sorrow, and if I bend for one I must bend for all. Six months, it is better than arrest, no?"

"Of course, Excellency, of course. I will endeavor."

"Do more than endeavor, Señor. Succeed."

The Marqués of Condera stood, indicating that the interview was over. Isidro had been standing the whole time, of course, and when the Marqués stood, Isidro bowed. The Marqués' hair gleamed black in the pale light; his red and gold brocaded jacket seemed to shimmer around the broad shoulders of the young nobleman. Isidro felt the weight of his fifty- five years settle on his shoulders as he retreated from the Marqués, though his own tall, slender build belied his advancing years.

"Your Excellency," Isidro tried once more, "if only, if you could ask that the accountants remain silent on this matter, at least until I can conclude it..."

"The accountants have reported to me. They need not report to the Viceroy until I am ready to make a final accounting. You may be assured of my confidence if you meet my goal. If you fail, the Viceroy will make his own decision."

Isidro glanced sideways at the recording secretary. The old scribe sat at his high desk, quill in hand, his face a blank mask of disinterest cultivated over forty years of note-taking in delicate negotiations. "He is completely in my confidence as well," the Marqués added. "He was my mother's scribe before me and holds our family's unstinting trust." The scribe showed no reaction to this accolade and Isidro felt his bowels churn.

CONSUELO

Consuelo pulled the heavy shawls around Leila and carried her into the carriage. She wrapped another *rebozo*, a long woven shawl, around her mother, almost losing that bird-thin body under the layers of cloth. If it weren't for the heavy wrappings, Consuelo thought, she could carry Leila with one hand.

Consuelo climbed in next to her mother. Though the carriage had curtains on either side the frigid wind blew through the drapery in occasional gusts. Nonetheless, Consuelo fanned herself to dry the perspiration that was beading on her forehead. Her heart pulsed in her throat and her hands felt unsteady and moist. The smell of the damp wool of their shawls filled the small, enclosed space, competing with the attar of roses she had rubbed on her mother. Consuelo breathed in the strangely comforting aroma, trying to still her jangling nerves.

The sky, bright blue for days, had acquired a grey sheen that morning and strange clouds massed in the north and east of the high plain. The wind had picked up in the last hour and it whistled damply around them as they headed to the Castillo hacienda.

"Keep your mother well wrapped," Isidro called down from his perch next to the carriage driver. "Unspeakably cold weather, terrible for a wedding," he added.

Consuelo kept silent for fear that she would explode into a disrespectful tirade but her lips trembled with barely contained anger. She had pleaded with her father to leave Leila home with a servant and not take her to the wedding in this cold, but her father had been insistent.

"Why? Why must she go in this terrible cold?" she had asked.

Isidro had looked away from Consuelo, his mouth pressed into a thin line, and she sensed for a moment a hesitation, thought she saw the smallest wave of fear pass through his eyes. But he had remained silent.

"She is not an ornament!" Consuelo had said at last. "Spare her the suffering of this journey."

"Be quiet, Consuelo. Your mother will enjoy the outing. Won't you, Leila?" Without waiting for an answer, perhaps knowing that the answer could well not match the question, Isidro had stormed from the room. "I will attend and my wife will attend with me."

At least she had prevailed in dressing her mother in sensibly warm clothing instead of in the shimmering satin gown her father had wanted. Beneath the woven wool Leila wore a heavy black embroidered skirt wrapped with a sash now that it was far too large for her shrinking frame. She had a white cotton blouse and a *mantilla* of black lace. Consuelo looked at her mother's face. She had indeed been a beauty and Consuelo could still see the fine golden skin, deep-set almond eyes, and full lips that Leila had rubbed oil into to keep soft. Even in her emaciated state the past was still visible in the bones.

Consuelo adjusted her own shawls. It was bitter cold. Her gown, a deep sage that set off the peach complexion she had inherited, was cut modestly at the neckline but Consuelo's full bosom and lithe arms and waist were clearly outlined by the rich material. She had pulled her chestnut hair to the top of her head. That mane was from her father's side, thick and shining, as was her height.

She looked at her father, still tall, his own thick chestnut hair now streaked with grey, and felt a twinge of something other than anger at him for the first time since her mother had become so ill. He hadn't always been a self-centered buffoon, she knew. There had been a time when he had been worthy of the beautiful Leila Argenta, a time when his own towering beauty, his gift of governance, and his spaniel-like devotion to Leila had been greater than his current obsession with his own standing. As his wife of thirty-five years slipped further away, as his own power ebbed with the rise of the new Marqués, he clung to what he had and what he had been. Consuelo could almost forgive him his failure to see Leila as she was when the reality was so desolate.

"Where are we going?" Leila asked, her voice muffled and weak.

"Joaquin Castillo's wedding to Lucía del Varga."

"Who?"

Consuelo held her mother's tiny hand. She didn't answer.

LEILA

How many times have I ridden in this carriage, my feet covered in a rich, embroidered rug, my Consuelo bouncing around at my side? And now I am covered to stifling and Consuelo sits stone-faced next to me.

It is cold in this cart. We are going to Josefina and Manuel's son's wedding. Which one? I can't remember, but not the fair one, nor the priest. Must be the oldest one. The fair one loves my Consuelo, but she, like her father, is blind to so much. I would give her my sight.

She is not wearing the blue dress I would have preferred for her, and her hair, that crowning glory so unlike my tight curls, barely has the luster I know it can show. I could not supervise her toilette, she escapes through my fingers so fast.

The words that come from my mouth are not attached to me. Once I was known for my quick wit, a word of apt jest. Now I listen and hear my own voice croak, disembodied, the contents coming from somewhere I cannot reach. But my throat can feel their passage and my lips their form.

My lips. They were supple once, and tender when Isidro kissed me. He was so tall, so handsome. His sons, had they lived, would have been like him. But Consuelo, my only, she is like him too—less vain, I hope, but intense, demanding, and with the will of God, as lucky.

CONSUELO

They arrived mid-afternoon and the courtyard was filled with carts, carriages, and other conveyances. Prominently placed were the carriages trimmed in green and gold with the large C for the Marqués of Condera embossed on the doors. Father had been right, she thought, the young Marqués and his entourage had indeed come.

It was a big courtyard bordered on two sides by high stone walls. To the right were fenced cattle enclosures, the nearest ones small, and growing more expansive as they ranged further from the house. A stable ran the length of the second enclosure and beyond that Consuelo could see chairs and a roaring fire pit set up for the day's events. The *charreada*, or rodeo, that traditionally preceded the wedding feast had not yet ended. By the look of the group of men relaxed and drinking Consuelo knew she and her parents had missed seeing the groom, Joaquin, ride the stallions, competing with the other men on horseback and bull-back. Only the roping challenges remained. Men and boys stood near the fire, laughing and talking loudly. A few women stood there too, warmly wrapped, holding mugs of steaming liquid, an occasional higher-pitched laugh joining the boisterous male ruckus. In the enclosure great horses milled and jostled, their nostrils and coats adding to the steam.

Ahead a wide veranda formed the front of the Castillo house, its whitewashed walls and large windows establishing it as the home of a wealthy landowner. Grand double doors of carved wood formed the entrance to the home. Smoke wafted from behind the house, spreading the aroma of grilling meats over the courtyard.

"Take your mother inside. I'm going to pay my respects to Don Manuel. What joy to be father of the groom. I don't want your mother to feel sad. Had any of your brothers lived..." Isidro trailed off, his eyes filming.

"Go, Father," Consuelo said tightly. "Mother won't even notice." She did not think she could bear watching him get maudlin over the past, or stand another one of his long, self-pitying speeches.

The cold wind whipped through the yard, scattering leaves and dust and blowing Consuelo's hair and shawls. She pulled the rebozo closer around herself and held her mother's arm firmly.

She watched her father walk towards the gathered men, her eyes searching intently. It was not difficult to spot the white-blond head amongst the throng of dark haired and olive-complexioned men. The sun, weakened by the greenish clouds that increased by the moment, absorbed and returned the unnatural glow of that otherworldly hair. Consuelo swallowed as Juan Carlos turned as if sensing her stare and looked back at her. It was too far for her to see the expression on his face but he clearly raised his hand in greeting. Unable to breathe she nodded back, her flush banishing the cold from the whistling wind.

Something soft touched her hand. Consuelo looked down to see her mother stroking her hand tenderly where she held her mother's arm in an unconsciously iron grip. "Thank you," Consuelo whispered, but the clarity faded once again to opacity in Leila's eyes. Consuelo turned towards the hacienda door. Small specks of white swirled in her vision and for the first time in a hundred recorded years snow began to fall in the high plains of Central Mexico.

CHAPTER 2

CONSUELO

"**ALLOW ME TO SEAT YOU**," Juan Carlos said in Consuelo's ear as she approached the dining table. He pulled out a chair. Consuelo stared at the chair placed far up the table, well above where she would have seated herself, and felt her face heating and her throat closing. "It's the new mode. A gentleman holds out a chair for the lady to sit down. Allow me," he repeated.

"I must sit with my mother, help her," Consuelo managed to eke out.

"I will take charge of your mother," her father's voice boomed, causing heads to turn. He had selected a chair at the Marqués' table, an audacious choice, but towards the middle, at least, rather than near the head. Consuelo felt the world spin.

"Then there's nothing stopping you from joining me at the table," Juan Carlos said. Though his skin was as fair as parchment he did not flush red, unlike Consuelo, who felt herself on fire. He was smiling, calm, and somewhere in those strange blue eyes there seemed to be laughter. She could not tell if it was mocking or merry.

The Castillo dining room's large double doors had been opened to include a sitting room and tables had been set throughout both rooms. The table where her father was now seated next to Leila was near the huge hearth and the fire within made the room bright and warm. The Marqués sat at the head, his red embroidered jacket seeming to reflect the firelight. Beside him the Marquesa, in a fog-colored silk, cooled her side of the table. Their host, Don Manuel Castillo, father of the groom, still strong and handsome, flanked the Marquesa, while his wife, Doña Josefina, quietly radiant, took the seat nearest the Marqués.

Consuelo looked anxiously at her mother, tiny and birdlike in her oversized woolen shawl, and felt a pang for the lost glory of her beauty. Isidro, at least, cut a masculine figure and for the moment was not talking.

Joaquin and Lucía, the newlywed couple, sat at a table for two directly in front of the fire. The bride was in a richly embroidered but distinctly old-fashioned blouse with a high collar and loose sleeves, unlike the more fashionable square neckline and tight sleeves of Consuelo's dress. Neither Consuelo nor Lucía wore the large bustles sported by the two golden-haired ladies who still stood near Doña Josefina, glowing as much as their jewelry in the firelight.

At the far end of a table in the candle-lit sitting room Consuelo could see her friend Maria Elena next to one of her brothers. She would have moved to sit with her but Juan Carlos was holding her chair, his hand firmly on her shoulder. She sat.

"I cannot resist a beautiful woman who has yet to hear my stories from Salamanca. I have exhausted the good will of my family and my new sister with my tales and seek a fresh victim."

"Have you been home long, that you've tired everyone with your stories?" Consuelo knew to the minute how long it had been since Juan Carlos had returned.

"Only a fortnight."

"Then they must be dull tales indeed." Consuelo found her tongue. "But since I have been no farther than the road to the Marqués' castle in the two years of your absence any stories will amuse me. You will not find me a judging audience."

"You are too kind," he replied, pushing her chair in gently and seating himself to her right. "However, you must promise to ignore whoever sits to your left and pay attention only to me." Again he smiled, his straight white teeth gleaming.

"No, she will not ignore me," a tall, slim man with smoothed back black hair said as he pulled the chair for himself. "She will find that my stories are vastly more entertaining and witty than yours!"

"My good friend!" Juan Carlos bowed slightly. "Consuelo, you have the honor or perhaps the misfortune to be seated between my fascinating company and the brilliance of the university at Salamanca's newest poet, the Honorable Leandro de Almidón, whose starchy name belies the grace of a swordsman who writes the most fluid of verses."

"At your service my good lady. And who is this flower of the provinces?"

"Good heavens, Leandro. Don't tell me that you've already forgotten all your *novatores* vows? Flower of the provinces! This *lady* is Consuelo Costa Argenta, daughter of the mayor of Tulancingo, Alcalde Isidro Costa."

"Señorita Costa, a pleasure."

"The honor is mine, Señor Almidón." Consuelo wondered what *novatores* were and determined to ask when the opportunity presented itself, but the conversation had moved on while she had that momentary thought.

Juan Carlos seemed to have grown taller in his absence though he was still only the width of four or five fingers taller than she was when standing. When seated he talked almost over her head to Leandro. Her height was mostly in her legs and Juan Carlos, instead, was magnificently proportioned. His broad, strong shoulders leaned into the space in front of Consuelo and his expressive mouth was close to hers as he laughed at Leandro's reply. She sat back to give him space and her eyes roamed over the room.

"It's beastly cold out there," Leandro said, addressing Consuelo as much as Juan Carlos. "As cold as a Madrid winter's night and not nearly as civilized. I was told that the climate was more temperate here in New Spain but like so much else I was told it has proven false." He smiled, leaving Consuelo confused. Was this a complaint to be answered with soothing words or a sally to be played back against him? Her conversations in the sickroom with her mother or with the apothecary who taught her to use the herbs and mixtures had none of the playfulness she had enjoyed with Juan Carlos years before.

"What other lies were you told?" she asked, choosing a neutral path through the verbal thicket.

"That the women were all ugly and unapproachable and that New Spain was the ideal land to heal my broken heart." He looked at her woefully, opening his brown eyes wide before bursting into laughter.

Consuelo smiled back. "And how would we ugly, unapproachable women help heal your sorrow?"

"But no, that was two lies in one! An ugly woman cannot mend a man's heart as she cannot replace his lost beloved, and yet these ugly women are devilishly hard to find. I have not yet seen one in the fortnight I have been here to test my hypothesis."

"Hypothesis? What a strange word."

"It is all the rage in Europe, outside of our backward and decaying motherland. It means an educated guess which you next set out to prove or disprove by experiments."

"Oh, well, I do that often in my apothecary work without such a fine word."

"Ah, a healer. Though not an ugly one. What shall I do?"

"I am not quite a healer, though the apothecary and the herbalists have taught me much. It is all grounded in centuries of knowledge and tradition, of course, but when the traditional remedies fail I frequently," she paused, "*hypothesis* a new remedy based on what I already know about the plant or the tincture."

"You hypothesize, but other than the word form you've got the meaning. And next you try it out on your suffering patient to see if it works, no? And if it works you have a new remedy. And if you don't, it was God's will!" Consuelo sat back, astonished. "Don't be alarmed. Such talk is common in the rest of the world. Only Spain remains in the dark ages. But perhaps there is hope, if beautiful women engage in sciences."

"Don't be misled by his flowery words, Consuelo. He's a rake and a heel." Juan Carlos interceded. "She's not used to such high palaver, Leandro. Salt of the earth, she is."

"You're throwing down a gauntlet, my friend," Leandro replied, with no menace at all.

"In defense of a beautiful woman."

Consuelo shivered lightly at the attention though she didn't know whether to be offended or pleased by Juan Carlos' intervention. He was much changed by his university education. "You're a landowner's son, Juan Carlos," she said. "But you talk like a Spanish grandee."

"And what would you know of grandees?" Juan Carlos asked.

Consuelo shrugged. "Tulancingo isn't a cave. We do have educated people, and the Marqués is more educated than anyone in this room, I dare say." They all three looked over at the table where the Marqués himself sat with Juan Carlos' parents as well as Consuelo's mother and father. She cringed. Her father was talking to Don Manuel, who had a distant look on his face.

Juan Carlos followed her eyes and then laid his hand briefly on hers. "Don't worry, Consuelo. My father can take care of himself."

The ladies retired to a large room warmed by a blazing fire. Consuelo wrapped another shawl around her mother nevertheless. So thin was she that Consuelo could feel the chill in her own bones looking at Leila. *We should leave,* she thought, *get mother home.* Resentment stabbed briefly at her throat. Juan Carlos' lingering touch, his whispered "When the dancing begins..." at the end of dinner, threatened to draw her from her duty, but only for an instant.

"I will only be a moment," she told her mother, who nodded, her eyelids drooping as she rocked in the chair in which Consuelo had ensconced her. One benefit of Leila's illness and decline had been her constant need for sleep and her early bedtimes, giving Consuelo her rare moments to herself.

She watched her mother slip into a state that was neither sleep nor waking. Other women, their needs relieved behind the privy curtain, lingered by the fire in groups. Chocolate would soon be served and some of the older women would remain to gossip, share news, or simply rest from the long, wonderful day. Those young or lively enough would join the gentlemen in the great room where Consuelo could hear the musicians tuning their instruments. It appeared there would be dancing until the early morning for those stalwarts who cared to extend the revelry. Such elaborate celebrations, along with the complex and foreign conversations she had heard at dinner, were not within her experience. Consuelo considered sitting for a moment to ponder the newness of what she had seen and heard and to relish the moments when Juan Carlos and Leandro had vied, however in jest, for her attention at dinner, but the strains of the music propelled her onward. Her duty was to find her father and prepare her mother so they could leave.

Consuelo passed through the entryway where already knots of people stood donning their wraps for departure. The strange weather had gotten worse and the cold swirling specks fell thicker. She saw a servant slip on the icy cobbles in front of the house. She turned away from the door and followed the sounds of the men's voices. She stopped at the doorway of a large room. This masculine study was Don Manuel's private domain, given over tonight to the invited gentlemen for their refreshment after dinner before returning to the great room. She peered in, hesitant to intrude in such a male arena.

"May I be of some assistance?" Ygnacio, Don Manuel's manservant, asked. The gray-haired, portly man stepped in front of her. Consuelo backed up.

"My father, Alcalde Isidro Costa, is he within?"

Ygnacio looked faintly disgusted. Consuelo wondered what social horrors her father had committed. "No, Señorita, he is not. Perhaps he has already gone to the great room. The music will be starting at any moment."

"And it's where you should be going as well," came a smooth voice behind her. She turned to see Leandro, his black hair more recently plastered to his head, removing his gloves. "Come," he added, holding out his arm, "let's go into the great room. The music has started."

Consuelo's mind stuttered briefly at his touch. "I must find my father."

"The, er, somewhat talkative Alcalde?" Consuelo blushed. "What's your hurry?"

"We must leave. My mother is tired, she is sleeping in the women's drawing room and she is not well. It is time to take her home."

"You can't leave yet, we've barely become acquainted. And what would Juan Carlos think? He specifically mentioned seeing you in the dance."

At the mention of Juan Carlos' name goose bumps rose on Consuelo's arms. "I have no idea what he will think," she replied stiffly. "Do you see my father anywhere?"

Consuelo was tall but Leandro was taller. He scanned the room, looking over the tops of the guests' heads. "No, nowhere to be found. Come, if your mother is sleeping there is no hurry. Besides, the roads are slippery and you people have no idea how to manage in the snow. The grandees have left, slipping and sliding down the road. It would be best to wait it out. Now, come. Let me get you some refreshment."

Snow. So that was what that was. Consuelo had read about it but never actually seen it. In paintings it looked soft and fluffy, like clouds. Perhaps there was a different kind of *snow* in Spain and France where the paintings she had seen were from. Leandro was right. There was no sense in taking the horses through such strange stuff, and if something happened and the carriage became stuck or turned over her mother would never survive. She allowed Leandro to lead her, in the new fashion, to the trays of sherry, and accepted a glass.

"Do you dance?" Leandro asked Consuelo as they carried their drinks to a corner of the room.

"No, nor do most of us, I see." The musicians were playing and people drifted in from the withdrawing rooms but there was no one dancing.

"Not yet," Leandro said. "The dances are formed in squares and sometimes as *longues*, where a gentleman and his lady partner dance the measures together in line with other dancers executing the same steps." He sipped his sherry and over the rim of the glass he looked into Consuelo's eyes. "At the end of the dance there is of course the kiss."

"Nonsense!" Juan Carlos said, coming up behind them. "Poachers are shot in this colony, by the way," he added to Leandro. "All this kissing and touching is fine for France but our beloved Spain will reel in horror, and here in New Spain all the more so for the gentry who aspire only to be as hidebound and backward as their patrimony permits."

"Firebrand! And I thought I was the one bringing the enlightenment to the colony!"

"The limitations of caste are alive and well here as well as Spain, and though the Indians and the Mestizos have no aspirations, the Criollos are dying to be Hidalgos and the Hidalgos to be nobility itself. And your poetry, Leandro, with its *novatores* tones, will be burned at the stake, the Inquisition lacking Jews to roast."

Consuelo found the opening to ask her question. "What are *novatores?*"

"A nasty word for the enlightened thinkers that hope, somehow, to bring rational thought to Spain," Juan Carlos said. "It signals that classical logic is to reign over absurd expressions of emotion. Reason and science triumph."

"Well, our Consuelo here is a scientist. She can probably even withstand your endless palaver about crop sciences. She's a *novatora* too."

Juan Carlos raised his blond eyebrows. "Are you, Consuelo? How strange that my good friend Leandro should know after a mere dinner's acquaintance, and I, who have known you since childhood, have no idea." The idea that Juan Carlos might be jealous gave her an unlooked for delight. "What do you study?"

"She hypothesizes, don't you my dear?"

Consuelo swallowed her answer as she caught sight of her father across the room, still attached to Don Manuel. "Excuse me," she said, "I have found my father."

The great room had filled up with guests and making her way across the room took more time than it should have. She dodged, greeted and avoided the elegantly dressed revelers holding glasses of wine or sherry, speaking in raised voices over the music or trying out their steps in anticipation of the first dance. "Consuelo," a young woman called out.

"Maria Elena," Consuelo smiled. As the Alcalde's daughter and as an incipient healer Consuelo knew many people but had few friends. Maria Elena was one she cherished, though their meetings were infrequent. Maria Elena's brothers were in cattle, like Don Manuel, and she kept house for them far out on the *llano* while waiting for them to make an advantageous alliance for her. Her father and mother were long dead and Maria Elena was known to be a serious, competent girl whose finances more than compensated for her plain looks, though no suitor had yet presented himself.

"Stop a minute! I tried to get your attention through dinner but you were monopolized by two handsome men," Maria Elena said, linking arms with Consuelo.

"I would stay but I am trying to reach my father." Maria Elena, lacking Consuelo's height, craned her neck to see over the crowd. The Alcalde could be seen above the heads and appeared to be receding. "I must go!"

Maria Elena released her. "After you have spoken with him return to me. I long for decent womanly companionship." Consuelo promised without thinking and continued through the maze of guests. At last she reached the spot where her father had Don Manuel cornered.

"Good evening, Consuelo," Don Manuel said. He was not as tall as the Alcalde but his shoulders were broad and his brown hair was still thick, though heavily streaked with gray. His smile, gentle and genuine, reflected in the green flecks of his brown eyes.

"Thank you for inviting us to your son's wedding. It is a wonderful occasion," Consuelo replied. "I have been unable to thank Doña Josefina as she is surrounded by such loving guests." She looked up at her father trying to signal him to step away from Don Manuel so she could speak to him.

"Josefina would love to talk with you," Don Manuel was saying. "She so enjoyed knowing your mother when she was well. I am sorry for her illness."

Gratefully Consuelo nodded. "My mother's friendship with Doña Josefina had been a source of pleasure to her in better times."

"Leila is quite on the mend," Isidro started, "and as you know..."

Consuelo interrupted. "Thank you, Don Manuel. It is in fact exactly what I must speak with my father about, at this instant, if you will forgive me. Father," she said, turning to the Alcalde, "if you could spare me a moment."

Isidro glared at her but with a small bow to Don Manuel, turned away to speak to his daughter. "What is it?"

"Mother is exhausted and is sleeping in the ladies' withdrawing room. We should leave, take her home."

"Don't be ridiculous. If she's sleeping then there's no reason to leave."

"Father, this cannot be good for her."

"You are not the one who determines what is good for her."

Consuelo bit back her answer. "Then I will go and tend to her until it pleases you to leave." She turned away, knowing there was no arguing with her father in a crowded room.

To her surprise he put his hand on her arm. "No. She needs no tending if she's in the ladies' withdrawing room. I am sure that our hosts have sufficient wherewithal to have a servant who will watch over her. I will speak to Don Manuel about it."

"Don't," she answered sharply. It was embarrassing enough to watch him clinging to Don Manuel's attention but to importune him with such a request would be humiliating. "I'll go back to her and sit with her."

"You will do nothing of the sort. I saw Juan Carlos speaking to you earlier." Consuelo's shoulders tensed at his words. He dropped his voice to a whisper. "Go back and be attentive. Who knows when you will get such an opportunity again."

"Opportunity for what?"

"Don't be a fool, Consuelo. You are my daughter; an intelligent, beautiful girl. Play your cards right tonight." Consuelo looked at him astonished. He returned her look levelly. "With luck we will stay the night," he added, and turned back to rekindle his one-sided conversation with his host.

The musicians had paused their playing and now guests were pairing up in a line, men with women, their fingertips touching as they stood side by side. Still blinking from her father's odd counsel Consuelo moved to the other side of the room, taking advantage of the space created by the dancers. Maria Elena joined her.

"Your father did not appear happy to see you," she remarked.

"No, since I tried to draw him away from the festivities. My mother is ill and should return home."

"The weather makes that impossible. I imagine that Don Manuel and Doña Josefina will be playing *posada* for us all tonight. Their home will be an inn."

Consuelo sighed. "Where will we all sleep? It's a lovely hacienda but there must be a hundred guests here. I can't say I expected such an elaborate wedding."

"No, Don Manuel is not known for lavish parties. But the bride's family, the del Vargas, are well known in the North. Estebán, Lucía's brother, is friendly with my brothers and both Jacob and Esaú have been to many a *charreada* at the del Varga hacienda that has lasted through two nights. And this dancing nonsense, it's become common at even the most traditional of parties. Do you know any steps?"

Consuelo laughed shortly. "Entombed in a dark room with my mother, day after day, and at dinner with my father, night after night, I have not yet learned to dance."

Maria Elena grimaced, lending her plain face a moment of character. "Nor I, though my burdens are lighter than yours, to be sure. In fact, I so rarely see anyone outside of my own ranch that I would be overjoyed to stay the night, and more, here."

"Well, I fear we will have little choice."

"And you will have little choice but to dance," Maria Elena added. Bearing down on them were Leandro and Juan Carlos.

Consuelo looked at Juan Carlos, his fair skin flushed lightly with the warmth of the room, his white-yellow hair gleaming. What caused such an odd coloration, she wondered, not for the first time. She knew, as did everyone in the area, that he had been born in a lightning storm, and that such occurrences could cause that pallor, but it was rare enough to make her think that other forces could be at work. She had heard once that a mating of a Spaniard and a Negro-Native mixed wife could result in a colorless baby but neither Don Manuel nor Doña Josefina appeared mixed.

"The bride and groom command you to dance," Juan Carlos said smiling. "Leandro, meet Maria Elena Albanil. She is the youngest of the three ranchers out at Hacienda Llano Oscuro."

"A pleasure. Leandro Almidón at your service." Leandro bowed to Maria Elena. Her narrow brown eyes opened wide.

"Señor Almidón," she replied.

"No, in the modern fashion you must call me Leandro and I must call you Maria Elena."

Maria Elena shrugged. "As you wish."

"Well now, Consuelo, we must teach the two of you to dance. Come, it's not difficult to do badly and impossible to do well. You take a step, once backwards and once forward." Leandro took Juan Carlos' hand and held it up pulling him backwards. "You see, even Juan Carlos can dance poorly."

Juan Carlos wrested his hand from Leandro. "Take a lady partner, my friend. Come, Consuelo, join me."

Leandro laughed and turned to Maria Elena. "My wren, will you dance?" Consuelo stiffened at the insult to her friend but Maria Elena seemed not to notice.

"Certainly, Sir Crow," Maria Elena took his hand.

Consuelo smiled. Maria Elena could hold her own with the poet of Salamanca.

They took their place in the line. Juan Carlos took her hand and she felt the giddiness of excitement up and down her arm. The music began; he pulled her back and then forth. "Step back, step up, another," he said in her ear, his breath making her shiver. "You are the most beautiful woman I have seen in two years," he added.

"Stop. You speak nonsense."

"Why is that nonsense? It is only the truth, though the excess of sentiment makes it sound quaint."

"You've been away for two years. Things have changed."

"What has changed, Consuelo? Have you found another? Step back and back again."

Consuelo concentrated on keeping her feet from tangling, willing her heart to slow. "Another? Was there a promise between us that I was unaware of?"

"What has changed?"

Consuelo stepped on Juan Carlos' foot. He stepped back and the pair behind them stumbled into them. "Sorry," he said. "My error." They disentangled themselves. "Come, let's walk outside, " he muttered to Consuelo.

"But Leandro and Maria Elena...," she started.

"Let them enjoy one another. It will do Leandro good to dance with a country girl."

"I don't want him to toy with her," Consuelo said as they reached the door of the great room.

"He toys with all women," Juan Carlos replied. "It would be a mistake to take him seriously."

Consuelo looked sideways at him. "It sounds to me like you are protecting territory that does not belong to you. And that the similarities between your friend and yourself exceed the differences."

Juan Carlos guided Consuelo through the hall. "Here," he said. "Let's go outside and look at the snow." He opened a closet and took out a heavy wool *rebozo*.

"Who toyed with whom?" Juan Carlos asked, wrapping the heavy woolen shawl around Consuelo's shoulders. When Consuelo did not answer he proceeded. "You let me kiss you before I left but you didn't come to the *tertulia* to see me off. You never asked my family about me even when you came to the *charreada* after the cattle drive."

"How did you know I came to that?" Consuelo was surprised.

"My mother wrote to me and happened to mention it."

"Notably, you didn't write to me once while you were in Salamanca," Consuelo remarked. His complaints warmed her more than the *rebozo*.

"University life is busy, not that you could ever know that. You live in town, you can't imagine how dull it can be here on the ranch

and how like a draught of sweet wine going to Salar
things there that could change our entire existence.

"What could change this existence? It is as it sh(

"No. You can't imagine. I have been speaking ...u my father.
He is traditional, but not hide-bound. There are ways to plant, for
instance, that if we changed what we do the crops would flourish. There
are rotations."

Consuelo forgot the cold and her mother for a moment. "How?"

"It's too cold to explain out here. But I would tell you. You would
listen. And without innovations I would die here of boredom."

"And you would die of boredom with a country señorita. My life
is hardly a ball in Tulancingo. But I live it, as that is the life the Lord
gave me."

"This conversation is going in circles," Juan Carlos said. He drew
Consuelo behind the horse barn. They could hear the beasts snorting
in the cold. Comparative warmth emanated from the barn and
Consuelo leaned against the wall. Juan Carlos put his arms on either
side of her, leaning on his hands. "I missed you."

She inhaled his lemon verbena scent, triggering memories of years
before. "You did not but it doesn't matter now, does it?"

"No. You're right, it doesn't."

Consuelo waited. She knew he would kiss her and she knew she
would let him. She closed her eyes and felt his warm, soft lips on hers.

Consuelo disentangled herself at last from Juan Carlos' embrace.
She pulled the *rebozo* back around her shoulders, the cold beginning
to seep into her exposed neck. "We must go in."

"I will keep us warm if we don't," Juan Carlos said, though he
too adjusted his clothing into a more presentable arrangement. He
put his arm around Consuelo. "You are as enticing as when I left, but
grown more womanly and even more desirable. And you were already
a draw to me as the moon to the forces of the sea."

"Leave that be," Consuelo said. "It would be just as good not to
speak of the past." She would blush if it were not so cold to think about
how free she had been two years before, how Juan Carlos' hands had

oamed over her breasts and thighs in the summer heat, there behind the same barn when she was but sixteen years old.

"You are a strict taskmistress beneath your soft velvet exterior," Juan Carlos remarked. "Then you refused to speak of the future and now the past is out of bounds as well. So we are left with the present." His hand trailed back down to her breast and she pulled away slightly. They had to go back in, they could not stay out so long. "I suppose only the present is available to us then, though I had expected otherwise."

"I have given you no reason to expect anything at all, nor you me." Consuelo heard her own words, her voice hard and unflinching. She kept her eyes straight ahead, increasing her pace.

"Cold, cold woman," Juan Carlos replied but kept pace with her. "I would let you be if I could, but I dreamed of you even among the glorious offerings of Salamanca."

Consuelo bit her lip but said nothing. The door was near and the lights shone through the windows onto the swirling specks of snow, giving them a glow of warmth they did not possess. "A false warmth," Consuelo thought, "an illusion of gold, like so many others."

As they passed through the entryway she could hear the music, now a lively country tune. Juan Carlos took his hand off her shoulder after turning them both towards the great room. The room reflected an inviting, warm brightness, and the guests' voices could be heard between the notes of the tune. The dancing had gone from the strange, confusing steps of the European dance to the more accessible circles that the *hacendados* and Criollos were used to.

"I see we've gone back to our rustic roots," Juan Carlos said. Consuelo glanced around the room. She could not spot her father though he was usually easy to find because of his height. Nor did she immediately see Leandro or Maria Elena. She shook off the moods of the outdoors with the snow from her hair.

"I am going to go look in on my mother," she said. "Though perhaps my father is with her."

"I must go and toast my brother and my new sister," Juan Carlos said. "It will surely be time that they retire for the evening, and though I am sure that Joaquin knows exactly what to do I might give him some pointers on finesse for his wedding night. God knows he might otherwise think he was roping cattle!"

"I doubt he needs your help," Consuelo said, following his glance to the newlyweds. They were standing together with glasses in their hands, toasting with Joaquin's rancher friends. "And she seems at ease." She dismissed the thought of Juan Carlos acquiring the "finesse" he boasted of as well as the disquiet she felt at his need to brag like a country boy.

"At least in that regard the Colony has come a long way. She hasn't been kept veiled and hidden all her life. I expect she's seen enough of the farm to know what to expect."

"If your brother heard you talking like that about his wife he would thrash you," Consuelo said. "Easily."

Juan Carlos nodded, not contesting Consuelo's evaluation of his brother's strength. Consuelo appraised the couple as they laughed and toasted. Joaquin's square shoulders, coffee-brown hair with glints of caramel, his green-flecked brown eyes, all came from his father. He was a born cattleman, loved the Hacienda, and would produce as many children as Lucía could bear. As Consuelo watched, Lucía threw back her head and laughed out loud. Consuelo felt a twinge of envy. She would never have the easy confidence that Lucía exuded, the sureness of her position and role in the world.

The music stopped, the tune concluded, and the dancers, breathless from their pleasant exertion, retired to the corners for refreshment. Consuelo saw Doña Josefina, her soft grey gown catching the light, seated in her chair at the side of her oldest son, her eyes upon him with evident delight. "I will go seek out my mother," Consuelo said. Getting no more than a distracted nod from Juan Carlos, who was scanning the room intently, Consuelo left as the musicians struck up a softer, slower song for the guests to rest by.

Consuelo peered into the withdrawing room. A table had been set up and four matrons were playing a card game and in rear of the room two elderly women rocked in chairs with blankets over their legs. Cayetana, Doña Josefina's *ama de llaves*, the head housekeeper, sat near the fire, reading. Consuelo shook her head. Doña Josefina ran a curious household, it was known, where her servants read and her three sons had taken their own individualized routes. Doña Josefina herself was a poet, Consuelo knew, and was reputed to be an intellect. Her two younger sons, Ernesto and Juan Carlos, had taken the cerebral paths, with Ernesto going into the priesthood and teaching in the northern mining lands and Juan Carlos, of course, studying in Salamanca.

Consuelo approached the servant. "Have you seen my mother, Señora Leila Argenta de Costa?" The older woman shook her head.

"No, Señorita. She was here earlier but I had supposed that she was with you or with your father the Alcalde."

Consuelo frowned. The servant appeared to know who she was and who her mother was. But where could her mother have gone? "Did anyone see her leave?"

The servant shook her head. "But let us go and look for her. Doubtless she has gone to sleep before the fire in some other room. I would make up a bed for her as I am certain that we will have guests spending the night tonight with this strange weather, but I have not consulted with the Señora about where they will all go."

The older woman put her book away carefully after marking her page with a feather and stood up slowly. "Come, Señorita, she cannot have gone far."

Consuelo stopped herself from answering and with growing despair, Consuelo ran along the hallway, looking in every room. She stopped at Don Manuel's study, where only a few old men dozed by the fire. The *mayordomo* was nowhere to be seen. Behind her she could hear Cayetana shuffling as she headed to the other side of the house where the kitchen and the pantry were. "I will check there, Señorita. Your mother may have gotten hungry and gone to the kitchen for a snack."

Consuelo doubted that but thanked her distractedly and hurried on. At the great room she craned her neck to see if her father had reappeared. At the far end Josefina still sat near Juan Carlos. His hair shone brilliant in the lamplight. Consuelo elbowed her way across to them disregarding the glares of the guests.

"Pardon me, Señora. I am searching for my mother. She is unwell, as you know. I must find her."

Doña Josefina shook her head. She turned to Juan Carlos with a meaningful look. He nodded. "Mother hasn't seen her but we can certainly send a girl to look for her."

"Quickly," Consuelo said, "she is not well in her mind and she could get frightened."

"Where is your father?" Doña Josefina asked in her slow voice. Consuelo managed a twinge of pity for her hostess's speech, damaged by a stroke when Juan Carlos was born.

"I don't know, Señora."

"Perhaps with your mother?"

Consuelo's hopes for that were quickly dashed by Ygnacio's approach. "Your father is looking for you, Señorita." The mayordomo's sneer was more pronounced.

"Is he with my mother?"

"No, Señorita," he said. "He believes that you are."

"Where is he?" Consuelo started across the room.

"I believe he has returned to Don Manuel's study," Ygnacio called after her, "where he continues to bend my good master's ear as he has done all evening," he added under his breath.

Consuelo did not look back at him though she heard his poisonous comment. "He was not there a few minutes ago when I looked in."

"Well, my master has now taken refuge there but has been unable to free himself from the appendage of this guest."

She barely turned when Juan Carlos caught her elbow. "Don't rush around like a fool," he said. "Let's organize a search. Most likely she is dozing somewhere warm." He kept a light grip on her arm, steering her through the guests.

When they were back in the hallway, Cayetana caught up with them. "She is not in the kitchen. I have sent two girls to look through the house."

"We need some men," Consuelo said. "We must look outside as well."

"No one would go out in this bitter weather," Cayetana replied.

Consuelo pulled away from Juan Carlos. "Where did we leave that *rebozo*?" she asked, remembering at the same moment folding it over a chair near the door. She grabbed it as she headed outside. "She may have wandered out."

"I hope to God she hasn't, " Juan Carlos said, following her.

They retraced their steps to the barn, seeing no one. The snow had blanketed the entire field and only the faintest traces of their earlier footsteps remained. "Is there somewhere else?" she asked.

"The store house," Juan Carlos answered. "Over this way." Again he took her arm, this time pulling her very close. "Your father has spent the entire evening beleaguering my *pater*," he added.

"I know that he is annoying but this is not the time to talk about my father."

"I hope not. Step flat," he added, tightening his grasp on Consuelo's arm as she skidded on the snow. "Your shoes are soaked."

Consuelo looked at her wet cloth shoes but she felt nothing. The swirling flakes blurred her vision, the wind blew knives of cold into her cheeks, but for the moment all sensation was obscured by a sweat of fear. She had caught sight of footprints, small and uneven, around the side of the storehouse. Jerking from Juan Carlos' grip she stumbled ahead of him, following the marks.

"Send help!" she cried as she rounded the corner of the adobe building. Huddled on the ground was a small curled figure in a swirl of black and white cloth.

Consuelo bent down but there was no question it was she. Leila's pale face was turned to the wall, her knees drawn up toward her chest, as she lay on her side in the dirt. The eave of the hut had kept the snow off her face and front, but her grey hair was frosted, as was her back, with frozen crystals.

Consuelo pulled off her own *rebozo* and wrapped it around her mother. Her feet slipped as she shifted her mother's form and she dropped hard on one knee. She lifted Leila into her arms folding the heavy wool around her. Lowering her own face to her mother's she lay her flushed cheek against Leila's icy one.

She was silent, she held her breath, though her heart thundered in her ears. She listened, hoping, until she heard the faint hiss of her mother's breathing. "Run!" she cried to Juan Carlos, but he had already gone.

"Mother, mother," she crooned to Leila. "Please, by the blessed Mary, please," she said, as the hot tears scalded her cheeks. "Please!" But though she prayed with all her soul for her mother's life she knew, even then, that if her mother survived it would ensure her mother's continued, intensified suffering.

LEILA

It is very dark here. I must go to my child. My Consuelo needs me now and I have to find the cart. I will saddle the horse myself if need be, but she is calling to me and I must go to her. She is my only surviving child. Where did they put the cart? It is very dark, and cold, too. It may not be here, I must go and find it. But these are my daughter's footsteps. She has gone on ahead. I will follow them until I find her. She must be cold out here in the dark.

I will find her. I hear her voice. She is near and all is well. Her cheek is warm. I was not too late.

CONSUELO

Their footsteps were muffled by the snow but after what seemed an eternity Juan Carlos returned with two men laden with blankets. Without words one scooped Leila from Consuelo's arms, wrapped her in a blanket and set off towards the house. Consuelo caught the sounds of the guests and servants as they gathered at the entrance to see the rescue. Juan Carlos offered his hand to help Consuelo up and handed her a blanket. She draped it around her shoulders and walked silently towards the house.

"She lives?" Juan Carlos asked.

Consuelo nodded. She could not feel her feet, her hands were frozen into claws and she felt nauseous. The guests at the door parted to let her through and she followed the man carrying her mother to the withdrawing room. A settee had been softened with pillows and placed before the fire. The man lay Leila on the bench and Cayetana put a fresh blanket that had been warmed by the hearth over her.

Maria Elena appeared by Consuelo's side. "Come, Consuelo. Let's get those wet shoes off you, get you something warm to drink."

Consuelo shook her head but her teeth started to chatter and she began to shake. "Give me another blanket," Maria Elena said to Cayetana. "Let's not lose this one too."

Too? Consuelo heard herself moan as she sank into the chair that Ygnacio had pulled up for her next to her mother. Her hands felt hot and icy at once, and her toes, freed from the wet shoes, sent needles of pain up into her legs. Her chattering increased, clattering against the goblet of warmed sherry that Maria Elena held to her lips.

"Drink this. It doesn't matter if it spills." Consuelo managed a sip and coughed. "Good," Maria Elena said. "If you can cough you can breathe. Up north it snows like this five times a winter. The only cure for you is warmth. Now finish the sherry while your mother thaws."

Consuelo did as she was told and felt some life return to her. Cayetana was rubbing Leila's hands and a bit of color had returned to her wan cheeks. Her father's voice was heard nearing the room.

"My wife! My beautiful wife! My God, don't take her from me!" he wailed. He threw himself at her feet. "Oh Leila, be strong. Come back to me. I couldn't bear to lose you."

Maria Elena and Cayetana backed away from the couch as Isidro took her in his arms. "We must put her to bed," Cayetana said. "There will be several ladies staying tonight in this room as we are going to house anyone who has not yet left."

Consuelo got to her feet, weaved unsteadily for a moment, then straightened up. "Father, let us put Mother to bed. She must be kept warm to survive this."

"You." Isidro fixed his daughter with angry eyes. "You let her wander outside."

"No, Father." Her voice cracked. She had indeed, through her neglect, allowed this to happen.

"We will speak later. For now, all that matters is your mother. Attend to her for once." He kissed Leila's brow, then placed her back on the settee. Pulling Consuelo aside he said through clenched teeth, "Stay with her every moment. She may rave when she comes to. Do not leave her for an instant."

"Of course," Consuelo answered.

A man lifted one end of the settee and two boys took up the other. "We will take her to the pantry," said Cayetana. "She will be warm there."

"My wife should not sleep in a pantry like a kitchen maid!" Isidro bellowed.

"Señor Alcalde, it is the warmest room in the house. And it is Doña Josefina's order." Cayetana swept past Isidro. "Come, Señorita. We will make you both warm."

Consuelo lay on the pallet on the floor next to her mother. The room was indeed warm and the fire glowed behind its wrought-iron screen, casting flickering shadows on the jars of preserves and spiced meats put up for the winter. Dry nightclothes, from Doña Josefina's own closet, and diapering cloths had been brought for Leila. Consuelo had changed her unconscious mother with tears in her eyes. Now she stared at the ceiling, unable to close her eyes despite the soothing aromas of the fire and the herbs hanging from the ceiling. At the far end of the little room, cloaked in shadow, was Doña Josefina's desk where Consuelo imagined that she had written some of the beautiful poetry that had been lauded throughout the land. It was also where she knew Josefina kept all of the Hacienda's accounts. It was well known that Don Manuel had no need for secretaries or scribes, notwithstanding the enormous land holdings and herds of cattle that he owned. His wealth had increased mightily over the years, and he was, with his son Joaquin, the largest cattle rancher in the Marquisate. With Joaquin's marriage to Lucía del Varga, the families' joint wealth was stupendous, and yet Don Manuel and his wife remained modest, kind people. The warm, sheltering pantry was the embodiment of the family's aura.

But Consuelo still could not sleep. She listened to her mother's breathing, raspy and uneven but at least constant, and she hoped that Leila had survived the worst of it. Provided the brain fever did not return, a day or two of rest would be enough for Consuelo to move her mother home. But that meant that she must, for the duration, stay at the Hacienda with her mother. If the roads were passable her father would leave tomorrow, for City business demanded his presence. Consuelo tossed uncomfortably. She would be spending at least another night under the same roof as Juan Carlos.

She shivered at the thought of his proximity. She felt again his kisses behind the barn. But if she hadn't gone out to the barn with him her mother would not have wandered off. She was derelict, it was her fault that Leila had gone into the snow. Consuelo could almost see her, distraught, disoriented, wandering about without a wrap, looking for her daughter. Consuelo writhed on her pallet. All those days of devotion by her mother's bedside were pittance against the enormity of her negligence. Her father's fury was justified.

It was justified even if he himself had pushed her to remain at the fiesta with Juan Carlos. It was mortifying the way he was cozying up to Don Manuel, almost shoving her into Juan Carlos' arms, so that even Ygnacio, Don Manuel's *mayordomo*, mocked him. Had he not virtually ordered her to be friendly to Juan Carlos? Had he not insisted that Leila was safe dozing in the withdrawing room?

Consuelo tormented herself, sliding like she had on the snow, from guilt to anger, to shame. And with shame came desire, desire to be kissing Juan Carlos once more behind the barn.

Morning came and with it came brilliant sunshine. Consuelo looked out the window of the dining room, shielding her eyes from the blinding light reflected off the white landscape. She could never have imagined this light from the paintings she had seen. The sky was a hard blue, like a sheet of melted turquoise, and little clumps of snow dripped water from branches onto patches of bare earth that formed beneath the trees.

"It's unbelievable," she said to Maria Elena. "Is it always like this?"

"Sometimes it snows for three days and the snow is higher than your knees." Maria Elena's family ranch was high in the mountains, to the north. "But usually, yes, it is this beautiful when it stops. I must be going soon, though, for when the evening cools all that melted snow will turn to deadly ice. How is your mother this morning?"

"Only vaguely conscious, but alive. A kitchen girl is sitting with her now while I get some breakfast. I have but a moment to eat before I return to her."

"And your father?"

"He left at the first light."

Isidro had rapped sharply at the pantry door, then had come in to see Leila. "*Don't leave her side. I dread what she will say.*" Consuelo had nodded from her pallet. No one paid much heed to an old, ill woman, she thought, but she knew better than to voice that to her father. They both knew that Leila's bizarre fixation with her candles and her ancient prayer had grown with her senility or her brain fever.

Consuelo recalled that in better days, after Grandmother Rosa had died, Leila had only taken the candles out once a year, but Consuelo remembered the dark secret ritual every Friday while Rosa lived. "We do this for you," Rosa would say to Consuelo, and Consuelo, only four or five, would feel sad. "Your mother lost all her babies, all but you. Only when she vowed to say the Sabbath Prayer did God relent and let you live. So this is for your life," Rosa would say. Consuelo still felt the old dread every time her mother begged for the candles.

One Friday night, when Consuelo was about seven years old, Isidro had returned early from the City. That was the first time he found Rosa and Leila lighting the candles, curtains drawn and servants dismissed for the night. He almost strangled his mother-in-law with the candlesticks. Consuelo had been polishing the candlesticks since she was three but she had not realized until that moment that her father did not know about the ritual. She had simply assumed it was women's business, like so many other mysteries. Now she knew better.

She drew her mind back to the present. There had been almost no Inquisition presence in Tulancingo that Consuelo had ever known. All of that was in the past. Nonetheless, it would be imprudent to let Leila rave in front of a superstitious servant. Consuelo kissed Maria Elena, wishing her a safe journey North.

"Come and stay with me," Maria Elena pleaded. "I can't say I am looking forward to another winter isolated on my brothers' hacienda. And bring that charming Leandro," she added with a giggle. "Now there's a sophisticate! I had no idea what he was talking about most of the evening but it certainly made a pleasant change from cattle!"

Consuelo watched her friend make her escape from the Castillo hacienda, leaving her alone with her burdens.

The day passed quietly, much like it would have at home, but with the hacienda full of guests bustling about outside the pantry door. Consuelo sat with her mother, listening to her breathe, checking her temperature for fever. Though she seemed stable, Leila seemed not to regain full consciousness and Consuelo feared a permanent coma. That would lead to death within the week if Leila could not be roused to take food or drink, a lingering week of merciless suffering. Unless Consuelo or Isidro wanted to transport an unconscious woman through the cold to die at home it also meant that Consuelo would be staying on at the hacienda until her mother improved or died.

In the afternoon a servant girl came to relieve her vigil so she could take a meal with the few remaining guests and the family. Doña Josefina sat at the long dark wood table with a cup of chocolate. There was a platter of cold meats from the charreada, left over spiced chicken and chiles, and a stew of beans and herbs to be wrapped in hot, tender tortillas. Consuelo took a plate and helped herself to some of everything, marveling at the complex aromas from the herbs.

"It is *yerba santa*, and cilantro," Doña Josefina said slowly when she saw Consuelo inhale the steam from the stew.

Consuelo had eaten little at the dinner the night before, too mesmerized by the presence of Juan Carlos and Leandro, and now she savored the rich and beguiling flavors. Josefina's naming of the herbs gave her an opening to ask a favor.

"Can you help me select some herbs that might revive my mother?" she asked.

Doña Josefina smiled, a slightly crooked smile that too was a result of the terrible stroke she had suffered when Juan Carlos was born. "I can. But you are a skilled healer."

"I am not yet skilled, though I do work with the herbs and other medicines from the apothecary. I want to take my mother home and I cannot transport her in her condition."

"She is welcome here. You can nurse her. You may use any of my herbs."

Consuelo thanked Josefina and finished her meal. "I will return to my mother now. Please let me come to you when you are free to show me what you recommend."

"There was an old Sister at the convent. She was a healer. I can send for her successor, Carmela."

"Sister Carmela de la Paz? I have never met her but the apothecary speaks highly of her. She is well known and gifted. I would be honored and grateful if she came, but it is a great imposition on you."

Josefina only shook her head. "It would be good for you to meet."

Back at the pantry the servant rose from the stool where she sat sewing. "Your mother has not stirred. But she lives, which is God's will."

"Thank you," Consuelo said, taking her place at the stool. "Could you bring me more diapering cloths?"

The girl lit the wall sconces to shed some light into the darkening room as the winter sun began to set. When the girl had left, Consuelo took a good look at the herbs hanging from the ceiling, drying in bunches. There were mint, anise, pennyroyal, and rosemary, whose culinary and medicinal uses were well known to her. There were other herbs she didn't recognize. Behind the herbs, on the shelves, in addition to the jars of preserved food, she noticed cinnamon, fennel seeds, and even bags of almonds. She leaned over the desk, peering at the jars of honey on the shelves behind it, amazed at the variety of different foods that awaited a winter's pleasure.

"Reading poetry or studying the hacienda's accounts?"

Consuelo jumped at Juan Carlos' voice, her surprise making her feel guilty of trespass that she had not committed. "Good afternoon, Juan Carlos," she said shakily. "Did you spend a pleasant day?" It seemed like an inane comment to make but she was too startled to be intelligent.

"Charming. The day after a wedding is always a delight. Head pounding, stomach souring, and conscience troubled by unremembered indiscretions. You?"

Consuelo stared at him. He was hanging on the doorway looking in at her in the far end of the pantry. Unremembered indiscretions could only refer to their kisses by the barn. "My conscience is clear, at least in regards to indiscretions, for I can think of none. My only guilt is over my mother's condition, which I am afraid is stable but no better. Hence the herbs, for if she does not recover consciousness she will die of thirst and hunger."

"Sorry," Juan Carlos said, "I am a boor." He let go of the doorframe and crossed the pantry to her. He took her by the shoulders, pulling him to his chest. "She will be better. I have brought my mother saffron from Spain. Maybe it has a healing property that I don't know of. Would you like to try some?"

Consuelo managed a small smile, touched by his effort. "I know saffron and it is indeed a costly herb, and delicious. Far more potent than our homey safflower. But of no use in this context."

"In this context what would be useful? Lovage?"

"We differ in context, then. I was thinking of my mother."

"Of course."

"A steam of rosemary, maybe, for her breathing. But I am at a loss for something to bring her 'round."

"I heard my mother is sending for a nun from the convent who may be able to offer some helpful nostrum."

"Sister Carmela. I hope so. But that would mean another few nights here."

"Is that so distasteful to you?"

"I don't want to be a burden to your family."

"Your delicacy must be inherited from your mother."

Consuelo shot him a sharp glance. "Meaning?"

"Well, it is said by the modern scientists that some features and traits are passed down from the mother, and some from the father, occasionally mingling the two into a third type. In your case, since your father was importuning mine for almost a half a day, your reticence and unwillingness to impose cannot have come from him." Consuelo felt her cheeks heat. "Importuning? Dare I ask for what?"

"Money, no doubt. That's what everyone wants from my father. It's the fate of the fortunate."

"We are certainly adequately provided for, Juan Carlos, and I am certain that he has not come begging. He is merely loquacious, and unfortunately self-important, but really the soul of kindness and generosity himself, and definitely not a borrower or seeker of other people's wealth."

Juan Carlos raised an eyebrow but said nothing. Consuelo glared once more, then turned away, unable to put aside the image of her father glued to Don Manuel at the fiesta. "I will see you at dinner," he said finally, walking out the door.

Consuelo sat down heavily. Her father had been absurdly insistent on sticking to Don Manuel, and had talked, as usual, incessantly, but she could not imagine that he would be asking for money. It had to be something else.

A wheeze from her mother's couch roused her. "Mother?"

Leila tossed her head back and forth. This first movement from her brought a surge of hope to Consuelo, but laying her hand on Leila's forehead dashed it. Leila was burning with fever. Consuelo knelt by her mother. "Mother? Can you hear me?" Her mother moaned, then quieted. Consuelo ran to the kitchen. "I need cool water!" she said to Cayetana, and then in a moment of inspiration, dashed to the kitchen door. She scooped up a handful of the crystal snow that had re-frozen as Maria Elena had predicted after the sun had set, and went back to her the pantry. "Make a rosemary tea, please?" she asked as she passed through the kitchen.

Back at her mother's bedside she put the snow on her mother's forehead. It seemed crazy, but she knew that the cold could counteract the heat of the fever. Her mother turned away from the freezing slush but Consuelo's hand followed her. The girl came in with the tea. "Señorita! What are you doing?"

"It's to chill the fever. Then the tea. Not yet. Bring more snow."

The girl shook her head, wide-eyed, but left. Consuelo hoped that she would do as she was told. Moments later she re-entered with a bowl of snow and a cloth. "Cayetana says it's all right." Grateful only for the obedience regardless of the source, she applied the cold compress to her mother, changing it when it warmed.

After several changes of compress Leila's pulse slowed to normal and her breathing became even and less raspy. The tea was cold but Consuelo gave it back to the girl to heat, then held the steam under Leila's nose and mouth.

It was past dinner when Leila's fever broke, but Consuelo could not leave her. The girl brought a plate with food for Consuelo and some water for washing. Shaking with relief and exhaustion, Consuelo ate a few bites, washed as best she could, and lay down on the pallet for another restless night.

She was sure she saw a light flicker before she actually heard the door open. She lifted her head, for a moment unsure of where she was. The aroma of the herbs and spices reminded her that she was in the Castillo pantry, an odd enough location to warrant disorientation, without taking into account her exhaustion after the stresses of the past two days. She waited silently, intending to let the approaching figure take whatever it was she was looking for. She assumed it was Cayetana, or even Doña Josefina, come looking for some staple from the pantry. Perhaps a green to make a tea from, to soothe a troubled tummy or a restless sleeper.

The figure turned to the side, going around the couch where Leila lay in deep, sound slumber, and Consuelo started with surprise. The figure was a male, and in an instant she had no doubt it was Juan Carlos. "What are you doing here?" she whispered.

"Shh." He put the candle down on the desk. Consuelo looked up from the pallet. It was on the floor of the pantry so she was at Juan Carlos' feet. She moved to sit, pulling the heavy blanket up with her. She was wearing only her chemise, and her long chestnut hair was braided loosely down her back. This was no way to receive a visitor.

Juan Carlos knelt on the edge of the pallet. "Shh," he repeated. "Don't make a sound. You will wake your mother."

"What do you want?" Consuelo said quietly.

"Consuelo," he said. She waited. "I've been gone so long. I didn't know what I would find on my return." He put his hand on her shoulder and she leaned her face into his arm. She felt her pulse race.

"There is time for this in daylight," she whispered.

"I leave at dawn." He stroked her hair. "Our futures. They are forever intertwined."

Consuelo held her breath, waiting for the words that would justify this visit. No further words came. "Is that what you want?" she asked.

His hand lingered on her shoulder, then slid down to her breast. Her breath caught in and her whole body tensed. "I think you know." He slipped his hand under her chemise.

"Are you out of your mind?" she hissed.

He put his fingers to her lips. "Your mother's hard won rest should not be disturbed. There are few guests left so she would be the only one on this side of the house who would hear us. We could go to my room but I am still sharing it with Leandro and I have no intention of sharing you as well."

"We are not going anywhere. You must have lost your mind." And yet she could not pull away from him. She felt her heart in her ears, her throat close. His hand trailed over her breast and she felt the tip quiver under his fingers, and the icicle of sensation travel down her body.

"You want me. I want you."

"This is madness. We can't."

"Don't be afraid," he whispered.

How can I not be afraid? My life, my world hangs in the balance. He bent down and kissed her on the lips. She pulled back, but his hand encircled her head, holding her to his kiss. She felt the pressure of his mouth, she felt her own lips part. His tongue touched hers and she again felt the caramel warmth of desire that she had felt at the barn. Her head tilted back of its own accord. When his hand returned to her breast, she arched forward, yearning for his touch.

He pressed her back gently on to the pallet, then untied the waist of his pants. Lifting her chemise, he pulled it over her head, tossed it aside, then lay down beside her. She closed her eyes and his lemony scent filled her. She knew with every fiber of her being that this was the wrong thing to do, and yet she reached for him.

She opened her eyes a bit to see his fair face and light eyes before her. He was looking at her, his gaze covering her naked body as she lay before him. He wasn't smiling, but his lips were open with desire. She shut her eyes back tight.

He caressed her, the length of her torso, and pressed her legs open. She had taken an irremediable step, and she opened her thighs, closing her mind to the world. Her body felt liquid. He was gentle and knowing, and she yielded to his mastery until the moment when pain made her stiffen and cry out. He did not stop, but pressed forward powerfully. She bit down on her lip to keep from uttering a second cry, and the worst was over.

Tears formed in the corners of her eyes, but she blinked them away. What was done was done, it was irrevocable, and the consequences of the action were unfathomable, but for the instant, having allowed this outrage, she gave in to the pleasure of desire.

Juan Carlos pursued his release smoothly, quickening towards the end until he too bit back a cry, then another, and sighed with relief. He lay upon Consuelo, spent. She stroked that incredibly bright hair, hair that even now glowed in the light of the single candle. He touched the side of her face but did not speak.

Consuelo moved a bit under him, trying to shift his weight, but he did not remove himself, but instead he rocked slowly back and forth. She felt pain, but now it was a warm hurt, and his movements soothed and excited her at once. A sensation she had never before experienced began to build where he entered her, the sting enhancing the tension that built with each movement. Unconsciously she began matching his movements, mirroring and shadowing, while his hands traveled over the rest of her body. When she felt she could withstand no more, an explosion of tremors burst inside her, and this time she was unable to suppress her voice of release.

They lay side by side, damp with sweat, breathing together. He put an arm across her bare torso, and soon she heard the light rasp of his sleeping breath. She was certain that she would not sleep. Now she could not help but give thought forward to the morning, and she knew that come daylight she would have to face what she had done.

She disentangled herself from Juan Carlos and found her chemise. She struggled back into it, feeling the dampness on her legs. She blew out the little candle that was guttering on the desk, and lay down again next to Juan Carlos. His warmth and his scent comforted her. *Our futures.* A future next to him every night, a golden future. But when, she could not know, not with her mother needing her close by. She replayed their conversation again in her mind. It had been a suggestion of a proposal, an insinuation of a betrothal. A suggestion, an insinuation, not an actuality. My God, she thought, now what will I do?

She heard Juan Carlos leave before the first light, and was grateful. She slept soundly then, waking much later to the kitchen sounds and her mother's thin, anxious voice. "Consuelo?"

Consuelo rose quickly, and hovered over her mother's couch. "Mother. Blessed Virgin! You are awake."

Leila struggled to rise. Consuelo helped her up, positioning her over the chamber pot. Her mother taken care of, Consuelo was aware of her own sharp need. Retiring to the farthest reaches of the small pantry, she noticed the blood stains on her chemise. She blushed in the privacy of her corner. That single gift was no more.

She cleaned herself with the water from the washing pitcher, though it was cold, and dressed as well as she could, for the third day in her wedding fiesta finery. The green sage material no longer looked festive, but tawdry with its excessive use without brushing or changing. She had nothing else, and had not been out of the pantry enough for Doña Josefina to offer her some change of clothing. She wrapped a shawl around herself, and then helped her mother to dress.

"Where is this place?" Leila asked.

"We are in the Castillo hacienda, Mother. You became ill. We will be going home today." She willed it to be true. The Castillo hacienda. Last night's events would change forever her relationship with this wonderful home. She imagined living here as Juan Carlos' wife. They had lain together, and she was not some slattern to be taken and cast aside, they both knew that. It could only mean a bid for marriage. But that final word had not been spoken between them.

She felt the chill of fear. She had given the one thing a maiden possessed, the gift to her husband, and she could never get it back. There could be a child. There could be the scourge of shame, she could be turned out of her home, sent to a convent. She thought of Juan Carlos' offhand reference to the "finesse" he could teach his brother. He could use a woman and never look back. Her head rang with terror for her transgression. And yet, she could not imagine that Juan Carlos would use *her* so. Perhaps Don Manuel would call on her father.

The thought of her father brought her sharply back to reality, and with reality, the mortification of memory of his behavior throughout the wedding fiesta. Don Manuel could well be loath to tie his family to hers, and the disparity of wealth, though not of status, could be a further barrier.

"Consuelo? Where is my husband? What is this place?"

"It's all right, Mother. We are visiting the Castillo hacienda and going home today. Would you like some breakfast?"

It would not be a great stretch to imagine the reluctance of the Castillo family to ally itself with hers.

After a quick breakfast of sweet rolls and chocolate, Consuelo made herself and her mother ready for the journey home. Isidro had ridden back in the small carriage, and so Don Manuel, through Ygnacio, had graciously offered the use of his for the journey. "And here is a letter for your father," Ygnacio said, the look of contempt only moderated by the presence of Cayetana. "My good master bids you deliver it immediately."

"Thank you, I shall," Consuelo said. She avoided looking at the letter, tucking it into the bag Cayetana had given her with some food for the journey. She kept her face neutral, but her stomach clenched with excitement and fear. "Please convey my thanks to Doña Josefina," she managed to add to Cayetana. "We are incredibly grateful for your kindness during my mother's illness."

"Of course, Señorita. It was our pleasure, and your mother's recovery is the greatest reward."

Consuelo looked at the two servants, two such different people. She knew that they were husband and wife, and had heard that Ygnacio had served for many years at the Marqués's court as the Marqués's father's own personal butler. That in itself explained his supercilious attitude, though he seemed to reserve the full measure of his contempt for her. She would not enjoy living in his household. Cayetana, on the other hand, was kind and practical. Consuelo addressed her, knowing that she would only solidify Ygnacio's low regard for her. "And Juan Carlos? Is he about, that I may say my farewells?"

"He went out very early this morning, with Señor Almidón. But I shall give him your best wishes," Cayetana replied. Ygnacio pursed his lips but said nothing. Consuelo felt herself grow warm but did not respond. Perhaps in Don Manuel's letter, there was something... Consuelo put a couple of sprigs of pennyroyal in the bag, in case there wasn't.

"Where is my husband?" Leila asked. Her moment of clarity was past. It was time to get her home.

CHAPTER 3

CONSUELO

ISIDRO TOOK THE LETTER EAGERLY and put it in his pocket.
"Leila, you seem quite recovered." Leila looked at him blankly. "Come,
let us get you settled. Did you speak with Don Manuel at all when he
gave you the letter, Consuelo?"

"He didn't give it to me. That haughty butler of his, Ygnacio, did."

"Pity. Well, come along. Get your mother settled."

Consuelo led her mother to the sitting room and opened the drapes.
"Are you hungry, Mother?"

"Thirsty, my dear. Could you give me something to drink?"

Consuelo covered her mother's legs with a shawl. "Father, could
you build up the fire a bit? The journey was cold and I believe that
Mother's health is still delicate."

"Why delicate?" Leila asked. "Why would my health be delicate?"

"You almost froze to death, that's why," Isidro replied as he added a
log to the blaze.

"Nonsense," Leila said. "Why must you always talk nonsense? I
don't understand you."

Consuelo left them to bicker and went to fetch some lemon tea
for her mother. The whole trip she had worried about the letter, felt
its possible contents almost shining through the bag. The night's events
came back to her in pieces, and she blushed and felt her palms grow
moist off and on through the journey, in alternating shame, fear and
elation. Don Manuel's letter could only be an offer of marriage on
behalf of his son.

She returned as her father was leaving. "Have you read the letter
yet, Father?"

He raised his eyebrows. "What interest is it of yours? Don Manuel and I have business to transact... unless something transpired that you have not yet told me."

In point of fact I have told you nothing, nor have you asked, she thought. "No, Father. Nothing has transpired. You seemed eager for the letter and I hoped that it brought you news you sought."

"What news would that be? Has someone spoken to you, Consuelo?" His voice was abnormally sharp. Consuelo chided herself silently. She normally would not have let herself be caught in this web. She never confided any of her own thoughts to her father for fear that they would make her vulnerable. There had been a time when she could have spoken frankly with her mother but that time had long passed.

"No, Father, I simply wanted to express my gratitude for being able to bring you a letter from someone of such great importance. Nothing more."

"Well don't take too much interest in my business. It's unseemly, and it takes you away from your duties. See to your mother, she's thirsty."

Relieved to be let off so easily, Consuelo quickly returned to the sitting room with her mother's lemon water. As Leila drank, Consuelo felt her spirit ebb. If the letter was just business then Juan Carlos had not spoken to his father about her. Unless he had. But no, he would not be such a cad as to use her and then tell his father. No, if she was nothing to him, she would not merit mention. She thought once more of the pennyroyal.

ISIDRO

Isidro broke the seal and tore open the letter. His hands were damp with sweat and his heart beat loudly in his throat. He was not a praying man, he had never been, but he begged God nonetheless. He stood near the window to get the light, and held the letter out almost at arm's length. His eyesight was less than it had been and it frustrated him to read small letters or lengthy works. Fortunately, Don Manuel's hand was large and firm, and the letter was as short as the writer was direct.

Esteemed Alcalde, I am able and willing to advance you the sum of two hundred escudos, with repayment within a year. In exchange I only ask that you allow your daughter to study apothecary arts with Sor Carmela, sister of the holy order of the cross, who serves the Marqués of Condera. IKYH Manuel Castillo

"Oh thank God," he said aloud. *The Lord is merciful.* Two hundred escudos was more than he had borrowed from the City. He could pay back the coffers, satisfy the Marqués, and make one last payment to those bastard sons of Satan that called themselves priests. He had not hoped for such largesse. His smooth conversation with Don Manuel had clearly impressed the man and led him to such generosity.

He re-read the letter. What a strange condition Don Manuel had imposed. Of course Don Manuel's wife, Doña Josefina, had studied with the nuns at the Marqués's castle in the days of this Marqués's father, and there she had learned her poetry skills that had made her renowned throughout the Marquisate. Perhaps Don Manuel hoped that Consuelo would become a famous healer.

That thought brought Isidro up short. Consuelo had been overly interested in the letter. What had happened at the hacienda in his absence?

Isidro stepped out of the small room he kept as an office in his home, a room where he could conduct business away from the City, and called to Consuelo. She appeared at the door to the sitting room. "Come. I wish to speak to you." He noticed that Consuelo glanced at the letter he still held in his hand, and that her color heightened. "Shut the door. Do not lie to me, Consuelo."

Consuelo took a sharp breath. *Aha! She is hiding something.* "Did you or didn't you speak with Don Manuel during your stay?"

"I did not, Father. What is this about?"

"And Juan Carlos? Did you speak with him?" *Perhaps that was it; perhaps she had made a plea to Juan Carlos to intercede for her, to have his father make this ridiculous demand upon him.* Isidro tried to remember if Consuelo had ever expressed any interest in going to the Marqués's castle. To his knowledge she never had. Isidro felt a tremor of fear. Had someone told Manuel why he needed the money? All Isidro had said was that he had suffered business reversals of a short-term nature and that he was being preyed upon by moneylenders. Jews with no conscience, under the cover of conversion, still lent money in Mexico City and funded most of the trade that provided revenue to the cities, so even the small ones like Tulancingo could be at the mercy of sharp traders.

Did Don Manuel think that Consuelo was going to be left dependent on her apothecary skills to earn a living? *Damn his arrogance. My daughter is beautiful and lively, and will make a fine match without having to learn a trade, and if not, I will provide for her.* Isidro took a deep breath. No sense in being angry with such a generous patron.

He had forgotten to listen to Consuelo's answer. "What?" he said, "repeat yourself clearly. Don't mumble."

"I said, yes, Father. I did speak with Juan Carlos."

"What about?" Consuelo stared out the window. "Out with it! What did you ask him for?"

Consuelo looked startled. "Ask him for? Why, nothing, Father! What is he saying?" Her voice rose, and Isidro took a closer look at his daughter.

She was indeed beautiful. She was still wearing that sage green dress she had worn to the wedding. Her form was slender but womanly, and with her height she was almost regal in her bearing. She had his thick hair and smooth skin, and her mother's beautiful, deep brown almond shaped eyes. And heavens knew she was intelligent. That was not always appreciated in a woman, but Isidro knew that as beauty faded an interesting companion made for a happier life.

If only Leila hadn't become ill. He could talk to her about this, get her wise counsel. It was the loss of her mind that pained him so.

Her beauty, for a woman of her age, was undiminished. He loved to look at her, remarking that a man's eyesight faded at the same rate that a woman's beauty waned, leaving him with the vision of a wife as lovely as she had been as a bride. If Leila had been well he would not have been vulnerable to those crows seeking to peck his eyes out. He was so alone, now, without her.

"Please, Father. Tell me what he says!"

"You are a headstrong and disrespectful girl. But you have impressed Don Manuel. Or more likely Doña Josefina. He asks that you be sent to study apothecary with the sisters of the cross, at the Marqués's castle. Why he would think you would want that is my question to you."

"Study? At the castle? I don't understand."

"You needn't understand. You simply need to go, and not disgrace yourself or your patron. We will make the arrangements. But who will care for your mother?"

"I am to go away?" His daughter looked near tears and suddenly much younger than her eighteen years.

"Who will care for your mother?" he said again. "For I cannot have strangers with her. That ninny, Pepita, has left. We will need to get a new girl, a strong, trustworthy girl that can take care of your mother. Leila could say something. Give herself away." And the problem would go from bad to worse. "Perhaps you may not go. Though I don't see how we can oppose Don Manuel's wishes."

"Why would he have anything to say about my life?" Consuelo exclaimed, then stopped and bit her lip.

"What? What have you remembered? Were you somehow indiscreet? I only asked you to be amiable to Juan Carlos while I did business with his father. You were not more than simply pleasant, were you?"

"Of course not, Father."

Isidro turned away. No, his daughter would never be more than amiable, never give away her precious virtue, of that he could be sure. One fear, at least, was spared him. A match, a marriage proposal, would have solved all of his problems, but that was apparently not within Consuelo's skill at obtaining. He had given her the hint and Juan Carlos seemed interested in her, but no, Consuelo would never be the kind of girl to snag a man for her own advantage. Too bad, he thought, it would have solved everything.

CONSUELO

Three weeks later, Consuelo still fumed over Don Manuel's letter. He had not sent a proposal. He had sent an order, an order that for some reason her father was bound to obey, to send her away. Consuelo wrung her hands, roughened by the cold and the dampness of tending to her mother through the winter.

At least the pennyroyal had not been necessary. Her monthly courses had come timely and she would suffer no permanent consequence of her night with Juan Carlos. Only the pain of realizing she had been used stabbed at her heart. She was to go away in a week, for reasons she did not understand, and she had heard nothing from Juan Carlos. Business or other obligations could be keeping Juan Carlos from writing to her, her heart whispered; but her mind mocked her heart. *False hope be damned, I will not delude myself.* Nevertheless, she kept a close eye on the post and the door.

She would be gone for at least three months, through the spring, and would need most of her clothes and bedding. A letter from Sor Carmela had assuaged some of her fear in its welcoming tone and details of what she would need for her stay. Her expenses were being borne by the Castillo family, she learned, and that further enhanced her confusion. At her father's request, she had penned a pretty letter of thanks to Don Manuel and Doña Josefina, but had received only a brief note from the lady, wishing her a fruitful study.

Consuelo folded her linen bedding and laid it in the bottom of her travel trunk. She ran her fingers absently over the beaten metal edges of the wooden case. It had been her great grandmother Rosa's trunk, the one she had taken from Toledo to the new world.

Across the room, Leila dozed in her chair, close to the hearth. Consuelo looked up from her packing and her face softened. How often her mother had told her the stories of her life, of Rosa's adventures. Rosa and Leila had shared the same high spirits, the curly hair with glints of auburn, and the lively dark eyes of a Spanish beauty. Rosa had been adventurous, and never spoke a word of regret about leaving Spain. Leila had charmed the town's boys, happily setting them against one another to woo her. Consuelo, instead, had her father's managerial talents and her grandfather's eye for detail.

Consuelo put the last of the sheets in the trunk. How she wished her mother were lucid now. Consuelo felt a loss in her heart, a deep craving for her mother's optimism. *It's like she's already dead.* Consuelo inhaled sharply, shocked at her own thought, and quickly crossed herself. She got up and went to her mother's chair. She knelt beside it, and like a child, put her head in the sleeping woman's lap. She felt her mother's gentle hand on her hair and she tasted the bitterness of her own tears.

The sound she had been waiting for came, at long last, two days before her scheduled departure. The bell on the outside of the house rang through the rooms as she was folding linens into her traveling case. She went to the door, expecting a messenger, hoping for a letter or other word, but never expecting Juan Carlos.

A horse was tethered to the post outside the wall and the gate was ajar where he had entered. The late winter sunlight tried feebly to warm the air, reflected weakly off the dark blue door. Juan Carlos' blond-white hair shimmered. He was dressed for riding, with a short black jacket, dark pants with an embroidered strip on the side, and high leather boots. He held his leather hat in his hand. He looked more the country gentleman, and less the sophisticated student, than when she last saw him.

Consuelo, on the other hand, had been working. The sleeves of her linen blouse were pushed up above her elbows and her thick woolen skirt was tied with a strip of red cloth. Her lustrous hair was braided, the long plait wrapped on itself and anchored with a bone comb. Her eyes widened at the sight of her visitor. "Oh," she said.

"Hello." They stared silently at one another. "Will you let me in?" he finally asked.

"Of course. Welcome to my home," she said. He had never been there, she had never had a male visitor for her before. She stepped back from the door to let him pass. She could not show him into the sitting room, where again her mother was dozing and not at her best. In addition, her clothing and underthings were set out for sorting and packing. The only other places were the kitchen and her father's study. A clatter of pots from the servant decided the matter for her.

"Can I get you some refreshment?" she asked.

He shook his head. "I can't stay long. But I wanted to speak to you."

Again they fell silent. Finally, Consuelo could stand it no longer. "You wanted to speak to me, and here I am. I was not hard to find, was I?"

"No. I was away at the winter cattle market with my father and could not come sooner. I was not sure," he paused, "I was not sure I could bear to see you."

Consuelo fought down anger. "No? And why not?" *Would he say that he was sorry? Would he dare apologize for the night at the hacienda?*

"You are brazen, aren't you. You got what you came for, and more."

"What on earth are you talking about?"

"I never took you for a coquette. You were an honest, honorable woman when I left. Now, now you are for sale. Oh, I know it was out of necessity, but—don't interrupt me—I know you believed you had no choice, but you could have been honest with me."

Consuelo stared at him. "I have no idea what you are talking about."

"Spare me the offended virtue. I just rode with my father to the winter market, remember? I know now why your father clung to mine throughout my brother's wedding feast, never letting up his barrage of self-serving, boring, aggrandizing talk. But I never suspected you of complicity. Did you even arrange your mother's illness? Lure her out into the cold?"

"You have lost your mind," Consuelo said sharply.

"No, I've lost my faith. My faith in your purity."

"Don't you dare malign my purity when it was you who stole it from me!"

"I stole nothing that wasn't freely given. And now I know it was for profit, not for love. I have known girls who would give their bodies to garner a marriage proposal, but you did not need to do that. And yet, that, at least, is more honorable than to give their favors for money."

"I don't understand you, Juan Carlos. You came into my bed. I did not chase you away, I will admit that to my lasting shame. But there was no money involved. If this is some strange, invented ruse on your part, to insult me to deflect any claims I may have upon you for the taking of my virginity, save your breath. I have no intention of calling you to task, of demanding honorable behavior from you. You promised me nothing, and I expect nothing."

"You're right, I made no promises. To my surprise, in retrospect, you made no demands. Had I thought about it then, I would have wondered. But I was the fool, deluded by our history, your position, your honor. But once I learned the truth, I realized my mistake. A virtuous woman would have at least extracted a promise. Too bad you were too proud to see that."

"Get out. You rode an hour to insult me, and I have no need your insults."

"Only my family's money."

"The pittance your father is spending to send me to the castle is not the measure of the value of my virtue. I didn't seek that favor, I did not ask for it. If you wish to retract that gift, if it is one, and not a command, do so. I would not be in your debt."

"Your behavior put you in our debt, not my father's kindness. He pitied you, having to sell yourself for your father's failures."

"Sell myself?" Consuelo's voice rose to a shout. "Sell myself? Your indulgence of your lust..." She stopped. "Your father pities me? You told him...?"

"No. At least you will be spared that shame. His pity no doubt comes from spending hours in your father's company and seeing you spend a lifetime with him. There were other ways out, Consuelo. A virtuous woman would have at least extracted a promise before spreading her legs."

"How dare you!" Consuelo cried, and slapped him hard across his face. Juan Carlos reeled from the force of the blow, but turned and caught her upraised wrist. Pulling it back above her shoulder, he grabbed her hair with his right hand. The bone comb that held her thick locks fell to the ground. The change in position arched Consuelo backward giving Juan Carlos the height he needed to bring his face to hers.

"Don't you dare hit me, you slut!" he said, his mouth close to hers. Then he pressed his lips violently to hers, crushing her mouth. She tried to pull away but he held her fast, grinding hard against her until she tasted blood.

When he let her go, she staggered back away from him. His face showed the red outline of her hand, his blue eyes were narrow with lust and anger. "Out," she whispered harshly. "Get out." He turned away and left the study without looking back at her, closing the door softly behind him. Numbly, she knelt to pick up the fallen comb.

"Consuelo!" She could hear her mother calling for her. The light was golden in its last moments before setting into darkness, illuminating the study with a final glow. Consuelo pulled out the next drawer of her father's desk, tossing the papers and quills onto the floor. She would recognize the thick parchment of the letter from Don Manuel and the seal that she had stared at for the entire length of the journey from the hacienda to her home. Unless her father had taken the letter to the City with him, it would be here.

"Consuelo! Come to me!" her mother cried. She could wait a bit longer. It had to be here.

Red wax caught her eye. She dove for the paper, pulling up the folded letter. Behind it was a page lined across and down, with figures and dates on it, in her father's hand. She ignored that and opened the letter.

"...*two hundred escudos...*" Two hundred *escudos*? A loan of that size was unthinkable. What on God's earth was this about? And then the condition that she be sent away to study.

Consuelo felt her stomach knot and her hands grow icy. It all made sense now. Her father's clinging to Don Manuel, his ordering her to stay, and be, as he said, *amiable* to Juan Carlos. The loan of this staggering amount. Juan Carlos' visit, the following night, taking as his right what was hers only to bestow on a husband, without the need for promises or banns. Her father's immediate consent to the condition of sending her away.

She had been payment, Juan Carlos had taken her virtue as payment for his father's largesse. And she was being sent away, whether out of concern for her future with such a father or in case Juan Carlos' visit had had inopportune consequences.

Her father had sold her like a whore.

"Consuelo! What are you doing in here? How dare you touch my papers!" Her father stood in the doorway.

Consuelo stood before him, breathing hard. "Consuelo!" her mother called from the other room. "Consuelo! I am in the dark! Come to me! The candles!"

"Oh my God, your mother! And her goddamned candles! How dare you leave her? And what do you... Give that to me!" He grabbed Don Manuel's letter from her hand.

She reached to take it back. "You sold me! You trafficked in your own daughter!"

"You don't know what you're talking about! Get out of my study." Her father's voice was shaking. She saw him glance down at the floor, where the ledger page she had thrown down was illuminated in the setting sun.

She picked up the paper. "Is that it? Am I a whore for your money?"

In a travesty replaying of her last moments with Juan Carlos, Isidro stepped forward, and with a stinging slap, sent Consuelo into the side of the desk. She crumpled to the floor, her hand at her bleeding mouth. Her father had never struck her before.

She did not cry. She did not sob or scream. For the second time in an hour she tasted her own blood on her tongue. From the floor she looked up at her father. It was Isidro who had tears running down his face.

"See to your mother. Light any other candles but her Sabbath ones. Tell her I will not be home for dinner." And for the second time in an hour, Consuelo was alone on the office floor.

CHAPTER 4

CONSUELO

THE ROAD TO THE CASTLE of the Marqués of Condera was smooth and well traveled. The same road connected Tulancingo with Mexico City, a two-day journey Consuelo had made with her parents yearly until her mother first fell ill, and so she was familiar with the route. The castle was at about the halfway mark between the cities and reasonable inns could be found along the way for rest and refreshment. The coach, and the City of Tulancingo's head groom, borrowed for the purpose, conveyed Consuelo in comfort. Her traveling trunk was wedged in the back of the coach, and Consuelo, miserable and silent, was ensconced in the seat in front.

She had not spoken to her father when he returned late that terrible night. She had dutifully attended her mother, served her dinner, and put her to bed as she did nightly. She had completed her packing and had remained in her room for the evening. Silence was the only sign of her contretemps with her father, a silence that poisoned the air and set her mother on edge.

Consuelo had carefully wrapped the silver candlesticks and put them away in the storage basement. Regardless of her fury with her father, and the claims of Leandro Almidón that the Inquisition no longer was a force to be feared, she knew that her father was right about the candles. Any word by a faithless servant, put in the ear of the wrong Franciscan, could bring horrors down upon the house. The fact that there had not been an auto-de-fé in her lifetime did not negate the history of cruelty and suspicion that shrouded the Holy Office. With Consuelo gone and Leila's care delegated to a new young servant girl, no precaution was excessive.

On the day of her departure her mother had questioned her. "Why are you sad?" she asked. "Where is my husband?"

Consuelo could barely answer, but it made no difference. Regardless of what she told her mother the same questions would be repeated in an hour, or in less time if her mother was troubled. "Why are you sad? Where are you going?"

The first two or three times Consuelo had told her. "I am going to spend some time with the Sisters, to learn apothecary."

"How wonderful, darling. When will you be back?"

"In three months."

"Where are you going?"

"To the market," Consuelo replied after a while.

"Oh. Bring back some vegetables for dinner, would you?"

Consuelo nodded each time. "Of course, Mother."

But despite her increasing dementia, her mother could still perceive emotions. "But you are so sad. What is wrong?"

"I will miss you."

"Where are you going?" And so the circle would begin again. Consuelo felt her throat close. It was true, she would miss her mother, and in the back of her mind she wondered if she would even see her mother alive upon her return. But the path had been chosen for her, and Consuelo was grateful when the groom finally announced that the coach was ready.

While at home, she had maintained an icy stoicism, thinking and speaking only of the practical needs of the upcoming journey. As the distance from home grew, though, Consuelo felt her anger heat up. She remained both incredulous and hurt that her father would use her as a bargaining chip with Don Manuel, and she hadn't dared ask him how he had possibly gotten into such debt that he needed to borrow an astronomical sum from the Castillo family. All she understood was that Don Manuel had made the loan, and Juan Carlos had assumed either the right to her body or that she had offered herself to sweeten the deal. She twisted in anguish in her seat. The memory of his hands, his mouth, and her explosion of pleasure added to her shame and fury.

And now she was being banished to the Marqués's castle, not at his invitation, but at the insistence of the family creditor. She was not going as a lady in waiting to the Marquesa, as Maria Elena had once done, but rather was being sent to the nuns. That was the piece of the puzzle that did not make sense. There was no reason Don Manuel would demand that, except as a somewhat kindly way of getting her out of the way of his son or of releasing any obligation Juan Carlos may have incurred by lying with a virgin. And yet, Juan Carlos had seemed hurt, or angry, as if he had been the one wronged.

Consuelo recalled an oft-quoted line from a well-known poem from the famous poetess, Sor Juana Inés de la Cruz. *Men fog the mirror, then its lack of clarity condemn.* It was unfair, but it was how it had always been.

After a brief stop at an inn for some hot chocolate and refreshment, the coach took the turn to the west and the sun shone into her eyes. She closed them, and the gentle jostling lulled her. She felt herself relax for the first time in a month, since the wedding. She was getting out, getting away from everything and everyone who had any part in this debacle. Perhaps she had a small part of grandmother Rosa's spirit: she too was starting a new life.

When she awoke, the sun was near the horizon. It was still the last of winter and the days were not yet long, but she knew the journey was almost over. A thrill ran through her. She realized that she had not been excited about the enormous change her life was about to undergo, that she had not appreciated the fact that an unlooked-for, unpredicted adventure had been vouchsafed her by this iniquitous situation. Suddenly she was nervous. She had never been to the Marqués's castle. When Maria Elena had told her the stories of being a lady-in-waiting she had described it in her deadpan way as grander than her own hacienda, and she had been imagining it as if it were the Vice-royal palace in Chapultepec. That palace was hectares and hectares large, with grounds that covered an area larger than the center of the City in Tulancingo. She almost laughed at the absurdity of her thought.

No, surely the castle was no more than a grand hacienda. But where would she sleep and eat? Sor Carmela had written that she would be housed with the nuns, and would take her meals with them as well, but what that meant she could not imagine. Perhaps it would be like a convent within a castle. Her excitement was quickly replaced by the barely forgotten fury. If she was being sent to a convent, like a girl from a good family pregnant out of wedlock, then Don Manuel had clearly misunderstood the situation. She shook her head. The time to have asked those questions had long passed. She had known she was going for a month and had asked nothing. This was no time to start.

The coach left the main road and Consuelo felt a tremor as the familiar sights receded. Her heart was racing as they rounded the turn and the walls of the castle were visible for the first time, glowing red from the setting sun. Even from a distance it was a sight that was far grander than she had imagined. As they neared the wall a large gate, as tall as a house, opened as the coach neared, and a boy in a green and gold livery waved excitedly to the coachman. "Hello, Gustavo!" the coachman called down to the boy. "Papi!" the boy answered. The coach drove through and stopped. The gate closed behind them and the boy clambered up into the coachman's waiting arms. Consuelo blinked back tears and the horses began a slow walk to the portico.

The yard in front of the entrance to the castle was much like a country yard, filled with dogs and men, and horses being led to and from stables. Consuelo thought for an instant about the Castillo hacienda, how similar the front yards were. The dust from the coach's wheels made her cough and she wiped her eyes. Two young men in livery similar to the boy's came out to take her trunk. "Is that all, Señorita? Just the one?" She nodded. How much could a person bring?

Huge double doors fronted the building and one of the young men opened them, bowing her through. She took a breath and stepped across the threshold into a dark hall. Her eyes took a moment to adjust, and she made out wall hangings to the right, a set of tall windows, and an enormous staircase leading up from the left.

A grey-haired nun sat at a desk in the front of a grand hall, just inside the door. "Good evening, Señorita Costa. *Bienvenida.* Abelardo will show you to your room. Abelardo!" A young man about her age approached. "Take Señorita Costa to the nuns' wing."

He raised his eyebrows and looked her up and down insolently. "Come, sweetheart. Let's go to your new home." Consuelo stared at him. No one had ever spoken to her that way. "I don't think you will mind the nuns, they're not too bad with girls of quality. And quality is what you are."

"Mind your words," she answered sharply. *How dare he?* She looked over at the nun at the desk, hoping for intercession. The old woman adjusted the monocle she was using to see the visitor's book she held in front of her, but said nothing.

"Oh, come on, darlin'. Don't go all prim and proper on me. You mustn't have been so high and mighty when your boyfriend came around at night, huh? I can see how a piece like you could get in trouble, a long tall drink of tart lemonade!"

Finally the nun interceded. "Abelardo, that's enough. I am sorry, Señorita. Abelardo, take Señorita Costa to the nuns' wing now, and not another word out of you."

"Yes, sister," Abelardo said, not the least bit meekly. "This way, my lady."

Consuelo lifted her chin and turned to follow him. They passed the tall windows, and the grand entry, open and cavernous, gave way to a smaller, stone paved hallway, with tapestries hanging on the whitewashed walls. There was a drifting aroma of candle wax and powder. They walked in silence past a set of tall double doors that stood open to a room with a pianoforte and comfortable looking chairs. "The music room," Abelardo said, gesturing to the piano. The next set of doors, even larger, was closed. "The library," Abelardo said. "More books than any one body should read." They made another turn and the appetizing smell of tortillas wafted by. Consuelo's stomach growled and she realized how hungry she was. She had consumed nothing but the cup of chocolate at the inn since breakfast.

"Got to feed the tummy, eh? Or are you still at the upchuck phase?"

"Silence, Abelardo," she said, as if to a barking dog. He laughed.

"You'll get plenty to eat, that's for sure. These sisters know all about eating for two. Soon you'll be waddling down the halls, unable to find your embroidery needle under your big belly!"

At last they came to a curtain. "Hello, good sisters!" he called. "I've got your latest sinner!"

"Oh my goodness, Abelardo, you fool. Shut your mouth and get back to the gate. I am so sorry," said a voice on the other side of the curtain. A hand reached around and opened the drape. A tiny woman, perhaps as high as Consuelo's elbow, with a grey veil and habit, looked up at her. "Señorita Costa?"

"Yes."

"Come in, my dear. Get out of here, fool!" she said to Abelardo. He winked at Consuelo and turned away. "Come in here," she repeated to Consuelo. "Ignore him, he's an absolute boor. Brought up by a footman from the era of the former Marqués. There's no dismissing him, he's a family servant, but he's a vulgar piece of work. I am sorry he was on gate duty when you arrived. But now you're here. Let's make you welcome."

The curtain drew back to reveal a short hallway with rough adobe walls, the quick-lime plaster gleaming white. Dark wood doors came off on the right, one after another, and continued along the wall after the hall had opened into a large, warm kitchen.

Center and left, the kitchen was dominated by a long table with a good twenty chairs, all pushed in neatly. The top shone in the last rays of the sun, which slanted through multiple windows up high. Below the windows, along the left wall, was the biggest furnace Consuelo had ever seen, its door open. A rotund nun fed wood into the open maw and flames burned brightly against the black iron enclosure. The top of the furnace was large enough to hold the four big pots that sat boiling and steaming on the cook-top, with room for several more.

A pump and a huge basin took up the farthest wall from whence the hallway continued back until it turned right and out of sight.

"This way," said the tiny nun, opening one of the first doors in the hall. "I am Sor Carmela. I have been awaiting your arrival."

Consuelo looked down at the miniature woman. Her features were regular, not distorted or enlarged like a dwarf's, and her brown eyes were huge in her small face. Her light brown skin bore no ravages of time or pox. Consuelo stopped herself from asking if this tiny nun knew the cause of her diminutive stature.

"Your room is near the entrance, but our study is further back. I am sure Sister Portress will have your trunk delivered by that fool, Abelardo, or some other gate help, soon."

Her sparse room's furniture consisted of a bedstead, an armoire, and a small desk, in plainest wood. A little stove filled a corner, and a crucifix on the wall was the only adornment. It would be easy to feel studious in these plain quarters. Sor Carmela pointed out a pitcher and a basin. "You may fill your pitcher with water from the pump and warm it with some of the heated water on the stove. We are fortunate here, the river is deep and our water is plentiful. Refresh yourself, then come and find me. Just walk back along the hall." Consuelo thanked the sister and pulled the door shut behind her. She sank down on the bed, exhausted from her trip and the anticipation of the unknown. *So, she thought, I will live like a nun for three months.* She fought conflicting waves of gratitude and resentment. Finally she shrugged, got up and took hold of the pitcher. If this was her new life, she'd best get started.

Consuelo found the routine behind the nuns' curtain not unlike her life at home, with some salient differences. Much like at home, she rose early, washed quickly, dressed plainly. But without Leila to care for, Consuelo's remaining time was spent in the apothecary, deep in the recesses of the nuns' wing.

Sor Carmela began with the elements, not unknown to Consuelo, but presented in a new light. Each element, whether air, water, earth, gold, had its uses and meanings, and these meanings themselves had meanings. Each plant brought forth from God's earth had its use and its prayer.

Meals were taken at the long table in the kitchen, and provisions were simple and plentiful. New flavors came from herbs that she studied for medicinal purposes, and were then handed over to the Sister Cook to add to soups, and a delightful caramel made by boiling milk and sugar together was a treat to spread on warm tortillas for supper. Conversation was as lively as the food was plain, as the nuns who studied, wrote, sang or played music at the castle had much to share when they were together.

When weather or curriculum permitted, Consuelo and Sor Carmela walked in the rear gardens gathering herbs. Occasionally she glimpsed others on the formal paths, ladies dressed in their finery strolling in the early spring sun, but the weather was still changeable, so she and Sor Carmela usually had the gardens to themselves.

Consuelo attended diligently and took samples back to her room at night to study, reveling in the excitement of knowledge. But her evenings were long. As the days themselves lengthened she thought back to her mother, to her old life. She felt shame at the relief of not having to care for Leila daily, not having to watch her slide deeper into oblivion. She hadn't chosen to leave her post, she reminded herself when emotion threatened to overwhelm her.

The nights themselves were filled with shadows. She remembered in vivid detail the last scene with her father and how she had lit every single candle in the entire house, finding every candlestick, lamp and sconce and lighting it as an act of spite and fury. She had covered with a thick layer of memory beeswax the final interview with Juan Carlos and the night at the hacienda, but it took very little scratching to penetrate that protective coating and have her emotions bleed once more.

She tried to sort her thoughts the way Sor Carmela sorted herbs, but it was as if the wind kicked up every time she laid her thoughts out on the table, blurring the lines and categories until Leila blended with Isidro, Juan Carlos, and herself.

* * *

On a sunny morning of her third week, Sor Carmela sent her beyond the curtains to the Marquesa's library in search of an old and very rare herbology volume. Consuelo stepped tentatively out of the sanctuary alone for the first time since her arrival, marveling at the richness of the wall hangings in the hall, art that she had passed unseeing on her first day but that now stood in vibrant relief before her. Three weeks of plain living had opened her senses to the colors and textures that now almost pulsated with intensity. She felt giddy as she walked through the hall, reaching out to touch a tapestry as she passed.

When she came to the large doors of the library she hesitated. The doors were carved with leaves and flowers, and gleamed with fresh oil. She felt she was about to enter a fantasy world and her hand trembled as she pushed the heavy wood open.

Consuelo had never seen such a vast collection of books. There were thousands by her estimation. After staring in awe for several minutes at the enormous collection she approached the shelves and pulled down the books closest to her. Some seemed ancient, with pressed leather covers elaborately embossed with gold, but many were new and sewn with long-stitch and glued in the modern fashion. There were poetry books, plays, collections of thoughts and essays, and even books on homeopathy, herbology and metallurgy.

Small work tables were scattered throughout, with candelabras on each for light in the evenings. In the nooks behind the entry door were more little tables, one with a man seated with his back to her, surrounded by books, papers and pens. Hearing the sound of pages rustling as she explored the books, he turned to face her. Startled, she took a sharp breath. He half rose when he saw her.

"Señorita Consuelo," Leandro said, "what a surprise, vouchsafed from heaven, to see you."

She stammered a stricken response. He approached, and bowing over her hand, he assured her though he had been at the Castle for two weeks he had heard nothing of her presence. Had he known she was there he would have come and found her earlier.

"You have actually left your home to study healing arts?" he asked incredulously, when she had explained her presence. "What an odd venture for a lady."

"Not here in the Colonies, it isn't," Consuelo answered, knowing nothing of the sort. It irked her that he would find her predicament odd, though she found it so herself, and her brief annoyance allowed her to regain a small measure of self-possession.

"You are right, the world is changing, Consuelo. The world outside of Iberia, of course." Leandro leaned back in his chair, holding aloft his quill. His black jacket, embroidered at the lapels with gold roses, was open to display a smooth, unruffled shirt and a plain, almost clerical collar. His thick black hair was brushed back, rather than cascading in curls like so many men wore at the court.

"You told me so at Joaquin Castillo's wedding," Consuelo reminded him, smiling to cover the pang of anguish the mere words *Castillo's wedding* sent through her. She pulled the white crocheted shawl across her arms. The library was cool, notwithstanding the morning sun that streamed in the enormous windows. Her grey dress, plain and warm enough for the herb room in the nuns' wing, seemed dull and inadequate in this spectacular room.

He held a book up to her now. "Here's a new issue I brought from Europe. It's prohibited in Spain and yet is as appealing as a children's story. It is a work of a French writer, La Fontaine. Let me read you a bit." He cleared his throat, and in a theatrical voice, he read, "*Maître corbeau sur un arbre perché, tenait en son bec un fromage. Maître renard, par l'odeur alleché, lui tient a peu près ce language.*"

"I don't speak French," Consuelo said, "but it sounds lovely."

"Goose. It's about a fox and a crow. But there's a clean tone to it, something we don't see in the romantic flourishes of our Góngora, or Calderón, or Lope de Vega. Perhaps you should learn French."

The names were only vaguely familiar to her. "I am not much for poetry, except as a distraction. It's the herbology and chemistry that attracts me."

"Chemistry? My goodness, woman, you *are* unnatural." His laugh made the comment flattery. "I thought a scientist lurked under that lovely form. You did threaten me with experiments at the wedding feast, I recall."

"I did no such thing! I only described my treatment methods, which, after a month under Sor Carmela's tutelage I see were elementary at best. I knew so little."

"Well then, you must learn French, and if you don't read La Fontaine or Molière in the original you could instead read Descartes." She frowned. "A mathematician, and a philosopher. We must see to it that your education here is complete!" He winked an eye at her. "Why don't you dine with me in the great hall tonight? It will make a nice change for you from the gruel you must be getting in the nuns' wing."

"I am well fed there, I assure you," she smiled in return. She felt a rush of excitement—it had been a long time since she had spoken at length with a man, and, except for the long-ago days with Juan Carlos before he left for Salamanca, never with such ease and pleasure. "Let me seek permission from Sor Carmela. How shall I let you know?"

"Send a message with one of the pages. They loiter around Sister Portress and they will carry messages for a centavo."

"Oh! I don't think I want to do that. My first encounter was also my last with those pages. A repulsively forward fellow, Adegardo or some such name, made terrible, lewd comments to me on the very moment of my arrival. A nasty welcome, I assure you."

"You must mean Abelardo. Yes, he is a character. His father worked for the current Marqués's father, as his privy keeper if you can imagine. Emptied the old whoremonger's chamber pots. The prior Marqués was a licentious sort, took pleasure in stealing the virtue of his wife's *menina*s and cuckolding the ladies in waiting's husbands. You know how the Marqués died, don't you?" Consuelo shook her head. "I'm surprised, given that you're an old friend of Juan Carlos' family." Consuelo flinched at the sound of his name. Leandro raised an eyebrow but went on. "His mother, Doña Josefina, it is said, cut his, ah, this is delicate, his *cojones* off."

Consuelo burst out laughing. "Oh, go on! Doña Josefina is a kind, gentle poetess, and can barely walk. She had a stroke when she gave birth to Juan Carlos and was never the same. When would she go around mutilating nobility?"

"That's the story, anyway. But Abelardo learned his nastiness from being in his employ when he was just a child."

"He was certainly uncouth with me. He suggested very unchaste motives for my visit."

"Ladies of standing usually come to the Court as ladies in waiting to the Marquesa, and rarely come to the nuns' wing unless they are in a compromised condition. He probably assumed the worst."

"All the more reason to be kind."

"A free thinker as well as a scientist! My dear, you could be burned at the stake!"

"I meant nothing by it," Consuelo said quickly.

"Nor did I take you to mean anything more than what you said. You're simply a delight to tease as well as to talk to seriously. But be calm. The Holy Office is busy hunting down *novatores* like me in Spain, and Judaizers here in the colonies, and finding little support for either hunt from the monarchy. The Inquisition loses power daily. They've run out of actual Jews to fry, and the king has neither the money nor the desire for them to delve too deeply into anyone's blood lines back home, looking for traces of Hebrew. He would lose all his best accountants."

Consuelo shivered. "Is that true here as well as in Spain?"

"Who knows? From what I have seen everything is watered down here. The Holy Office has not yet awakened to its loss of power, but it has not yet noticed the coming of the Enlightened world, either. So it twiddles its ecclesiastic thumbs, minus the thumbscrews, of course, and strong-arms good citizens who fear exposure of their ancient blood taint."

"There cannot be many with impure blood here," Consuelo said cautiously. "I have never met any." The lie tasted dirty on her tongue.

"Oh, but you have! There are more *conversos* here in New Spain than there are pure Christians. You would just never know it. But it's the *marranos* they're really after."

"*Marranos?* Hogs?"

"Comes from pig, as in forbidden pork. They're the ones still following the God of Moses, behind drawn drapes and closed doors, eating their nasty special foods and saying their black prayers to candles dripping wax made from boiled babies' bones."

"Nonsense!" Consuelo exclaimed. "Who would think such a thing?"

"Ever listen to an auto-de-fé? Those are the ones the Grand Tribunal is after. Of course, they dread catching them almost as much as they hate letting the Judaizers go free."

"Why? Why would they dread catching them?" Consuelo fought down nausea, the glow of the earlier conversation now gone entirely.

"Because they would have to start up the whole damned machine, get the scribes and the torturers, take the testimony, meticulously keep their notes for a trial, record their findings, and destroy the economic fabric of the entire New World. Who do you think steals the land from good Christians with false papers and assumed names? Who keeps the King's books, lends the King money, and runs the major trading companies? Pure Christians? Not a chance!" Leandro laughed and Consuelo caught a bitter note.

"Yes, my dear," he went on, "all the silver in the entire Colony is in the hands of the Jews. Current, converted, past, what's the difference? They all keep their books from right to left. They've got us all by the purse strings and will never let us forget it."

*   *   *

"The alchemy is only good when accompanied by prayer," Sor Carmela said.

"Have you tried it without prayer?" Consuelo asked.

Sor Carmela looked up at her. "My dear, what a question. Every tincture, every salve and balsam, tea or tonic, is only good when accompanied by thanks to our eternal Lord. These elements are gifts to us from the Lord above, and if we fail to thank Him, to seek his blessing upon our work, how could those elements act on our behalf?"

Consuelo nodded. Of course, it was right to thank the Lord for His mercies, but was it a necessary component of the alchemy? "But if you don't pray..."

"If you don't pray, your work will be in vain. Try to imagine the tree of this flower," she held up the deadly, dangerous yellow flower of *hediondilla*, "growing in the wild fields, unplanted by man. Unblessed, and without prayer, a man stumbles upon it, and admiring its color, eats it. What would happen?"

"Stomach cramps, vomiting, diarrhea, and death, if he took too much. A purgative of other poisons if he took but a bit."

"But with prayer, and through prayer comes knowledge, he would know what measure of the plant to eat, for the Lord would lead him through it."

"The Lord is to be blessed," Consuelo said aloud. *But it is the measure of the plant, and not the prayer, that effects the cure,* she finished silently.

Sor Carmela fixed her with her sharp brown eyes. "Consuelo, a mind open to knowledge is a wonderful thing provided that it is not also open to sin and sacrilege. Beware of false teachers who would fill your mind with soul-damning thoughts while fooling you into thinking you are learning. Now, here is pennyroyal. It brings on the menses, but without prayer, can be the murderer of innocent babes and the damnation of a wanton mother. Let us consider the proper dose."

Consuelo thought back to the sprigs of pennyroyal she had taken from Doña Josefina's pantry. She already knew what pennyroyal could do. And perhaps Sor Carmela was right, without being right for the right reason. She would have taken it without prayer, had she needed it. She smiled slightly, recognizing the phrasing of her thought. Right for the wrong reason? She was starting to sound like Leandro.

"Sor Carmela, would you permit me to dine with the Marqués's guests tonight?"

Sor Carmela nodded. "You must be lonely for company of your own age and class. Of course, you may dine with them as often as you wish, as often as they wish, rather, so long as you do not neglect your studies. Your sustenance here is being paid for you to learn, not to engage in social play. And be careful. Some of the young men, especially those recently arrived, are full of strange and unchristian ideas. I do not want your mind polluted with them or you will not learn the skills that I am bound to teach you."

"Of course, Sor. I will not let such blasphemy or foolishness infiltrate me."

Sor Carmela gave her a sharp look but Consuelo was studying the *hediondilla* as if she had just stumbled upon it growing wild in the fields, unblessed.

Consuelo changed from her grey cotton dress to a finer one of green and black muslin with silk trim at the square collar and sleeves, caught up at the elbow with a black bone hook. She could not match some of the finery she had caught sight of on the occasions when she had seen some of the current ladies who waited upon the Marquesa walking in the gardens, but the chance to get out of the grey tones of the nuns' wing obliterated any concerns she had about her level of fashionable attire. She had never been excessively interested in the mode. She had even less opportunity to know about it as her world had become more and more circumscribed while she cared for her mother.

She shook her head to clear it. Her life was different now. A month ago her world had centered on her mother, her needs and her growing dementia. Her father's moods and grating monologues had been her largest irritant, and a matter of focus and anger for her. Her visits to the apothecary of Tulancingo had provided her with stimulating learning and contact with the world, and her rounds of the market, the butcher, the milliner had been her major outings.

Today she was at the Castle, a student of the art of healing. Tonight, she was to dine in fine company. She would not think about her mother. She felt a pang of guilt and a greater blow of sorrow. She would write again tomorrow.

For now, she had a dinner to attend.

ISIDRO

Isidro paced the floor of his study. He had done wrong, he thought, to allow the thugs to come to his home. *Allow*, he thought, was a misnomer, for he had very little choice in their methods. He had sent a message to the priest who called himself Father Bernardo and had received the courtesy of a letter, inviting him to name his meeting spot. That was a change from the summonses he had received in the past. He had not relished the long walk through the darkened tunnel under one of the old market buildings, to the barely lit cave-like room where he had been received in the past. Father Bernardo had kindly acquiesced to meeting him elsewhere to receive the final payment and to give him the signed release that acknowledged the "debt" paid in full.

It was curious, he thought, as he continued his pacing. The priest had suggested that very mechanism, and Isidro, for all his financial and municipal experience, could not see why. Father Bernardo had advised him in his letter: "You will certainly want something to show any pretenders that you have paid the Holy Office all sums due and owing. This way they cannot say that you are still in debt."

But I was never in debt to you in the first place, Isidro had thought. He hardly could consider blackmail to be a debt, but if it prevented the Holy Office, if indeed this was from them, from blackmailing him again, it would be beneficial. Besides, it was clear that Father Bernardo would be giving him this document whether he wanted it or not.

I should have met them at the City. Now they will know where I live. Isidro smiled bitterly. They already knew. And if any of the clerks or supernumeraries, or worse yet, his arrogant deputy at the City had seen the thugs, gossip would fly more rapidly than at a women's gathering. Word would get back to the Marqués, and from his castle to the Viceroy's prison was a short walk if the Viceroy decided that Isidro had been corrupted.

He wiped a film of sweat from his brow. He had asked that the meeting be late, well after the evening meal. As long as Leila slept there was no danger that she would cry out, say something that would incriminate him again. The new Indian girl who took care of Leila was not at the level of Consuelo, she did not labor out of love or duty, but for the regular pay that kept her entire family well fed and clothed. Perhaps that was the more honorable way to proceed but Isidro felt a pang for Consuelo.

At least she would not be here to witness or overhear the meeting. He suppressed the image that came to his mind, Consuelo on the floor of his study, right where he was standing now, her mouth bleeding from where he had hit her. He shut his eyes tight to stop the tears that rose to them. The thugs would be here momentarily. They could not catch him crying.

He heard sounds from the window and hurried to the door before they could ring the bell and wake the entire household. His heart thrummed in his ears as he opened the deep blue door and the last thing he saw before darkness overtook him was the mask of a crow and its large, black wings.

CONSUELO

The magnificence of the grand hall, filled with ladies and gentlemen in their finery, made Consuelo's head spin. Men with frilled blouses and coats decorated with gold and red braid, their long hair loose around their shoulders, conversed with beautiful women, their arms and necks uncovered, silk gowns rustling over wide petticoats. Consuelo was glad she had changed into one of her better dresses but felt truly outclassed in a way that she had never experienced.

Leandro came forward to greet her. "Only a dozen or so at dinner tonight," he said. "I am sorry that your first dinner with the nobility and their sycophants should be so underwhelming."

"You jest, I am sure. I have never seen such grandeur. What does *sycophants* mean?"

"People who surround someone in power and make him, or as often her, feel even more powerful by agreeing with everything they say. For example, Doña Maria Isabel, there, in the light blue silk, is busily agreeing with Colonel Vasco Jimenez de la Huerta, he of the extensive decoration, all because he has more money than God. And the Colonel will willingly nod at anything his host, the Marqués, says, even though the Marqués holds very modern ideas about the futility of endless military campaigns that suck the treasury dry and leave widows and orphans at the mercy of charity."

"Obviously you are no sycophant yourself, then, if you dare express such contempt for the guests here."

"Not contempt, my lovely, but a realistic, unromantic assessment. As you are known yourself to do."

"I do nothing of the sort. I am a well bred daughter of a City mayor and have been exercising restraint of my views since I could talk."

"For you likely never got a word in edgewise."

"Now you are rude! And self-contradicting, I might add. I am either given to unvarnished opinions or stifled, but not both."

"Both, both. You have the clear eyes of the Enlightened and the manners of a lady. How could a man complain?"

"No one has, that I have been told."

Consuelo saw a sly look on Leandro's face when he turned away, smiling. "Come," he said over his shoulder, "let us give some of these fancy guests the opportunity to find something to complain about."

Consuelo trailed after Leandro and felt the stares trail after her. "Why is everyone looking at me? Am I dressed wrong?" she whispered to Leandro.

"No, it's just the novelty. People have been looking at one another since Ash Wednesday and are starved for a new face. Lent is a dull season and any form of meatless entertainment is welcome."

"Since I have been sequestered in the nuns' wing I have not noticed the Lenten sacrifices. The good sisters only eat meat on Sundays and the rest of the time we are sustained by tortillas and prayers."

Leandro smiled. "You see? You would not have said that at the wedding fiesta, would you?" Consuelo had to agree, all the while wishing he had not mentioned the fiesta. "And speaking of Juan Carlos," he continued.

"We weren't."

"Ah. My apologies."

"There is nothing for you to be sorry about. I was only correcting you. Perhaps it is I who should apologize."

"In my search for candor I must say that I find your response lacking. If I pained you with a mention of Juan Carlos, I am sorry. No," he stopped her from disagreeing, "no need. In any case, all the more reason you should be forewarned. Juan Carlos and his mother come here next week for an extended stay. Doña Josefina is a favorite of the Marquesa whom you have yet to meet. The Marquesa is a poetess herself, though not on the level of Doña Josefina, and they enjoy intellectual conversation on the highest level that a woman can muster."

"I did meet the Marquesa, briefly, at the fiesta."

"True, though I thought it best not to mention that since the reference pains you."

"Enough! I will confess Juan Carlos and I had a disagreement and we are not on easy terms. Are you happy now that you have extracted this from me?" Consuelo's voice shook and she felt her skin flush.

"I would be since that tells me that the road is clear for me to advance, but I cannot be, having caused you sorrow."

"You are a dandy!" Consuelo exclaimed. She would turn his comment over in her mind later. She forced a smile. "My mother and Doña Josefina also enjoyed an intellectual relationship, back before my mother's mind was devastated by her illness. Though Doña Josefina can only speak slowly what she had to say was always worth waiting for. We visited her often in those bygone days."

"I writhe in jealousy that I was denied knowing you while you were growing up but rejoice in knowing you as a woman." Consuelo laughed at the absurdly flowery language, drawing a raised eyebrow from Leandro. "Come, we have missed the socializing by keeping to ourselves. Dinner is being served and we must be seated. Over here," he added, guiding her to a chair. "You will enjoy meeting Don Patricio Mendez. Don Patricio, this beauty is Consuelo Costa Argenta, of Tulancingo."

Consuelo smiled at Don Patricio, an elderly gentleman with lively green eyes and what hair he had left swept back from his face. Don Patricio took her offered hand and raised it to his lips. "My pleasure, Señorita. I know the name, wait, it will come to me…"

Consuelo cringed internally, waiting for Don Patricio to remember why he knew her name. "Ah yes, the daughter of the Alcalde Isidro Costa, right?"

Consuelo nodded, searching his face for the contempt that Leandro had shown. But she saw none. "He is a fascinating man, always full of stories. It is such a pleasure to speak with him. I much prefer dining with a talkative companion. There is nothing worse than having to pull conversation out of someone, don't you find?"

Consuelo smiled gratefully. "Of course, Don Patricio. And I hope that though I am far less amusing than my father I will prove a good dinner companion to you tonight."

"Very prettily said, Señorita. Of course in a woman, silence is often a virtue."

Behind him Leandro rolled his eyes. Consuelo bit back a laugh. "Oh, yes," she answered, "quite true, Don Patricio." *Sycophant*, she thought. *I am agreeing with him without meaning to.* "Are you visiting for the Lenten season?" she asked, hoping that she had phrased the question right.

The older man threw his head back and laughed, a cackling sound that caused some of the other guests at the table to turn and look.

They went back to their conversations, though, evidently used to the sound of his mirth. "Oh, my, no! I am here all the time. I am the Marqués's confidential secretary and scribe. I have been here for fifty Lents, before the young Marqués was even born, and hope to be here for another fifty."

Dinner was a welcome feast after the austerity of the nuns' kitchen. Meat was served, crackling pork and chiles, rice with cumin and bits of cilantro, strips of beef grilled and seasoned with powdered pepper, and for the final course, dried fruits and *acitrón*, its jellylike texture and mild sweetness lending a gentle ending to the generous repast. After dinner Leandro took her arm and led her away from the grand hall. They walked along the hall, past the music room and the library, until they came to large double doors with windows in each side. Leandro opened the doors and led her outside.

"You are certainly familiar with this castle," Consuelo said. "You walk about and go where you please, as if it were your own home."

"I do, I admit. It is my nature. I am not one to wait for permission." He put his arm around her waist. At his touch, Consuelo shrunk back. "Do I offend?" he said.

Consuelo thought for a moment, resisting the temptations of quick answers, either in the negative out of politeness or the positive out of modesty. "Let me think a moment," she replied.

Leandro looked at her, surprised. "You are taking this rationality a bit too seriously, Consuelo. Appetites of the body and of the heart won't withstand such logical scrutiny."

"Well, in this case they must since I surprised myself with my reaction and seek to understand it better before I try to explain it to you."

They walked further along a garden path lit by a newly risen moon, just past full. "It is beautiful, the way it washes the garden with its silver," Consuelo said.

Leandro laughed. "Leave the poetry to me."

Consuelo looked away, embarrassed. She had not intended her description as an attempt at poetry. She felt foolish and fell silent. Leandro seemed not to notice. "What kind of flowers are these?"

"The first of the *manzanilla*, good for soothing teas." Relieved to be on familiar ground she bent and picked a tiny white flower from the rows of chamomile massed as a low border along the path, and pinched it between her fingers. She sniffed it and held it up to Leandro. "Oh, yes. My mother used to drink that for her nerves."

It was the first mention of his family. "Where in Spain are you from?"

"Granada, the last stand of the Moors. But fear not, I am pure of blood. No *morizco* in me, nor even a hint of Portuguese or Jew. Nor in you, I take it."

"Of course not," she answered, careful not to speak too quickly.

"No. I saw you eat that pork tonight with relish and seem none the worse for having enjoyed it. A Jew would vomit or faint from it, I am told."

Consuelo shivered. "Cold?" he asked. She nodded, for it was true, though the sources of her chill were varied. Leandro put his arm around her again and this time she did not pull away. The warmth of his hand penetrated her sleeve and his scent mixed lightly and pleasantly with the aromas from the garden. "You are beautiful," he said quietly. "And you are interesting, so much more interesting than the other ladies I have met in the New World."

"You are interesting too," she answered. "And perhaps not ugly, as we were led to believe."

"What? Who said that?" Then Leandro burst out laughing. "Of course. I remember that idiotic remark I made at dinner at— at the first night we met. I thought I was being witty, you understand. Of course, wits and fools are closely related."

He was interesting and definitely not ugly. She looked at his dark brown eyes, so lively and knowing. She had never before had conversations like the ones she had with him. He bent his head and his mouth came down gently on hers.

His lips were soft and tasted slightly of the port he had drunk at the end of dinner. He did not insist with his kiss, only moving lightly over her mouth, his tongue touching her lips in a feathery caress before retreating. He pulled back and smiled a little. "Let's go back in before your reputation is spoiled. This is Mexico, not Salamanca, and the residents are far less enlightened than the university denizens."

Juan Carlos had said he was a rake and a philanderer. He was wrong, she thought. Leandro had taken more care for her reputation than Juan Carlos had, certainly, and had shown far more restraint. She allowed him to lead her back through the garden towards the doors. When they passed the *manzanilla* borders, he inhaled. "I will forever more associate this scent with this moment, Consuelo."

"I had better not," she replied, breaking the spell. "I administer it so often, for every common small ailment, and so would be forced to think of you daily. Too distracting from my work, I would say."

He pulled her close, then let her go. "I am happy to be such a distraction!"

*   *   *

"Pay attention, Consuelo. If you are dosing someone with any kind of medicine you cannot have your head elsewhere lest you poison your patient."

Consuelo nodded, acknowledging the nun's gentle chiding. Distraction did not begin to describe the whirlwind in her head. *The road is clear for me to advance...Juan Carlos arrives next week with his mother...A Jew would vomit from it, or faint...You are beautiful and interesting...* She knew nothing, really, about Leandro Almidón. Who were his people? Pureblooded Spaniards, he said, though he raised the issue so often she felt doubt creep in. And what were his intentions? If a proposal were forthcoming would he still want to marry her if he knew that her mother secretly lit candles and chanted an old Hebrew poem? Or more truthfully, that she did these rituals herself, for her mother...

And if a proposal was not forthcoming, if Leandro was as much of a rake as Juan Carlos had intimated, was he toying with her for his temporary amusement? She no longer had her virginity to lose. If his intentions were honorable that was a condition she could easily disguise. Her family history was harder to conceal. As long as her mother lived she was at risk. That led to even more disconcerting thoughts.

"Go to your room and rest. You are not present at this moment and I will not have you dreaming over your lesson," Sor Carmela said.

"If you are mooning over that young poet, Señor Almidón, kindly do so elsewhere."

"I'm sorry, Sor. I am not completely myself, I will admit. I am troubled and not concentrating properly."

"You are not, indeed. If this happens again you will not dine with the ladies and gentlemen as long as you are entrusted to me for education. If you wish to change courses and live on the other side of the curtain you may inform your patron. Otherwise, today you will be given a pass on your lack of attention, but tomorrow you will not."

Consuelo was surprised at the force of the rebuke. "I truly am sorry."

"Your apology is accepted, as I said, under condition that the lapse not be repeated. You will find me a stern teacher when you are a lax student. It is rare that I take on a student at all, outside of the convent, but I did so at Doña Josefina's request. She has been a generous patron of the Convent and was a special friend of my mentor, Sor Inez. But certainly Doña Josefina will not want my time or her generosity wasted."

Consuelo nodded and went to the spare cell that was her room. She hung her shawl on the bedstead, smoothed the bedding over the mattress and blew on an ember in the stove to ignite a flame. The plain, unvarnished furniture, the lonely cross on the wall, seemed more markedly stark after the sumptuousness of the furnishings on the other side of the curtain. She pulled the un-upholstered chair up to the table serving as a desk, a concession to her studies, and stared at her alchemy book without seeing it.

Taking a sheet of paper from her writing book she made a line down the center. She would write in cryptic notes, for what she needed to think out was not something she could bear to have found or read by anyone. On the one side she made a mark for the sensual pleasure of Juan Carlos's kiss. On the other, a parallel mark for Leandro's.

She made two marks for Juan Carlos's wealth. In Leandro's column she wrote nothing for she knew nothing about his family, his finances or his lands. Looking at the list she added another mark in Juan Carlos's column for wealth since it was greater even than she could imagine.

In Leandro's column she placed a mark for a possible proposal. In Juan Carlos's, she placed none, as he would never marry her after the scene they had had in her father's study. She held her pen up. Was there a mark to be made for his use of her body? How did she account for that? As a positive, for the pleasure of it and her desire for him, or as a negative, for what decent man took a virgin, a woman of family and quality, and then abandoned her? Leandro, on the other hand, had kissed her, but tried no more intimacies when she invited none.

She looked at her tally and laughed out loud. She had taken this rational thinking too far, Leandro had said. Indeed, this was the silliest thing she could have done and something she never would have thought of before she had learned of the new kind of thought. If Leandro proposed it would be up to her father to determine his financial security. If he didn't, she had better not let him take any more liberties with her. One mistake, with only a broken heart as consequence, was sin enough, without adding another to it.

She crumpled up the paper and put it into the stove. It was a huge waste of a page but it would be even more foolish to leave such scribblings, even if they were undecipherable, for someone to find. She vowed to be more attentive to Sor Carmela and to avoid any more of Leandro's kisses. She stood up, resolved. And when Juan Carlos arrived she would be busy with her studies and keep him at a cold and formal distance.

ISIDRO

Isidro woke with a violent headache. He sat up and before he could wonder where he was or what had happened to him he was sick on his pants and on the floor. He struggled to get on his hands and knees, to keep from vomiting again on himself. Each retch, each gag made his head throb with red, flashing pain. Finally there was nothing left to bring up and nothing even to gag upon. He knelt, heaving, until his breathing evened out. Then he rocked back on his heels and moaned.

"All cleaned out?" Isidro heard the voice of Father Bernardo behind him, but he did not turn around. Why do so, he thought, when the pain is so great? "Isidro, you have messed your clothes." Bernardo came around to the front looking down at him. Isidro shifted, not wanting to be on his knees before his enemy. He tried to rise. The room swirled and he sank back down on all fours.

"Give yourself time, Isidro. That was quite a party you enjoyed last night. All that wine and carousing. No wonder you feel awful."

Isidro tried to think back. He was in his study. He opened the door, a crow enveloped him and all was black. He had been hit on the head, he thought, though he couldn't remember it happening. He reached up and touched a swollen lump near his temple.

"Yes, Isidro. When you drink too much, you fall down and hit your head. A university boy knows that much!"

Isidro ventured a look around. He was in the cave room where he had met Father Bernardo the other times, where he should have gone to meet him this time. But he had let him come to the house instead. The small window at the top of the wall showed light. It had been night. It must be morning. "What do you want from me?"

"Nothing today, my friend. You are all paid up. That's what we were celebrating last night, remember? You have paid us and we tried to give you a receipt. The Holy Office is nothing if not meticulous in its records and we wanted to share our records with you. And you insisted on drinking almost a half a cask of wine with us in honor of your good fortune."

"What good fortune is that?" He did, as it became clearer, remember drinking. It came back in wavy thoughts. He had regained consciousness to find himself wrapped in heavy black cloth on a hard stone floor. He felt the panic again as he remembered struggling with the cloth, freeing himself only to find himself on the floor of a dark room. A single candle burned in the corner.

"Welcome to the party," Bernardo had said. "Nice of you to wake up." He had handed Isidro a cup with wine. Isidro remembered standing up, throwing the wine on the floor. "Now, is that any way to thank your hosts? Elizonte," he had said, "help our guest get comfortable." The thug had appeared from the shadows. Isidro remembered his surprise: Elizonte was left-handed. Isidro had blocked the hook punch with his own right arm and had slammed his left fist into the thug's nose.

He recalled Bernardo's chuckle. "Elizonte, you are dealing with a fighter. Come now, Isidro. Take a drink." He had refilled his cup and held it out to him. Elizonte, his nose running blood, grabbed Isidro's hair and pulled his head back. His other arm wrapped across his throat. Isidro could barely breathe. Bernardo handed Isidro the cup. "To your health," he said. Elizonte's arm tightened. Isidro knew he had no choice. He drank.

Bernardo had refilled the cup, again and again. Finally, he began to sway, held up by Elizonte's relentless grip. He drank one more cup. The priest removed Isidro's belt, untied the knot to his pants. He pulled them down around his ankles. Elizonte laughed and pushed Isidro to the ground. He remembered nothing after that.

"What good fortune?" he repeated.

"Your memory is addled from your excesses, I see. Let us review then. Your wife, the Judaizer, has not indulged her passion for black prayer in a while. You have paid her fine in full. She must now only recant her foolish adherence to the God of Moses who has been discredited by our Savior's crucifixion and your daughter will be able to make an advantageous match. Of course, if your wife persists in her heresy all the silver in the world will not save her."

Isidro felt the chill. His wife. His daughter. And here he was, helpless, in a room with a thug and a priest. "What do you want?"

"I told you, at this time, nothing. In ten days, fifty *escudos* for the expenses of interrogation. Your wife will be brought before the private tribunal at which time she will be interrogated. If her answers are those of a good Christian and if she confesses her Judaizing and promises never again to indulge in her heretical acts, then you will be free of worry and concern. Your position as Alcalde will be safe, your daughter's reputation will be unsullied by the taint, and you, having paid the fine in advance, will retain your material goods."

"She is ill. She cannot be interrogated. Why are you tormenting me?"

"This is not torment, Isidro. We can show you torment if you would like."

His pride warred with his fear. He was conscious of the position they had put him in, soiled, bruised and helpless. But he also knew that the Marqués was unaware of the horrors being perpetrated in his Marquisate. He had repaid the money he had taken from the City till, thanks to Don Manuel. And his daughter was safe in the Marqués's castle. Only he and Leila were exposed to these criminals. He would go to the Marqués. Surely, if he were armed with the truth he would protect him. He needed to buy some time.

"I want your promise in writing," he said to Bernardo.

Bernardo laughed. "*You* want...?"

"Yes, I. The Church, the Holy Office, is known throughout the world for its careful records. Take me before the tribunal and let me have the order and receipt in writing. Give Leila another month to heal from the terrible effects of her freezing and I will bring her before the tribunal."

Bernardo shook his head. "I am amazed by your audacity, Isidro. You did not become Alcalde by virtue of your reserved modesty! Two weeks I will grant you. In a fortnight you and Leila—"

"Señora Argenta de Costa, if you please."

Bernardo smiled thinly. "Señora Costa, then, will appear before me along with two other priests as it is customary and shall give testimony. If you fail to bring her or if you or she disappears you will learn exactly what torment means. Is that clear?"

"It is." Isidro waited. He knew there would be more for it was unlikely that this reprieve would be without cost. He did not have to wait long.

"You may go." His pants were covered in vomit and urine. Isidro looked around for his shoes and his coat. "It is not a long walk from here to your home. Perhaps a quarter hour. Surely your feet and your pride can handle it."

CONSUELO

Consuelo was true to her decision. She was more than dutifully attentive to Sor Carmela's instruction. She filled her notebook with the incredibly vast knowledge the sister was imparting. "I am grateful, Sor Carmela, that you have seen fit to teach me so much. I knew of the aloe, for burns and cuts, but knew nothing of the *caléndula*."

"Yes, the sweet marigold, the flower of the Virgin's crown, will heal and soothe, but with the prayer to the Blessed Mother it will save fading eyesight and prevent internal growths."

"And it can be found in the garden," Consuelo smiled. She had been spending every afternoon walking with Leandro in the gardens, talking and kissing. As the week had worn on his kisses had become more passionate but his hands had remained chaste. They spoke of poetry, or rational thinking, flowers, art. Leandro teased her. "How does a healer see flowers differently from a poet?"

"How does a poet see the healer?" she smiled back.

But when she asked him about Spain, he was reticent. "Your home, Leandro. What does it look like? From a poet's point of view, of course!"

"Ah, home. May it always be near you. Naked we came into this world, and naked we leave. Would that we spent some time like that in between!"

Consuelo blushed, her peachlike skin taking a rosy hue. "You are getting bold."

"Indeed, Consuelo, I have been most well-behaved. My dear friend and fellow student Juan Carlos has accused me of being something of a rake, you know. I hope I have shown you otherwise."

"You have, Leandro, and I am most grateful for your respectful behavior." She flinched less with every mention of Juan Carlos. As his arrival date neared she felt more equal to seeing him. Her daily walks with Leandro gave her confidence. "I have seen paintings of Granada, the castle of the Moors, but know nothing of the city. Do you live in town or is yours a family of landholders?"

"I am a poet, and a man of leisure. Neither farmer nor municipal servant but a creator of verse and rhyme for my lady's pleasure."

CHAPTER 5

CONSUELO

JUAN CARLOS ARRIVED WITH HIS MOTHER, and Consuelo wondered if she would have the daring to continue her walks in the garden with Leandro. The idea of Juan Carlos coming upon them unawares made her almost sick with nerves. Her entire being was rigid, she noted, with a strange mix of anticipation and trepidation. The first afternoon after his arrival, Consuelo went to the music room as had become her habit before walking with Leandro. The days had grown warmer and longer, and the air was sweet with flowers and sunlight. This time not just Leandro but Juan Carlos and several others were in the music room when she arrived.

Her resolve trembled, her steps faltered. Leandro came forward and took her arm. "Consuelo, you have arrived to make our party complete."

Juan Carlos nodded at her and she saw his eyes stray to Leandro's hand on her arm. She smiled, her confidence bolstered by the surprising realization that Juan Carlos might be jealous. "Welcome, Juan Carlos. It is strange, isn't it, for me to be welcoming you to the Marqués's castle rather than the other way around?" She held out her free hand to him, amazed at her own brazenness.

He had no choice, she knew, but to take her hand in his for the moment. Leandro's eyes sparkled as he slid them sideways to hers. She smiled back at him slightly, then turned to see Juan Carlos' lips pressed into a thin line. "You had a good journey, I hope?"

"Indeed."

"And your mother came with you, I understand. I am locked away in the nuns' quarters, as you may know, studying, but I hope that the

Marquesa will grant me a visit or more during your mother's stay."
Her voice was without tremor.

Juan Carlos simply nodded. She knew that if he behaved churlishly
the rest of the castle would gossip. She pressed him maliciously,
wondering at the source of her malice. Some of Leandro's style had
rubbed off on her, she noticed. "How long is your stay?"

"A fortnight, I hope."

"Hope it is as long, or hope it is only a fortnight?" she laughed.

"You have grown daring," he finally said quietly.

"No. You have grown shy."

Leandro laughed. "That's something none of the misses in Salamanca's
parlors would ever have said about you, Juan Carlos! Cat got your
tongue?"

Others were watching with growing amusement. "Señorita Consuelo,
I am glad you have emerged from your apothecary for more than a stroll
with Señor Almidón," a woman commented, raising her eyebrows.

Consuelo racked her brains for the lady's name. She was a pretty
woman with light brown hair drawn up in the back and falling in
curls down her back. She had green eyes and a wide smile. "You do
know Elisabeta del Gaspar," said a voice at her elbow. Don Patricio,
his old face lined with a lively smile, extended his hand to her.

She took his hand gratefully. "Yes, Don Patricio, Señorita Elisabeta
and I met at dinner the time I met you. Señorita," she said, turning
back to Elisabeta, "I have been too immured in the nuns' quarters to
enjoy another dinner with you but I am certain that I will be able to
join you more often."

"You have put your studying time to good use, I hope," Juan Carlos
said stiffly. His pale face turned red at the laughter from Leandro,
Elisabeta and others.

"I don't know what they find funny," Consuelo said with a toss of her
head. "I have been almost a ghost here!" She joined in the others' laughter.

"Irony now," Juan Carlos said bitterly. "What else have you picked up?"

"Come, there are refreshments," Don Patricio said, taking Elisabeta's
arm.

"Consuelo?" Leandro offered his arm. She took it. "Come along,
Juan Carlos. You don't want to face dinner without a glass of port or

two to steel you. The ladies' conversation can be vicious without sustenance."

"I am not thirsty," Juan Carlos said shortly.

"Don't be petulant. It's unbecoming a *hacendado*," Leandro remarked, leading Consuelo away.

Her legs felt weak as she fought the desire to go to Juan Carlos. She couldn't. Not in front of the other guests. And, she thought with sinking despair, possibly never again. She turned back. Juan Carlos was looking straight at her, his blue eyes hard. The tenderness he had always shown her was missing. She looked right into them, holding them for a moment before turning away. She could still feel the contempt he had shown in their last encounter. Had she hoped for something else? It didn't matter if she had. She had to show him that he meant nothing to her, that if he thought he could embarrass her or drive her back to the shelter of the nuns' wing, he was sorely mistaken.

Consuelo and Juan Carlos feinted and parried, she being cool while burning inside, he being cool and heaven only knew what inside. Leandro watched with an ironic look on his face, his strong jaw thrust forth in an arrogant announcement of his triumph.

"Juan Carlos seems to resent our friendship," he said to Consuelo the third evening. He had drawn her aside in an attempt at private conversation.

"That surprises you?"

Leandro laughed drily. "I had no idea I was poaching in his preserve. Actually, I would have more right, I hope, to feel he was the one poaching."

"He is doing nothing of the sort. I belong to no one."

Leandro smiled. "You are really remarkable. Of course you belong to someone. You belong to your father, poor darling. And perhaps one day you will belong to me."

Consuelo caught her breath. "Don't speak ill of my father." But the second part of his declaration rang in her ears.

Leandro threw a quick look around the room, then, taking Consuelo by the elbow, steered her out the door and down the hall. He opened a door she had not noticed before and they slipped in. Leandro shut the door quickly and threw a hook lock across.

Consuelo looked around. The room was very small, no larger than a closet, with stone walls and a single window through which the red rays of the last of the evening sun shone, illuminating dust motes dancing in the air. There were no wall hangings or adornments and the furniture consisted of a single daybed.

"It was a place for a lady to withdraw, to rest, in days gone by," Leandro said. To Consuelo it had a more sinister aura. "Are you tired? Would you care to rest?" he said with a smile.

Without waiting for an answer Leandro gently pushed Consuelo down onto the daybed. He wrapped his arms around her, and unlike his gentle kisses in the garden, this time he pressed his mouth firmly on hers. His hands slipped behind her head and he moved her head back. Her lips parted and his tongue pressed between them. She reached for him with her hands, half to stop him, half to hold him.

As her mind shouted to her to stop this madness before it went beyond stopping, a stronger power blinded her, washed the voice of reason from her mind. His mouth felt like fire on hers, fire that left a wake of desire.

The sting of Juan Carlos's rejection of her after taking her virtue was nullified by Leandro's tongue, his lips, and soon, his hands. His fingers went to the back of her gown, and he pulled the collar. The buttons slipped easily from their notches and her bodice fell open around her shoulders. He slid his hands under her chemise to her breasts. The sensation as he brushed her nipples tingled in her thighs and her head dropped back. He pressed forward upon her and she leaned back in the day bed.

He grew more insistent, lightly pinching her nipples as they grew taut. He pulled the chemise over her head, leaving her bare from the waist. He lowered his head and suckled her breasts, first gently, then harder as she moaned. Her fingers entwined in his hair as she pulled his head to her.

"Consuelo," he said hoarsely. "Lift your skirt."

"No, we mustn't."

"This is not the time to say that," he said, and lifted her skirt himself. He knelt between her legs and pushed her dress to her waist, pulling down her pantalettes and leaving her naked to his eyes. "My God, you are beautiful," he whispered, his hands going to her.

"No, Leandro. We can't." She knew she could not give twice what was only hers to give to a husband. She struggled, against him and against her own desire.

He pressed her down, his hand intimately holding her in place. He was flushed and his breath was ragged. "You're right. We can't. But we will. Oh, Consuelo, let me look at you for a minute before we stop." He pushed her back against the day bed and took a long, lingering look at her with her dress bunched around her waist and her stockings at her knees. "I want this image emblazoned in my mind."

She felt the mortification of exposure and pulled up the top of her dress. Her legs were still parted by his knees but she pulled the skirt down over her nudity. He smiled. "This will be mine. Every part of you will be mine, to look at, to touch, to possess." He bent and kissed her lips, this time a quick kiss. "Get dressed. You can't leave the room looking like a well-used whore."

She breathed in sharply but knew enough not to reply. No decent woman would have permitted this and she deserved the rebuke. He stood and re-knotted his collar and watched her struggle back into her chemise, pull up the pantalettes and straighten her skirts.

"How quaint. I had heard that colonials wore *zaragüelles* under their dresses but I did not believe it. I am sure your father will be amenable to a good match," he added.

"Don't speak ill of him," she said softly.

"I will not speak ill of him, but if I can get a word in edgewise, I will, I hope, speak seriously to him about you." Consuelo forced herself to look into his eyes. "As long as Juan Carlos doesn't get there first."

Consuelo dropped her gaze. If he only knew.

The next afternoon after her studies Consuelo arrived at the music room to find it empty except for a stranger. In the middle of the room, with the sunlight pouring in, a man in a grey cloth smock stood before an easel. He wore a white hat, which was odd since he was inside, and his dark blond hair was tied in a tail. His hands were white but splotched with color from his palette. She could not see his face since he was facing away, towards the windows, though she could see the picture. He appeared to be painting a family portrait but without the sitters. She backed out of the room.

At the gathering before dinner she saw Don Patricio speaking with him. "A painter has arrived," Don Patricio said to her. "This is Juan Rodriguez Juarez, the famous artist from Mexico City. He comes from the Viceroy, Duke of Linares, to paint here."

"My pleasure, Señorita. You must let me paint you sometime for the pure delight of your beauty."

"Oh, good heavens, Rodriguez! Don't be such a rogue!"

Both men laughed, the older Don Patricio wheezing slightly at the end. The artist bowed slightly. "I apologize, Señorita. I was simply overwhelmed."

"You should be honored, though, Señorita Consuelo," Don Patricio went on. "Usually Don Juan only paints for profit."

"Commission," the artist corrected.

"Commission, then. He has a remarkable mandate from the Viceroy. Don't you, Rodriguez? Tell her. She's very scientific, being a healer and all."

The artist raised an eyebrow. The other eyebrow stayed flat as if there were no connection between the halves of his face. He was an odd-looking fellow, Consuelo thought. He should paint himself.

"A healer? Well. How do you feel about the mixing of races?"

"My goodness," Consuelo replied. "I know nothing about it." He was as odd in his speech as his visage, she thought.

"Have you ever mixed the pollen from one plant and another?" She nodded. "And you get a plant that has some of the powers of each, right?"

"Or none."

"Exactly!" he said, beaming at her. Half his face rose up in a smile, the other side went down in a frown. "And with people it is the same thing. You mix an *Español* and a Black, you get a *mulato*, right? And an *Español* and an Indian native? A *meztizo*. And so forth. But what happens when you mix a *meztizo* and a *mulata*? Or an *Español* and a *mulata*? Then what? There aren't these problems in Spain, you know. You are either Spanish or Moorish, or deep down, Jewish!"

"He's an artist, not a poet," said Don Patricio, as Don Juan laughed at his own rhyme.

"But I am commissioned by the Viceroy, Duke of Linares, to paint all of the combinations. Happy families they are, or might be, but not of pure blood. And the Viceroy wants to send a chart of the myriad combinations we have here to his Royal Highness so he can better understand the differences that affect governance out here. The Marqués has generously offered me the chance to get away from the hurly burly of the Chapultepec Castle so I can complete my commission."

They turned at the sound of more people entering the music room. "What have we here?" he exclaimed, his voice rising in excitement. "Don Patricio! You didn't tell me!" Both sides of the artist's face were working wildly.

"Another beauty for your collection?" Don Patricio asked.

"Not at all!" Don Juan was breathing hard. "Over there!"

He was pointing at Juan Carlos, who had entered the great hall with Doña Josefina leaning on his arm. "Juan Carlos Castillo?"

Consuelo felt herself grow cold. She knew what he was about to say but there was no way to stop him. "Speak gently, Don Juan," she said. He nodded, not taking offense at receiving instruction from one so junior.

"Yes, I shall, you are right. But Patricio, what a find! An actual albino! The product of an *Español* and a *morizco,* a blend of Black and Spanish. Which one of his parents is a mix? Not that lovely *dama* on his arm. His father, perhaps?"

Dinner was grander than all of the prior meals, Lent notwithstanding. Consuelo was honored to sit near Doña Josefina, with a shy young man between them. She tried to engage the youth but he simply colored and ducked his head, spooning fish in *escabeche,* new greens, and fried onions yellowed by *achiote* into his mouth at a terrifying pace. Consuelo leaned around him and asked Doña Josefina about her visit.

"I come every year now that the boys are grown," she said. As always, she spoke slowly. Consuelo waited. "Usually for the weeks before and after Easter. Such a beautiful time. Inspirational."

"Do you write when you're here?" Consuelo asked.

"No. It is my inspiration but I need the time for the images to coalesce in my mind before they go on paper."

Consuelo smiled. Another beautiful word. She was learning so much from all of the poets. "What do you think of the new poetry, the *novatores*?"

Doña Josefina raised an eyebrow slightly and smiled. "You have been listening to my Juan Carlos and his friends. All very good for young people to try new things." She paused. "We must not fear innovation. But their images, in my mind, lack detail, and their poetry fails to move the heart and soul. Moving the mind is not enough."

"In my work moving the body is sufficient," Consuelo smiled.

"An apothecary may save a life and a poet may make that saved life worth living. We must have both."

"Juan Carlos is not a poet," Consuelo remarked.

"A rancher feeds the poet and the apothecary."

"Is he going to ranch with Joaquin, then?"

Doña Josefina shrugged slightly. She waited a minute before responding, regaining her energy for a long response. "I do not know. He has studied but is not eager to return to Salamanca or to make his mark as a writer. He says he is caught between worlds, where he longs to think but has the need to ride with the cattle. He believes he can find a new method for raising the feed crops. He will find his way but I don't know what that road will be."

Consuelo's mind flashed back to a moment in the snow, a moment when Juan Carlos had been the child of her youth. *I can tell you. You would listen.*

"Your three sons could not be more different."

"True. Joaquin was a cattleman from birth, and Ernesto, my dear, sweet Neto, was a dreamer." Doña Josefina's dark brown eyes grew misty. "He has gone north to serve the Church in the mining towns and heaven only knows when I will ever see him again. But he writes weekly and I receive his letters when the messengers come south." She shook her head and again paused. When she was ready she returned to the original topic. "And Juan Carlos, he has always been a little of both."

A little of both. Consuelo pondered the thought as the plates were cleared and the sweets were served. A poet who did not write poetry. A cattle rancher who studied at Salamanca. A lover who didn't love. An albino.

The dinner was over and there would be music in the music room. Don Juan had moved his easel to the side but the smell of the paints was still strong. Juan Carlos escorted his mother into the room and found her a seat. She lowered her rounded form into the chair and arranged her skirts. She smiled across the room at Consuelo as Juan Carlos joined Leandro. The painter approached Consuelo.

"I wish to paint the albino," he said to her. "And you. You shall pose as his wife, the pure *Española*. Though I caution you not to marry him in real life or your babies will be black as carbon!"

"What a ridiculous idea!" she exclaimed.

"That you should pose or that you should not marry him?"

Consuelo glared at him. "You are shockingly impertinent."

"My goodness, lady. You know nothing of artists! We have Papal dispensation to be as shocking as our muse commands us. I am as banal and polite as they come. Let me show you my current painting."

He led her to the canvas that was turned to the wall. He lifted the easel and turned it so that she could see. It was a large board, covered in painter's canvas, almost as tall as she was. It was divided into sixteen boxes, and there were small portraits in each box. Each depicted a man, a woman and a child. Some were colored and adorned, others barely more than charcoal drawings.

"Each one represents a pairing, a family," he said. "Here is the purest of blood: a Spaniard and a Spaniard. Their child, perforce, is pure as well. Next, we have two Indians, also noble and pure. Their child, of course, is pure Indian. But what have we next?" He pointed to a square. "Say this lovely Spanish child were to mate with this Indian girl. Their child would be a *meztiza*, right? Here is their depiction."

The boxes completed thus far were intricate and detailed. She peered into the faces. They were lifelike in their colorings and expressions. The Spanish woman, dressed in a lace *mantilla*, or head veil and rich gown, had a pious expression that could have come directly from the communion rail. The little dog at her feet could have sat up and begged.

"Your painting is beautiful," she said. "So lifelike."

"That is why I need you to pose," he said. "I can only paint from life. Lusty life mates with fecund imagination and brings forth art.

When you paint from imagination alone you bring forth only flat, dull work. I have no models here yet, though there is a vast array of *Españolas* to choose from."

"Then choose another. You don't need me."

"But you would best complement that albino. On the painting, of course. We would need a black child for the issue, though. Where shall I get that? You wouldn't have a black baby somewhere, would you?"

"You are an outrage, Señor! And I will not model for your painting!"

"But the fire in your eyes is most captivating and I would test my talents to paint that!" he added to her retreating form.

She walked towards Leandro and Juan Carlos. Standing together, the two were a study in contrasts, and not just in their opposite colorings. Leandro, she thought, though taller, was not nearly as broad in the shoulder as Juan Carlos. But he moved with a fluidity and speed, she recalled with a blush, that could take a woman by surprise. Juan Carlos, for all of his university training, exuded the power of the cattle ranch, the strength of hard work.

She was relieved at her ability to stand near Juan Carlos without trembling. Leandro took her arm. "That painter seems to have his eye on you."

"Everybody does," Juan Carlos said drily. Leandro snickered. "What, Leandro? Are you not also smitten with our country girl's charms?"

"The mayor's daughter can hardly be called a country miss," Leandro said, neatly sidestepping the import of the remark.

"And if I am country, what are you?" Consuelo said to Juan Carlos. "You were born on the *hacienda*, your father is a cattleman and your mother is a poet, and you have studied at Salamanca, yet you have no knowledge of who you are or what your life's work should be."

"You have been speaking with my mother," Juan Carlos replied blandly, and Consuelo felt ashamed. "I do have a hypothesis, though. I believe, and others do too outside the limits of Spain, that the way we farm is wrong. We can get more from the soil by changing the crops every few years."

"Oh my blessed saints," Leandro laughed. "Please, for the love of beauty and all that is holy, don't go off on that again. Consuelo, you can have no idea what it was like to cross an entire ocean with this crop business in my ear. Speak poetry, man! The ladies do not want to hear your nonsense!"

Consuelo caught the fleeting disgust on Juan Carlos's face before it faded to a mask of indifference. She opened her mouth to tell him to continue, but the moment passed.

"My mother gave me an inquiring mind and my father the gift of land and hard work." Juan Carlos reached for a glass of sherry from the sideboard. "I am the product of so much bounty I don't know yet how or where to funnel it. Is that a tragedy?"

"Indeed, it is what I am most curious about, sir." The artist was upon them. "Juan Rodriguez Juarez, your servant." He bowed from the waist in mock obeisance.

The men introduced themselves. "And you obviously have met Señorita Consuelo Costa Argenta," Leandro said, his hand proprietarily on her shoulder.

"Indeed, I have had the pleasure and I am eager to paint her. To that end, Señor Juan Carlos, you have a most interesting coloring. An albino, I believe? I have never actually seen one, although of course I have heard all about them. Though your eyes are not pink, I see," he added, peering into Juan Carlos' face.

Juan Carlos took a step back. "You are mistaken, Don Juan. I am not an albino but a full *Criollo Español*. I was born in a lightning storm which accounts for my fair coloration."

"If you say so, Señor. Though I doubt our beautiful scientist would agree."

Juan Carlos glared at Consuelo. "And what opinions have you been offering?"

"None!" Consuelo felt her heart constrict in alarm. "Don Juan, I must remonstrate. I said nothing of the sort. It is well known that Juan Carlos was born in a lightning storm."

"And does your science say that lightning causes such pallor? Surely Señor Juan Carlos was not the only soul born during that storm, or the only child to be born in any storm, of all of the people you have met. And yet, it is only he who was bleached by the light!"

"And exactly what are you implying otherwise?" Juan Carlos stood straight, his broad shoulders eclipsing the artist as he took a step close to him.

The artist held his ground. "Science tells us that when you mate one type with another, you get a cross-type. Here in Mexico we have seen more types mated and crossed than anyone has ever seen before, and we can show conclusively that people are like animals and plants. Cross a horse and a donkey, you get a mule. Cross a mule and a donkey, you get a burro. Cross a burro with anything, you get nothing. People are the same."

"And what do you suggest Juan Carlos is a cross of?" Leandro said. Consuelo shot a look at him. He widened his eyes innocently.

The artist looked from Juan Carlos to Leandro. "I have no idea," he said, backing up.

"Good answer," Leandro said. "Come, Juan Carlos, don't let this colonial *novator* upset you. We all know what you are." His words, in themselves soothing, fell like poison on the group. The artist quickly bowed and walked away, inserting himself in the group over which Don Patricio and the Marqués presided.

Leandro, still holding Consuelo's arm, turned her away, steering her towards the corner where the Marquesa sat with Doña Josefina. His voice had a bitterness she hadn't heard before. "In this colony every white man thinks he's an Hidalgo. It's Don this, and Don that, and Your Mercy and Your Exaltance! In Spain, Hidalgo still means what it should: *hijo de algo,* son of something. Here a hectare of land and you're a Hidalgo, son of nothing!"

Juan Carlos remained alone, his fair face flushed, staring blankly towards the canvas in the corner.

*   *   *

Consuelo nodded her thanks to the *menina* who had escorted her to the Marquesa's drawing room. She had been at the castle for over two months and had never before been invited to wait upon the Marquesa. "I did not even know this whole wing was here," she had told the *menina* as they walked down the thickly carpeted hallway. The walls were adorned with art in crafted iron frames, with mirrors and colored glass. The air was warm and redolent of Spring, and Consuelo's dress, in peach tones, was her favorite.

Consuelo entered the room and was stunned by the light and beauty before her. Doña Josefina sat in a chair, her blouse richly embroidered with brightly colored birds and flowers. She had a white crocheted shawl around her shoulders and her hair was dressed in a twist with a silver comb on top.

Next to her was Sor Imaculata, whom Consuelo knew from the nuns' wing, and then two young women, also in springtime gowns. A large window stood open and birdsong enriched the atmosphere. The sister motioned to her. "Join us, my dear. Consuelo, this is Señorita Elisabeta del Gaspar, and this is Doña Blanca de Cáceres. Señorita Consuelo Costa Argenta."

The young women held out their hands. "Señorita Consuelo and I have met," Elisabeta said.

"Have you recently arrived?" asked Doña Blanca.

"No, I have been here all of Lent. But I am studying with the nuns and so this is my first time waiting on the Marquesa."

"I remember my first time," Doña Josefina said with a dreamy look. "I had come from our *hacienda*, but it was not so large as it is now. I wanted to study poetry. I was so dreadfully ignorant."

"I have read your essays about your visits," Señorita Elisabeta said. "They are one of the reasons I begged my father to let me come. *Only during Lent!* he said." She made her voice deep and commanding. "I think he was afraid I would be corrupted here!"

Doña Blanca laughed, showing pretty white teeth. Her dark complexion set off her smile and her black hair glistened in the light. "And you have been, Elisabeta! You should see her with the gentlemen! All sparkles and smiles."

Elisabeta laughed back. "And you, Blanca? Your husband will barely know you when you come back, so erudite and poetic."

"Yes, we have both been enjoying the wonderful hospitality of our Marquesa. It will be a shame to go home after Easter, though I do look forward to joining my husband again!" Both women laughed, Elisabeta coloring a bit.

Doña Josefina smiled slightly. "It is very different from when I came here twenty one years ago. Then it was rare, almost suspect to want to study. But now, it is the norm."

The door opened and all the women rose except Doña Josefina. The Marquesa entered, attended by another woman all in black. The women curtseyed.

"Good morning, ladies," the Marquesa said. Consuelo took in her blue brocaded gown, square necked and trimmed in white lace, gathered on the sides to create a widened figure below the waist, and falling in folds to just above her white kid shoes. The Marquesa's soft-looking neck and round face were pale above the blue, and her hair, light brown with streaks of gold and grey, was gathered much like Doña Josefina's, into a silver comb. "And welcome, Señorita Consuelo."

Consuelo curtseyed again. "Thank you."

"Times have certainly changed," Doña Josefina said. "I recall the day I met her ladyship, the Marquesa." She spoke slowly and carefully. "The mother of our honored Marqués, Miguel Angel. I was absolutely terrified. This Marquesa has made the castle a most welcoming place, Consuelo, and you can grow and blossom here without fear."

"Josefina, you are too kind," the Marquesa said, holding her hand out to Doña Josefina. "Though my *suegra* was kind enough to allow me to study, and she allowed you too, you must recall. But I remember the fear too and have striven to make this a refuge for study and writing. Of course, my good husband the Marqués has most generously allowed it."

"I will never forget what Sor Juana Inés de la Cruz said to me," Josefina said. All were silent, fully riveted on her slow speech. The words of Sor Juana herself were about to be quoted. Consuelo's heart pounded with excitement. "She said she could not abide the idea of being *permitted* to study. For her it was as if she were begging permission to live. That was the reason she did not marry."

The Marquesa smiled. "Yes, the good Sister felt that to study was as much her right as the right to breathe, and not merely a favor to be begged from an indulgent husband."

The women nodded sagely. "It is sometimes not a choice," said Sor Imaculata. "We either serve our kind masters as wives or as devotees. If they are kind, indeed, we may study, or if they are not, we perish. As happened to our Sor Juana."

There was silence in the room.

The Marquesa broke the mood. "Shall we have some chocolate? Let us not be morose in our memories. Have you all met the artist in residence? He is painting *casta* paintings for the Viceroy."

"He is a most unusual fellow," Elisabeta said. "Half his face goes up and the other down."

"Perhaps he suffered the stroke of God's hand as I did when Juan Carlos was born," Josefina said. "I could only move one side for a time."

"Fortunately for him his right arm moves well enough to paint," Consuelo said.

"And the rest of him seems to move just fine too," said Elisabeta. "He has importuned me most lasciviously."

"And did you comply?" asked Doña Blanca.

"Nasty, aren't you today?" Elisabeta replied. "No. He is not as attractive as the Hidalgos and sons of *hacendados* that fill this place."

"He would paint you, you know. You could model for the goddess Venus."

"Blanca, you are outrageous today!" Elisabeta laughed. "I would not take my gown off for him for all the paintings of Venus in the world!"

"Certainly not during Lent," Consuelo said in a deep voice, eliciting a giggle from Elisabeta. They all turned to her.

"Has he asked you to model, too?" Josefina asked.

Consuelo nodded, regretting her sally. It was amusing to joust with the other women with wit, something she rarely had the opportunity for in her regular life, but she had to be careful. "But of course I am here to learn apothecary," she bowed her head to Josefina in acknowledgment, "not to model for artists."

"Of course. And your father the Alcalde would be most displeased if you did."

She thought of her father, blustering and speechifying at Joaquin's wedding, and flushed. She looked up to see Josefina looking at her with a keen eye. "Come to my rooms this afternoon, dear. I would like you to report on your progress."

"What does that artist want from you?" Josefina asked, comfortably ensconced by the window of her room. Consuelo had been amazed to see that the extent of the castle was even greater than she had learned that morning. There was an entire wing devoted to the ladies who visited the castle for a season, as well as a dining room for when they did not dine with the gentlemen in the great hall. Josefina had a nice suite of two rooms, a sitting room and a bedroom connected through a small dressing area.

"He wants me to pose for one of his *casta* pairs," Consuelo said, looking down.

"There is nothing shameful about posing for a portrait, provided you are modestly dressed," Josefina replied. Consuelo remained silent. She could not tell Doña Josefina the real reason for her disgust with the artist. "My son, Juan Carlos, was similarly approached."

"Will he pose?" Consuelo looked up, surprised.

"No. He was furious. Now, shall we get to the truth of the matter?"

Consuelo's eyebrows rose in surprise at such a direct approach. She was not yet ready to match it. "The truth?"

"Don Patricio sees almost everything that happens in this castle, and despite his advancing years, he hears much too. His report to me has given me some misgivings."

Consuelo shifted in her seat. To what should she admit? She had so many sins to which Doña Josefina could be referring and she did not want to voice regret for something that perhaps her sponsor was as yet unaware. "You are silent. In most incidences, the truth is easier to manage than a web of lies. Secrets fester in the soul and destroy it. What did the artist want?"

"To paint me as Juan Carlos' wife."

"You are fond of him, or you were at one time, and he of you. You have known each other since you were children. Why would that be offensive?" Her slow speech prevented Consuelo from reading much into the tone, but she thought she heard a hardness in Doña Josefina's voice.

"Because he wants to paint Juan Carlos as an albino. Which, in his deranged science, means that Juan Carlos is the product of a Spaniard and a mulatto. Which is an insult to you, my lady." Consuelo lifted her chin, looked straight at Josefina. She had demanded the truth, and there it was. In part.

Josefina laughed. It was a soft sound no louder than a whisper. "Silly girl. It is only art. Juan Carlos is not an albino, but if his fair looks help the artist picture an albino for his painting, where is the harm?"

"You are not offended?"

"He is not the first to imply some strange progenitor for my son. I have become immune over the course of twenty one years. What else is troubling you?"

"Doña Josefina, forgive me, but some secrets are best kept."

"There is a time for that, this is true, though the truth may come out at some inopportune time unless you tell it yourself."

"The truth can be fatal. Doña Josefina, some might doubt," Consuelo took a breath, "some may think that a lightning storm will not produce a pale child."

Josefina sucked in her breath. Consuelo held Josefina's eyes with her own. She could not look away or she would never be able to look up again. "As I said, I have become immune to the ravings of those who would harm me. But why would you wish me, or wish Juan Carlos ill?"

"I don't! I truly don't, though I cannot say that Juan Carlos feels much kindness towards me."

"If you have become attached to another, as rumor would have it, it is not surprising that his regard might cool."

"If his regard has cooled, as you say, Doña Josefina, it may not be solely because of Leandro's attentions to me. And despite whatever rumors you or Don Patricio have heard, Señor Almidón's attentions have been completely honorable."

Consuelo despised the wounded virgin tone of her own voice, and worse, feared squandering this precious private audience with Doña Josefina, but she felt at a loss to stop the course of the conversation. She pressed her lips together.

"Don't. It will age you prematurely." Doña Josefina smiled slightly.

Consuelo relaxed her mouth and felt a wave of longing for her mother. Not as she was now but as she had been two years ago, before the brain fevers started. The longing softened her anger with herself, allowing her to look again at Doña Josefina.

"Juan Carlos may know a truth."

"You are speaking in circles, Consuelo. Explain yourself."

She used the same words Juan Carlos had used that night out by the barn. *Speaking in circles.* And she was back where she had started, now sullied and heartbroken.

"Juan Carlos believes that I, I--" she could not say what she had done, what she had permitted, "I pretended to be in love with him so my father could borrow money. I believe he used my father's desperation and your good husband's generosity to try to take advantage of me."

"Did he succeed?"

"No." There was a time and place for a lie. "And you sent me here to study and I am grateful, I truly am, but was it to get me away from your son?" To her horror, tears began to run down her cheeks.

"I sent you here because I saw something of myself in your yearning. And to give you time and leave to establish yourself outside the constricting forces of your home. For as Sor Juana said, in some women, the need to study or learn coexists with the need to breathe, and you will die without breath." She paused to gather her own breath. Consuelo held hers. "But as to my son, Juan Carlos loves you, Consuelo. He respects you, and at one time he trusted you. Your rejection of him—no, stop, do not interrupt—your rejection has made him angry and bitter."

"Then let him tell me himself. He does not need his mother as messenger."

"You are bold, indeed," Josefina said softly, but she was smiling. "I was once bold too. Boldness may at times end badly, but I don't regret my past. I hope your boldness has better results."

ISIDRO

Isidro drove the cart himself, the City groom no longer being at his beck and call. *It is impossible to govern under these conditions,* he thought. Someone, and he had no doubt who, had undermined him so drastically that when he called for his deputy to bring him a bottle of Madeira from the City cellars the deputy had laughed in his face. It did not seem wise to order the groom after that.

Before he left he ordered the new girl who was charged with Leila's care to keep the doors locked and open them to no one. For any reason. She stared at him. *"Si, Señor Alcalde,"* she had answered. They were some of the few Castilian words the girl spoke. Let the Inquisition priest try his best Nahuatl on her. He had not seen the damned candles since Consuelo had left, praise be God. Perhaps it was better with her out of the house. Leila could rant all she wanted about lighting candles and the Indian girl would just think she was afraid of the dark, like most of her kinsmen were.

The daylong journey was tiring. Isidro stopped at an inn and ordered a light meal. He fished out an eighth of an *escudo,* tossing it to the innkeeper's wife. She glared at him as it fell to the ground, then turning her back on him, she showed him her wide rump as she bent to retrieve it. She walked away without so much as a thank-you. *Society is disintegrating,* Isidro thought as he remounted the cart.

The indignities of the past several days were erased upon his arrival at the Marqués's castle, however. The nun at the door welcomed him immediately, and as at his last visit, he was led by the obsequious page, Abelardo, directly to the Marqués's chambers. If he was dismayed to see Don Patricio, the scribe who had witnessed his humiliating meeting with the Marqués when the loan he had taken from the City was discovered, he would give no sign. He greeted the old scribe with the aloof condescension that was appropriate to his rank. "Good afternoon, sir. The Marqués will be with me soon, I expect."

Don Patricio smiled. "Señor Alcalde, he will be, with all due speed. He has received your letter and its urgency has been impressed upon him."

Isidro simply nodded. Notwithstanding the horror of the past ten days Isidro had taken the time to craft his letter seeking an audience.

Your Highness, it started, *I am in need of your good counsel. I find myself at a crossroads in my governance, which office I of course owe to your largesse and kindness.* He hoped it was clear that the governance, and not the crossroads, was owing to the largesse, but if not, let the Marqués wonder how he had caused a disruption in municipal government. *The extreme and outrageous urgency of my appeal cannot be underestimated, and I crave--* he had labored over that word, "crave." Was it too strong? Or too humble? He could not decide, and so continued with a more dignified word as well, so as to balance the two-- *I crave, and yet require, indeed, your most immediate attention. I shall wait upon you this Thursday, the fourth day of April, in the late afternoon. KYH, Isidro Costa Argenta, Alcalde of Tulancingo.*

Nothing could be clearer than that. "His Highness, the Marqués," the scribe intoned, and the Marqués entered. "Señor Alcalde," he said, "welcome." The Marqués was not particularly tall, and now that he was nearing forty his rich dark brown hair was feathered with grey at the temples. He wore his hair loose, but without those ridiculous wigs that the French style of the King had been making popular. Isidro had seen those at Chapultepec in his last visit to the Viceroy's palace—it was unfortunate that the visit did not include an audience with the Viceroy, although under the circumstances of the year that followed, perhaps that was for the best.

Isidro ratcheted his attention back to the Marqués. This wandering mind problem only arose when he was under great stress, he knew, and so he corralled his mind sharply. He must be at his most charming to convince the Marqués to help him.

"Your Highness, thank you for receiving me. The urgency of my mission cannot be underestimated, but alas, nor can its confidentiality. I ask that we be private." He threw a sidelong glance at the scribe.

"As I told you in our last audience he is my confidential scribe, and if he attends or not I shall dictate my observations to him afterwards. It is better for him to have the impressions from your own mouth, no?"

Isidro knew he would not prevail, and so yielded. "It is regrettable, but if you must so order then so shall it be. Now, may I have your ear?"

The Marqués nodded. "You come in dire urgency so let us not waste another moment in palaver. What is distressing you, Señor Alcalde?" Faced with the need to explain, Isidro felt the chill of uncertainty. It had seemed so right until that moment, but what if the Marqués instead reported him to the Inquisition? Ah, he reminded himself, the Inquisition already knew. There was nothing they could learn. "Your Highness," he began, "my family is a good Christian family." The Marqués raised an eyebrow. Isidro swallowed hard. "An old Christian family." He who repeats himself defeats himself, he thought. "But I am assailed by false accusations and so I need your protection."

The stunned look on the Marqués's face gave Isidro hope. Clearly he was not privy to the machinations of the Holy Office, or of its outpost in Tulancingo. "I am the subject of vicious rumor, subornation, harassment and blackmail. My wife, who, as you know, is suffering from a cruel illness that has robbed her of her memory but not of her bodily life-force, heaven be praised, is being threatened with examination by a priest who claims to have the backing of the Holy Office, but whose honorable, if terrifying, methods he ignores."

He grew more confident the larger the Marqués's green-brown eyes got. "I have come to throw myself at your mercy. The money I borrowed from the City, which as you know I have repaid in full, was to pay the blackmail of these disreputable scoundrels who called themselves men of God. But now, they want Leila. She is weak, she is dying, and they want to take her from me. If they do half to her of what they did to me, she will die. And she will die at their hands. We all die, Your Highness, but my Leila was meant to die in my arms, as my loving wife, not at the hands of a crow-masked torturer!" And forgetting his dignity, his supercilious pomposity, Isidro fell to his knees before the Marqués and cried.

CHAPTER 6

CONSUELO

CONSUELO EAGERLY TOOK THE NOTE brought to her by the young page. Her interview with Doña Josefina had left her both confused and elated. Her joy that Juan Carlos might yet love her played unaccustomed havoc with the pleasures of Leandro's courtship. She tore open the seal.

"No! That cannot be possible!" Consuelo stared in disbelief at the note from Don Patricio. Her father, here? Good Lord, why? Her mouth dried. Her mother. Her mother must be dead. But the note said that Don Patricio wished her to go to the Marqués's public rooms immediately, for an audience with him. He would not need to do so simply to give her the sad news. "Sor Carmela, what is this?"

"I do not know, dear. Perhaps you should brush your hair and put on a shawl and go and see."

"Could you come with me?" Consuelo asked in a small voice. "He is probably here to take me away and you could tell him how well I am attending to my studies." She was surprised to realize how much she wanted to stay. "Unless," she paused, "unless someone told him otherwise. You have not found me lacking, have you, sister?" she asked.

"No. Or perhaps better said, I did not write to your father to complain. You have been distracted, haven't you, by the gentlemen of the castle. But I doubt that anyone has sent complaint to your father. Anyone with concern for your progress would have come to me. Now go, fix yourself up, and see what his visit is about. It could be that he missed you. You have written regularly, haven't you?"

Consuelo didn't have the heart to tell the good sister that she had only written a few times in the months she had been at the castle. "I have been so self-centered! I did not think—but perhaps my mother..." She could not finish.

"Now go."

Consuelo nodded, quickly retwisted her hair into the bone comb, and took her white crocheted shawl from the bedstead. She left the nuns' wing hurriedly, and only when she got to the Portress did she realize that she had no idea where the Marqués received visitors.

"Abelardo, take Señorita Costa to the Marqués. And this time, no nonsense from you. You would not want her reporting to the Marqués that you were fresh to his visitor's daughter."

"No, sister," he replied, winking at Consuelo. "Had I known that the gentleman I escorted earlier was this luscious piece's father, I would have asked him for her hand in marriage!"

"Be gone, and come back immediately. I have other errands for you that won't be nearly so pleasant if I hear you have misbehaved."

"Come, gorgeous," Abelardo said.

"Quiet!" Consuelo said sharply, recalling from her first day that this was the only effective way to deal with Abelardo.

"Sorry, Señorita," he said. "This way. Your father is quite the fine gentleman," he added. "He tipped me very generously for my troubles. I told him all the gossip I could fit into the short walk to the Marqués's chambers. Had I realized to whom I was speaking, I would never have mentioned your walks through the garden with Señor Almidón, or Señora Blanca's enjoyment of the fine wine the Marquesa offers at her soirees. Or is it your enjoyment of the albino, and Señora Blanca's walks after dark, when you have returned to the chastity of your nuns' cell, with Señor Almidón? Oh, who cares? Of course, I didn't mention names thinking they would mean nothing to him, but if I can't have you to wife, Señor Almidón should continue to enjoy your favors, perhaps lawfully!"

"You are a fool!" Consuelo said angrily.

"Here you are, my lady. Fool I may be, but I am not the only one."

Consuelo had no time to react for Don Patricio came immediately to the door. "Get out of here, Abelardo. You are a troublemaker, that is certain. Señorita Consuelo, has this ninny been rude to you? Your face is flushed and you cannot greet your father this short of breath. Get out!" he repeated as Abelardo stood there, leering.

"No, I am fine," Consuelo said in a shaky voice. "We just walked here rather fast in my haste to see my father again."

Don Patricio raised his eyebrow in what Consuelo had learned was his characteristic habit when he did not quite believe something, but he said nothing. He ushered her into the room. It was decorated with rich wall hangings. A large desk with heavy, carved wood legs, and topped in embossed leather, took up a portion of the room. A smaller desk, very ornately carved with roses and bearing gold trim, took the side nearest the door. Large chairs flanked the fireplace, and arched windows open to the warm spring evening gave the room light. The curtains billowed in the wind and the back of the room was in shadows from the contrasting sunshine. Her father sat in one of the chairs, his head bowed.

"Father," Consuelo said, her voice thin and reedy. "Father. Is Mother— tell me, Father."

"Your mother is well," he answered as though far away.

"Thank the merciful Lord," she said with uncharacteristic piety.

Isidro looked up sharply. "Have you deepened your faith here?"

Consuelo pursed her lips. "I have been studying. Are you well?"

They eyed each other uncomfortably. *I had thought I had reconciled my heart to his, but I have not. Nor, evidently, has he to mine.*

"Your father finds himself in a difficult situation," Don Patricio intervened. "I did not know that you two were on such formal terms, for he speaks of you as his one true jewel."

Both father and daughter stared at Don Patricio. "So, Señor Alcalde, do you wish to speak with your daughter alone, or with us?"

Consuelo looked around, perplexed. "Father, what is going on?"

"Alone, if you please."

The Marqués spoke. "We will withdraw." Consuelo started. She had not noticed him standing by one of the windows, looking out, concealed by the bright light and the curtains.

"I am sorry, Your Highness. I did not see you." Consuelo curtseyed.

He sketched a bow to her and he and Don Patricio left the room by a small door in the back.

"Father?" Consuelo looked down at her father, still seated in the large chair.

"Sit," he said, motioning to the other chair. "I have much to tell you."
Consuelo felt her heart skipping and her hands were cold. She sat.
"You recall the night I found you reading my letter?" His voice
was tentative. Consuelo nodded. The memory of that day, the worst
day in her life, could be pressed down but not eliminated. "I never
meant to strike you, Consuelo. I never had before, though it was my
right as your father, just as I never touched your mother in anger.
But circumstances, circumstances overwhelmed me. You see, that
letter, from Don Manuel, saved your mother's life, at least for a time."

"Mother's life? From your business reversals? How so?"

"Who said anything to you about business reversals? Who talked
about this?" His voice was high.

"Juan Carlos. He said, he accused me... he said you had begged
the money from Don Manuel to cover business reversals. What kind
of business reversals cost you two hundred *escudos*?"

Isidro covered his face with his hands and was silent a moment.
Consuelo waited. She had never known her father to be at a loss for
words. At last he sighed. "I will explain. But I am going to tell you
something I didn't even tell the Marqués."

"The Marques is involved in your business reversals too? Oh
Father, what indiscretions have you committed?" Consuelo felt her
anger rise. "And how did this involve Mother?"

"Watch your temper, child. And if you can be quiet a moment, I
will tell you." Consuelo put her lips together. "Your mother's candle
lighting has come to the attention of the Holy Office."

Consuelo's eyes grew round. "The Inquisition? How?"

"I believe that one of my rivals suborned the maid who used to
clean for your mother, and that she told him, and he went to the
Holy Office."

"Pepita? Why would she do that?"

"For money, child. But I do not know this for sure. All I do know
is that the Holy Office got word of this and sent a priest to interrogate
me. He fined me one hundred and fifty *escudos* which I had no way
to pay. So I borrowed it."

"From Don Manuel." Isidro looked as if he would speak, but was
silent. "For business reversals, since you could not tell him what

you needed the money for." He nodded. "And how does this involve the Marqués?"

"They want more. And they want to take your mother for interrogation. I must stop them. She would never survive an interrogation."

Consuelo was silent. An interrogation. "Father, did they hurt you?" she said, finally, softly.

He nodded. "But you know me. I am stronger than a bull. I can handle it, but your mother is frail. She would die."

"Will the Marqués help you? Did you tell him about Mother and the candles and the prayers?"

Isidro sighed again. "No. I cannot. I don't know if he will take my side about the Judaizing. It could put him at risk. That has to remain our secret. But I asked him to shelter your mother here, and, er, lend me a bit more for any fines as I cannot well afford more."

"I am so sorry, Father. I am sorry you suffered, and that Mother is at risk. When will she come here?" Consuelo could see her freedom coming to an end, but her mother's life came before anything else.

"I am sending for her now. As soon as possible."

"I am glad." She noted her own selfish thoughts. No more walks with Leandro, no more messages from Juan Carlos, and no more studies with Sor Carmela. But then again, the endless hours of nursing her mother would not be as dark here at the castle. She lowered her head. "And will you be staying here too?" She tried to suppress the dread she felt at the answer.

"No, I must attend to City business. Though somehow they have gotten into the City as well and my days as mayor may be numbered."

They sat quietly for a bit, Consuelo sorting through the new information. Finally Consuelo spoke. "Father, with all due respect, a couple of things you said don't make sense. First, why did you borrow two hundred *escudos* from Don Manuel when the fine was one hundred and fifty? And second, why did your rival, whoever he is, learn about the candles? How would he know to bribe Pepita unless he knew Mother was doing something she shouldn't? Who told him? Do you know which rival?"

"You ask a lot of questions, Consuelo, it is unseemly. And I don't know the answers. I asked Don Manuel for a sum to cover my debts without specifying the amount. He lent me what he thought was appropriate."

"And what did you say about me? Why did Doña Josefina send me here?"

"That I can swear to, Consuelo. I never said anything about you. I had hoped, you know, that you and Juan Carlos might find yourselves sufficiently comfortable together for him to propose a match, but that was for your safety and happiness. Though from what I have heard when I arrived there is another nobleman whose eye you may have captured. That is all to the good. What Don Patricio said is true, Consuelo. You are my gem. My precious, precious jewel." Once again, and to Consuelo's astonishment, he began to cry.

Don Patricio and the Marqués reentered the room. Their timing made Consuelo wonder if they had only concealed themselves behind a curtain. If so, they now knew the darkest of the family secrets. Consuelo waited to see their reaction.

"Have you spoken sufficiently with your father, Señorita, to understand his situation?" Don Patricio asked.

"I believe so," she said.

He raised his eyebrow again. "I hope so. Your father will be spending the night here and returning for your mother tomorrow. It is an arduous journey to make twice in a week and Easter is this Sunday. No Christian would travel on Easter." He let the words settle. "We will make your father comfortable tonight. Sir," he said, turning to Isidro, "please follow me. I will have that rogue, Abelardo, show you to a room. When you have rested, please join us in the great room for dinner. Consuelo, ask leave of the nuns and join us as well."

Consuelo nodded and rose. "She has to ask leave to eat with us?" Isidro asked.

"Of course, Father. I am here to study, not to mix with the gentry. I will see you at dinner."

Isidro rose as well. "I am glad to hear it. You are an intelligent girl and times have changed. You will do well to attend to your studies, and with your mother safely by your side, I will be able to rest easy for the first time in months." He reached his hand out to Consuelo. Lowering her eyes, she took it. He lifted it, not to his lips, but to his heart.

With trepidation Consuelo observed her father. He had already buttonholed a gentleman whose medals eclipsed the embroidery on his lapels, and Isidro seemed to be filibustering into the man's ear with equal joy on both sides. Maybe he would find likeminded people here at the court. Leandro approached her and bowed.

"I see your father has arrived. How fortuitous."

"How so?" Consuelo asked, just barely above a whisper.

"A girl must not make life plans without her father's blessing."

She looked for irony in his face and found it. "Don't jest, he's apt to take you seriously."

"I may be, Consuelo. I just may be. Sir!" he said, advancing on the older gentlemen. "Señor Alcalde, I am dying to present myself. I am Leandro Almidón Garza, of Granada. I have heard your praises sung and cannot believe the incredible good fortune that has blown you across my path." He bowed to Isidro.

"Señor Almidón, the pleasure is all mine." He looked Leandro up and down, then returned the bow, not quite as low. "From Granada, you say?"

"Indeed, land of the Alhambra, so graceful and white, and so brilliantly emptied of its Moorish masters. A rocky, craggy city, not as beautiful by half as some of the municipalities I have seen since arriving in the New World."

"You find our cities to your liking, then? Have you visited Tulancingo?"

"Ah, not yet, although I have heard from one of its inhabitants that it is the pride of the country, run like fine clockwork. I do know that it produces flowers of rare beauty."

Isidro colored slightly, and Consuelo, within earshot but not where her father could observe, turned away so as not to laugh. It wasn't nice of Leandro to mock her father, but her father seemed blissfully unaware of the game.

"You are obviously a man of refined taste."

"The most delicate, I assure you."

"But not a delicate man, I hope."

Leandro smiled. "I see where this flower gets her wit as well."

"Where is my daughter?" Isidro asked, looking around. Consuelo stepped up to him just as he turned in her direction, carefully timing it so he would not know she had been eavesdropping. "Ah, my dutiful girl. Come, let me admire you."

Consuelo schooled her face into a pleasant expression, avoiding Leandro's eye. "Father, I am glad to see you well rested. You have met Señor Almidón?"

"Yes, my dear. A most refined gentleman. How do you occupy your time away from your lands, Señor Almidón?"

Consuelo turned to watch Leandro's response. "Oh, my good Sir. Please simply call me Leandro. I am enough your junior to be your son and not so highly placed that you should honor me so."

Nicely sidestepped, Consuelo thought. "Leandro, how *do* you occupy your time here?"

"Unlike you, Consuelo, I am not of a studious nature. I write poetry, Señor Alcalde. It is the preferred avocation for the idle in Spain."

"Best not to be too idle," Consuelo added. "You leave your mind open to temptation."

"Consuelo! What an odd thing for a young lady to say to a gentleman!" Isidro attempted a surreptitious aside, turning his shoulder so he was slightly facing Consuelo while pretending to adjust his sash. "Don't be unladylike!" he whispered behind his hand. Consuelo saw Leandro turn away to hide his chuckle.

The guests moved towards the table to be seated for dinner. Leandro took a seat on one side of Consuelo and her father took one next to Leandro. She shrugged to herself. If her father made a fool of her, it was out of her hands. She looked up as Juan Carlos joined her on the other side. *The tableau is complete. Dinner may as well end in tears as in bloodshed.*

"I did not have time to greet your father," he said. He leaned forward and said across Consuelo and Leandro, "Señor Alcalde. What a pleasure. What brings you to Court?"

"Juan Carlos! I had no idea you were here. Is your father with you?"

Juan Carlos shook his head. "No. Papa never comes, he abhors the Court. He would rather spend his days riding with the cattle. I come with my mother almost every year around Easter. Are you here to see Consuelo?"

Consuelo smiled slightly. Juan Carlos had known her family since they were children. He was relaxed around Isidro and Consuelo, clearly enjoying his easy familiarity. "You are kind to my father," she said quietly, "to tolerate his pompous manners."

"They are but one element of his person and he has at his deepest a good heart. And besides, he is your father."

She looked searchingly at him. *Let him tell me himself.*

"Señor Alcalde, you must come to the music room after dinner," Leandro said. "There is an artist here, a man commissioned by the Viceroy himself, who is making most interesting paintings of the natives of this colony. I am sure a man of your understanding and erudition will find them amusing, at the very least, if not instructive."

"Instructive? How would one find art instructive?" Isidro asked. Consuelo tensed and felt Juan Carlos draw up next to her.

"It is of the modern type of art, full of scientific import. But again, one of your experience would possibly open up its meanings to me. I would enjoy sharing your appreciation of the works."

The soup put an end to the conversation but Consuelo found little appetite despite the flavorful broth in her bowl and the luscious cream sauce on the fish on her plate. "That Leandro is mocking your father," Juan Carlos said quietly to her.

"I know. But he asks for it."

"It is rude to provide the mockery even if it is asked for. Leandro is putting himself forward, or so it appears. Why? Have you reached an understanding with him?"

"What right do you have to ask?"

"You know perfectly well what right." Juan Carlos moved back angrily. "Or is there something of an even more unsavory nature going on?"

"How dare you?" Consuelo exclaimed. Heads turned and Consuelo blushed deeply. The guests, misinterpreting, chuckled indulgently.

She felt her breath come short. The insinuation was unbearable. Did Juan Carlos think that she was up for sale again, this time to Leandro? Her outrage was not yet complete. She felt a hand touch her thigh. Leandro, under the cover of the table, squeezed her leg, then caressed her. Having already drawn attention to herself she could not move. She put her hand in her lap and tried to push his hand away. Instead, he pressed towards the center, between her legs. She clenched her thighs together horrified at Leandro's groping, and at the reaction that started within her.

"Señor Alcalde," he said smoothly, pressing his hand more intimately, "I would very much enjoy showing you the paintings." He squeezed her thigh tightly.

In the music room Leandro stayed close to Isidro, pointing out the various guests and whispering tidbits of information about each one. "You are a very observant young man," Isidro remarked.

"It is the role of the poet to see, hear, and transform the mundane into art. And speaking of art, come Sir, and let us admire Don Juan Rodriguez's production." He guided Isidro to the painting which had gained yet another square.

"You see here, he is illustrating the various combinations of people resident in the colony and classifying their issue. Here, you see, an Español and a *mestizo*, half Indian and half Spaniard, producing a *castizo*. The beauty of the painting rests not in its science, though it is illustrative of a modern concept, but in the particulars of each household. Note the clothing, the different animals and flowers, attending each."

"They look happy," Consuelo said. Both men turned and looked at her then wordlessly turned back to the painting.

"That is the heart of the painting!" Don Juan, the artist, had appeared before them. "Your daughter is a girl of great artistic sensibilities. I have asked her to model for me," Don Juan added.

"What? That is an insult!" Isidro sputtered.

"No, Father. It is not. An artist needs to paint from life and I believe I would exemplify a Spaniard quite nicely. Now, let us go to the pianoforte. Doña Blanca is about to play."

"Juan Carlos Castillo has also been asked to model," Leandro informed Isidro as they moved to the pianoforte.

"Well, then Consuelo must be right, it is an acceptable thing these days, though who would have ever known that. Will you be starting a new one, then, that you need more Spaniards?"

"Oh, Juan Carlos wasn't asked to model a Spaniard, Señor Alcalde," the artist said. "I need him to model for the albino, the issue of a cross between a Spaniard and mulatto."

"How absurd," Isidro said, turning away. "I know both his parents."

"It is the look, not the actuality that the artist seeks," Consuelo said quickly, with an angry glance at Leandro.

"It is to be hoped, since as the artist depicts, a cross between an albino and a Spaniard will produce a baby as black as coal!" Leandro laughed as Isidro's mouth dropped open like the maw of a Soul's Day skull.

ISIDRO

Now that he had a plan Isidro felt life in his veins again. He would leave at noontime to fetch Leila. He had four days before the deadline from those demons at the Holy Office and ample time to get Leila behind the sheltering walls of the castle. There Consuelo would once again be her caretaker, lifting that burden from his shoulders. He must remember before he left to tell Consuelo that her duty was to be returned to her. He smiled, his heart beating a regular beat. Consuelo, yes. He had one more trick up his sleeve.

At breakfast he sought out that young Leandro. Handsome devil he was. Clearly he was a cultured man, and with land in Spain, in Granada, that famous city, he must be well situated. Perhaps he was even richer than Juan Carlos' family. He was grateful to Don Manuel, he would never forget his kindness, but Juan Carlos was the third son, and although he would never lack for funds he would not be in control of the family wealth. At least this was not the English or Basque system that set all of the property on the oldest son, but rather the Spanish rule, where all the males shared in part but the eldest son retained the control. As an *alcalde*, Isidro prided himself in knowing about such things.

Nevertheless, Juan Carlos was not Joaquin. And what if he was, indeed, an albino? Isidro shook his head. That was not possible. That artist was a fool. Don Manuel Castillo was as much a Spanish pureblood as he was.

Leandro seemed fond of Consuelo and eager to pursue Isidro's acquaintance. Such acquaintance would be desirable of its own accord, Isidro was certain, but no doubt Leandro had some interest of a serious nature in Consuelo.

"Young man, I would speak with you."

Leandro left his breakfast plate with alacrity. "Of course, Sir. Would you like to walk in the garden?"

They left by the large double doors that came off the main hall and walked onto the path that curved away from the house. The plants were flowering, the air was sweet. "Leandro, I have a very serious question to address to you."

"And I to you, Sir."

"Indeed. Does it pertain to my daughter?" Leandro nodded and Isidro felt a rush of warmth. This could go very, very well. "Are you fond of her?"

"I am, Sir. Most fond. And my intentions most honorable."

"As am I. But she is my only child, you must understand, and I must be sure that she is well provided for. Have you spoken to her?"

"Not about anything serious. I wished first to speak with you."

"Very fitting, very proper." Isidro liked this fellow more and more. "But you know, my Consuelo, she has her own mind. Not that she would disobey me, of course." She had better not, he thought. But it would not do for this prospective husband to know how little he controlled his only daughter. "She is the model of daughterly piety."

Leandro snorted. "Forgive me, Sir. These strange spring plants make me sneeze."

Gachupín, Isidro thought, then started in surprise at his coarse thought. He would never use the word that the lower classes employed for Spanish-born Spaniards. "As I was saying," Isidro went on, "she will do as she is told but a marriage is happiest when both sides share a desire to wed."

"I hope that I can assure you that Consuelo and I have enjoyed the most chaste and proper, yet delightful, companionship during the time we have been here. She will no doubt be happy to obey your orders."

"I should hope so. But let us talk as men." Isidro raised an eyebrow. "Your family's lands are in Granada, you say. How many sons does your father have?"

"You do move quickly to the business at hand, Sir. Are you sure you have no Jewish blood in you?" Leandro spoke with a smile and Isidro forced a laugh.

"Consuelo is my only child. All of my estate shall be settled on her. And as you know, what a wife brings to a marriage may, by contract, remain within her family at death. But she has no one but me. And her mother, of course, but she may not be long in this world."

"I am sorry to learn that, Sir. And yet I hear the good Señora is being brought here."

"Yes. I go today to fetch her back. We will be here again before Easter. And you, Leandro, do you come from a large family?"

Leandro chuckled. "Large in number of sons? No. I have two brothers, two sisters, and my mother. My father no longer lives."

"Who manages your lands? Your estate? Your finances?"

Leandro shook his head. "I don't know. I am, after all, a poet. My brothers, certainly, know more than I."

"I would need to know your finances. Perhaps," Isidro took a deep breath, "perhaps you can offer a bond." Or some gold, he thought, or silver.

Leandro smiled. "Sir. I am not the one to speak of all this. I shall contact my financier in Mexico City, who can advise you of all of my assets. As to a bond, I have no more than to live on at my disposal. Surely you have sufficient access to ready money?"

"Of course, of course," Isidro said quickly. He did not dare imply that he was desperate or scrambling. Perhaps the Almidón holdings were so vast that this young poet had no reason to know their extent. Isidro would pursue the details in due course. "We will leave it as gentlemen for now. I will speak to Consuelo, ascertain her agreement, though of course she will obey me, and we can finalize particulars later. Ample time for that, ample time."

They shook hands and Isidro resisted the impulse to rub away the pain Leandro's grip had caused.

CONSUELO

Isidro sent word to Consuelo. "I wish to speak with you before I go retrieve your mother. I will await you in the hall." Consuelo arrived to find him smiling. He took Consuelo's arm and steered her to the unoccupied music room. "I have good news."

"Tell me!"

"Young Leandro Almidón wishes to marry you." Consuelo sat back in her chair. She felt hot and cold at once. "So, Consuelo, our problems are solved. Your mother will be so pleased."

Consuelo stared.

"Don't you have something to say? *Thank you, Father,* for starters. Or are you going to be so strong willed as to oppose this match simply because I have arranged it?"

"I do not oppose it." She felt the room spin. She did not oppose it, she could not. Not for Juan Carlos, though he had done so much more. She had to wed Leandro. He had looked at her naked and that in itself was enough to compromise her. She had let him, she had desired him. She felt herself blush with the memory.

"Ah, I understand. Your modesty is proper and becoming. I wish that your mother were well, Consuelo. She could advise you on all such matters as I cannot. Perhaps one of the Sisters—oh, that is a foolish thought. Maybe Doña Josefina, Juan Carlos' mother, could act in her place."

"No. I will not need their counsel." She spoke too quickly, reacting to his mention of Juan Carlos. She caught herself. "No, I will seek counsel from some of the married ladies I have met here. But Father, what are his holdings? His lands? Will I have to go to Spain?"

"I have not inquired fully about that, Consuelo. I will do so as soon as your mother is settled. And remember, not a word to Leandro about your mother's, you know..."

Consuelo's rebellious anger rose. "Of course not, Father. For if he learns of that he will not have me. He has the highest contempt for anyone with the smallest taint of blood. He would throw me on the doorstep."

Isidro frowned. "Nonsense. He will never know." He stared into space, his lips pursed. "How do you know that about him?"

"He has said as much, and more. He is highhanded and a snob about his nativity. As he was born in Spain he regards himself as higher than we are."

"Unfortunately, he is right. The one thing we cannot change about ourselves is where we were born."

Or whom we were born to. "Perhaps it would be best if I simply joined the convent," she said, her voice childish and petulant in her own ears.

"Don't be a fool. What a ridiculous thing to say!" Isidro exclaimed "And besides, they would not take you if they knew of the taint of your mother's blood."

"Of course they would. Convents would be empty and poor without women with a drop of Judaism in them."

"Well I am not going to give you a dowry to spend it on a nunnery. Leandro can do much for us, I believe, and for that reason alone you will marry him."

"You cannot force me!"

"I can and I will!"

"You sold me once, for your two hundred *escudos.* Yesterday you called me your gem, your jewel. Yes, a jewel to be auctioned to the highest bidder! You will sell me again and without even knowing what the man's price is!"

"You are mine to dispose of as I see fit!" Isidro shouted. His voice echoed in the empty room. "But you are my jewel, Consuelo." He sighed. "I thought you liked him." He put his hand on hers.

I mustn't be contrary just for the sake of disagreeing with my father. But the truth of her words, and his, laid bare the reality of her plight. "I do, Father. But he is forthright without being honest. He despises anyone who isn't him. And we know nothing about him. How can you give me away for the rest of my life to a stranger?"

"That's the nature of marriage, my dear. We bind our lives to strangers, never knowing the future. Well, the banns cannot be read until after Easter, so we can learn everything possible between now and then. I posit that you will enjoy the next several days in courtship!"

Consuelo looked down. She had known Leandro had honorable intentions towards her, and she had encouraged him, but now the reality was daunting. She would have to live with her secrets forever, and worse, give up the last of her dream of Juan Carlos.

The truth came starkly. She wanted Juan Carlos, not Leandro. But Juan Carlos did not share her desire. She was for sale, that was clear, and she would not be the one to choose her buyer.

ISIDRO

Isidro was at the courtyard waiting for his cart and horse when the messenger rode up. He had been contemplating his surprising lack of satisfaction with the outcome of his conversation with Consuelo. While he had not been expecting an outburst of joy he had certainly not predicted her vehement anger. Selling her? Hardly. He was seeing to her future the only way he knew how. Where on earth had she gotten such strange ideas?

"Señor Alcalde?" The messenger intruded on his thoughts.

He took the rolled paper from the young man and fished in his pocket for a *peso*. The messenger dismounted. "I am to await your answer."

Isidro broke the seal and unrolled the paper, which had been tied with a leather band.

"You have run off, leaving your precious wife unattended. We can only think that you are hiding from us and care nothing for Leila. We have asked, and she has answered. She is a brave lady in extremis. Do not play us false if you wish to keep her safely at home for her few remaining days. Her fine is set at one hundred escudos. On Friday, Our Lord was sacrificed by the Jews. On Sunday he rose."

Cold sweat ran down his face. "A brave lady in extremis." Good God above, what had they done to her to test that bravery? "On Friday..." His nausea threatened to choke him. "Consuelo!" he shouted. He rushed sobbing into the castle.

CONSUELO

Consuelo had not yet left the great hall when she heard his cries. She ran to him. He clasped her to him, heaving unabashedly heartfelt sobs. "Father, calm yourself!" she said, stroking his back. "Take some breaths. What is it?"

He handed her the letter. She unrolled it, noting somewhere in her mind that the paper itself was thick and sturdy, meant to last. The lettering was fine, like that of a priest or a scribe, and she expected word that her mother had died. The message, however, was a far cry from a condolence, and was unsigned. She read it twice.

Isidro's sobs had quieted but he did not meet her eye. "Come, we will go somewhere completely private," Consuelo said and took her father by the arm. She led him to that small stone room where not a week before she had lain with Leandro, their lust not consummated but enflamed. She put the image out of her mind. "Sit down," she pointed to the day bed, "and tell me everything."

"I have told you all I can."

Consuelo locked the door and stood waiting quietly. The room made her shiver but she did not budge or speak. After a bit Isidro looked up. "If I am going to tell you, sit at least." He moved over so there was room for her to sit next to him. "What is this room?"

"A resting place. The stone walls will keep us from being overheard and the lock will deter visitors. It is a haven for ladies when they feel ill."

"I must begin with something I wish I never had to tell you."

"There is no more time for secrecy, Father. It is Maundy Thursday, tomorrow is Good Friday. From the letter there is very little time. What on earth is going on?"

"Most of this I have spoken of before. But I am afraid I must go back a bit further. About two years ago I was accosted at the City by two fellows, a priest, evidently from his cassock and the large red cross of his order upon it, and his body guard. It seemed that someone had found irregularities in the City accounts, which I, as mayor, control. I believe it was my faithless deputy who had stolen City money but I could not prove his falseness and so I was powerless.

"Less than a year later, shortly after your mother had fallen ill, the priest and his henchman returned. This time they had a warrant for me and led me to a chamber underground, somewhere beneath Tulancingo. At the time I had no idea where it was, though I was to learn it later. This room, with its stone walls, is an unwelcome reminder of it. I cannot imagine ladies finding solace here."

Nor could Consuelo but she let it pass. "Go on, Father."

"I had launched an investigation into the accounts and had figured out exactly how the theft of City funds had been done, and so craftily that it had gone unnoticed until now. When the warrant came I thought I would be able to explain to the priest how my deputy had stolen money and receive their reward. Instead, as you already know, they announced that Leila, that your mother, had been caught Judaizing and that she would be called to testify before the Holy Office's Tribunal."

"You told me about Mother yesterday. It was about the candles."

"I suppose, though they never told me exactly what the accusations were. In this and in other ways they were unlike everything I knew the Inquisition to be. No witnesses, no hearing, no questions and answers. Just the two, the priest and the thug. They levied a fine of one hundred and fifty escudos."

"Which you borrowed from Don Manuel. I know," she sighed, "you told me."

"Not exactly." Isidro dropped his voice more. "Remember that I had figured out how the deputy had stolen the money from the City. Well, he is crafty, but I am much smarter than he. And so I devised an even better method and used the City funds to pay the fine."

"My God, Father. You could hang for that."

"And your mother, and you, could burn for those damned candles."

Consuelo looked at the stone floor. "Father, there has not been an auto-de-fé in my entire lifetime. I am told that the Inquisition has less power than ever, and less money from the Church and the Viceroy to fund its investigations. Why would they persecute you, or Mother, or me?"

"Who tells you this? Why would you ever be discussing the Inquisition?"

"Leandro told me. He and Juan Carlos, and many others now, speak openly about things that matter. They apply logic and reason to things, not just feelings, emotions, or even, God help them, faith."

"Well, these young men do not know everything. Even an outpost of the Holy Offices, like Tulancingo, needs money. And where there has been quiet, a need is festering. And even if they are right, perhaps the Holy Office is going to reassert itself in an effort to retain its dwindling power."

"So it was money that they wanted," Consuelo said, bringing the conversation back to the issue at hand.

"Yes."

"And you stole it from the City."

"A harsh way to put it."

"And you borrowed it from Don Manuel. Why both?" Isidro shuffled his feet like a servant caught stealing a spoon. Consuelo's anger boiled over. "Why? You were a thief, I understand, to protect Mother. But why involve Don Manuel?" *And by extension, me?*

"I was caught," Isidro whispered, "by the Marqués's auditors."

Consuelo buried her head in her arms. *Juan Carlos knows, the Marqués knows, who else? Doña Josefina? Leandro? Am I the laughingstock of the court?*

"The Viceroy, Duke of Linares, has decided to clean up corruption. What a Sisyphean task. The Marqués, in an effort to control his own Marquisate, offered to send his own auditors in to all of the cities ahead of time. Hopeless, but he has the most sophisticated auditors in New Spain. They caught me, reported back to the Marqués, and I was ordered to pay back the money in six months."

"When was that, Father?"

"About the time of Joaquin Castillo's wedding. As you know, Don Manuel was most generous. All was quiet for a time, but again, as you know, the Holy Office came calling. They mistreated me but I cannot be intimidated that easily. But they threatened Leila and gave me ten days to pay an additional fifty escudos. That was why I came here. I could not take City money again, even for such a worthy cause as your mother. I came for mercy and the Marques granted it. But the *pendejos* jumped the deadline and seem to have approached her before I could get her here." He covered his face with his hands. "Poor Leila. Poor thing."

"You must tell the Marqués. He will put a stop to this. It cannot be the Holy Office. This is a blasphemous blackmail and ransom. You must tell him!"

"I cannot. If I tell him, he could sympathize with the priests because of the Judaizing. Or he could send me to prison for corruption."

"But he already knows about the theft."

"Yes, but not about the loan from Don Manuel or the deputy's dishonesty, which I was bound to confess."

"Why didn't you?"

"Unless I could prove the deputy's falseness I would be responsible. And would you believe me if I told you I had stolen from the City the one hundred fifty *escudos* but not the previous one hundred?"

"You could prove it. But you are right, they could sympathize with the Holy Office and persecute us all for the Judaizing. Is there more?"

"I cannot go on."

"Tell me."

"The priest, his henchman, they humiliated me. I cannot tell the Marqués about it. We must find another way to save Leila."

Consuelo was silent. She could not guess what had happened to her father but it was clear he wasn't going to tell her. "Go back home, Father. If you cannot speak to the Marqués then you must take care of Mother, and go get the money you have left from Don Manuel's loan and bring it to the priests as appeasement. Bring Mother here and we can plead with the Marqués to charge these men."

"I do not have it all. In fact, there is almost nothing left. This disturbance at the City has made if very difficult to get my money from our investments. I will have to go to money lenders, pledge our home as collateral."

"Then go do that. Do something. I will see what is possible here."

"Perhaps, perhaps you could go to Leandro. As you are to be betrothed to him, maybe he will lend me the money."

Consuelo shuddered. "If he hears that there is Judaizing in our family I can assure you that he will not marry me. As to the money, I don't know." They looked at one another. "I cannot marry a man who would hate who I am."

Isidro nodded. "But we can't let your mother burn." He took her hand. "I will seek out Leandro and take up the issue of money. I will not say a word about the candles."

Consuelo shook her head. "No. Leave it to me."

Leandro met her in the library. "Come, walk with me," he said.

Consuelo put on her best face. "Gladly." She took his arm. He patted her hand. Perhaps the interview with her father had gone well.

They stepped out into the garden. "There is a nice path this way that we have not explored," Consuelo said, leading him away from the house. They walked in silence for several minutes, winding deep into the garden, past the roses and marigolds, entering a grove of papaya trees. The large leaves shaded the ground and made patterns on their shoulders.

"I have spoken with your father," Leandro said.

"I know. He told me. Are you pleased?"

"I should be asking you that. We have not settled the question yet."

"No, but he seems well inclined toward you."

"And you, Consuelo? Are you well disposed to marry me?"

Consuelo looked at the ground. She gave one last thought to Juan Carlos, his white blond hair, his blue eyes. She thought one last time of the day he handed her his sword to try, trusting her with his most precious possession. Then she put the thought away, thought of her mother's life hanging perilously in the balance. It was now or never. "Yes, Leandro."

He bent his head and lifted her chin. His lips covered hers. "Soon I will know what I could only glimpse." She pulled away, ashamed. "Ah, a little belated modesty. Better late than never. We can make our announcement at Easter and have the banns posted. It will take less than the two weeks for my financiers to make a marriage settlement with your father. We shall return to Spain after the wedding. You will like Granada, I am sure."

Go to Spain? She had never considered this new terror, that she would have to leave her homeland. "You would not consider living here?"

Leandro laughed. "Among savages? No. It has been an amusing visit and your father's assets will be welcome, but no. We won't be living in Mexico. Come, let us enjoy our new status. You must learn to obey me like a good wife." He kissed her again, this time caressing her breast. She shivered. "You like that? That's what sets you Criollas apart from the true Spaniards. Your life among the indigenous people has made you earthy and passionate, unlike the convent-bred misses from Spain."

"There is one additional thing we need to talk about, Leandro," Consuelo said, her heart pounding. She was about to sell herself.

"At least one, if not a hundred."

"True. But one now. As I am to be your wife would you be able to advance my father a sum to be repaid along with my dowry? Nothing excessive. Something along the lines of fifty *escudos*?"

"What?" Leandro stepped back.

"A small loan, to be sure." She caressed his arm, letting her hand linger as it reached his waist. She was not breathing.

"What, have his creditors chased him here?"

"Oh, no. Just some business reversals. A temporary matter, of course, until he can get back to the City."

"That's a day's ride, Consuelo. What is going on?"

"As I said, a simple matter of business. You could take it up with him. But let's not talk about that any more." She had failed. Mortification overwhelmed her.

"We certainly won't. Now come," he said, "Lie down with me under this tree."

"We must get back. Sor Carmela awaits me."

"You need not study anymore, as you are to be married."

"Oh, no, of course not," she said quickly. "But until it is announced I must continue."

"No. I said lie down, and you will lie down here now. And take it as a lesson, for when I tell you to do something, you will do it. Understand?"

Consuelo attempted a coy look. "I am sure you will enjoy teaching me that lesson, but for now let us take it as begun and not ended." She walked quickly away from Leandro, breaking into a trot. He strode after her and caught up just as the path crossed the way to the herb garden. Doña Blanca and the artist came around, laughing and kissing.

Each couple stopped short. "Aha!" Doña Blanca said. "Caught you in the act!"

"I believe it is you, madam, who has been caught," Leandro said.

"Consuelo, my dear, I understand that formalities are in the wind."

Consuelo forced a smile. "Until the formalities are formalized they are but in the wind."

"My goodness," the artist said. "Poetry seems to be rubbing off on you. Let's hope nothing else is rubbing!" He cackled at his witticism. "At least now you'll be spared little black babies."

Leandro chuckled at the sally and Consuelo stiffened. She felt his eyes upon her and cursed her failure to dissimulate.

Doña Blanca laughed again, covering the awkwardness of the moment. "I am at court to become refined, and what is more refined than a study of art!" She linked her arm with the artist and with a wink at Consuelo walked off towards the papaya grove.

Consuelo took advantage of the diversion to reach the garden doors. "Come, Leandro. I must get to my lesson. I will see you at dinner." Hastily, she made her escape.

Abelardo caught up with Consuelo as she hurried back to the nuns' wing. "Lady!" Consuelo turned. *What could this fool want at a time like this?* "Señorita. I have important messages for you."

Consuelo held out her hand to receive them. Abelardo took her hand and attempted to raise it to his lips. "Knave!" she said, snatching her hand away. "Give me the messages."

"Oh, I don't actually have them personally. I am only to come and get you."

"Well who has them?" Consuelo said impatiently.

"Sister Portress." She rushed away from him towards the door. "No *peso*? Not even a few *centavos*? You are certainly not as generous as your honorable father who gave me one of them." But Consuelo was already gone.

"Sister?" she said breathlessly.

"Señorita, your father leaves word that he has departed for home. He said he was certain that you would understand, and further wished you Godspeed. Odd, in that he was the one traveling, but that was his word."

Consuelo nodded. She did know what he meant and was glad. She offered a quick prayer for his safe journey, pushing away from her mind the images of priests and thugs lying in wait for him on the road. *May he get back in time to guard Leila.* Somehow she had to get the money.

"One other matter. After he left, the messenger who had earlier delivered a message to your father came to me. He was unpleasant and most insistent, demanding that your good father furnish an answer to his note. I did not permit him entry as your father had already left. That was when I sent Abelardo for you."

"Where is the messenger?"

"Gone, Señorita. He was furious to learn that your father was no longer within and when Abelardo did not return instantly he left."

"Lord have mercy on us," Consuelo said.

"Is there anything..." Sister Portress looked sadly at her.

She shook her head. There was nothing the sister could do to help. There was nothing anyone could do. She looked for someone to blame. "If only Abelardo had come to me immediately. But he would not have known where to find me."

"Oh I know where you were, Lady! I always know where everyone is! You were out in the garden with that gentleman. I didn't want to disturb you, you know what I'm saying?" He winked.

"You must find me immediately, wherever I am and whatever I am doing, when there is something important to deliver!" Consuelo turned away to the Sister, furious. "Why does the Marqués keep him on?" she said angrily. "He should be kept as a boot-black, not a messenger! How can you tolerate him?"

The sister shrugged. "It is God's will. And besides, he is my son."

Maundy Thursday went slowly by. The Holy Week, normally a time of contemplation and anticipation, was treated almost cavalierly by the Castle's lay occupants. There were Masses daily, of course, and prayers in the castle chapel, but by Thursday it was evident that most of the residents and guests were eager to get Good Friday and Glorious Saturday behind them so Easter could come and all the beautiful gowns could be worn and rich foods eaten with abandon.

There were no musical soirees, no genteel dancing in the great hall. Only the nuns seemed to enjoy the pall that had fallen on the Court. "It can be a time of study and devotion," Sor Carmela instructed. "Your time with us is almost up so we should make the most of the quiet. Now, bring me the tome from the library with the pictures of the plants. We will review your knowledge, for as you know, mistaking one beneficial herb for a poisonous one is the biggest mistake you could make."

Consuelo went back to the library. It was late afternoon, when most of the guests were resting, but not all. In the previous weeks she had met up with Leandro quite a few times in the quiet hours before dinner. Then she had looked forward to their meetings. Now she dreaded finding him again. To her relief the library was empty.

This could be the last time I come here for a book. The two months had been a whirlwind. From unwilling visitor, she had become a Court habituée, soon to be formally betrothed to the son of an old world Spanish family, or so it seemed. She felt the weight of an uncertain future on her heart. No, not every marriage was a leap into the unknown, as her father had said, but many truly were.

As she looked around the Marqués's library, she recalled the story she had been told of the Marquesa's betrothal. The young girl had been only fifteen when her father and the former Marqués had made the marriage compact. She said she had only seen a portrait of her intended and she had been brought to the castle to serve the strict and demanding Marquesa for several months, to learn the ways of the family she was about to join.

But that marriage had been a fortuitous one; it was a happy one. Consuelo reflected on the fact that she knew far less about Leandro's family and the home she would go to than young Felicitas had known at the time of her marriage to Miguel Angel, then the future Marqués. Leandro appeared to have a home in Granada, in Spain. He was handsome, witty and commanding. But he expressed no regard for her thoughts and would despise her family if he knew the truth about her. Perhaps he was taking as great a chance on the unknown as she was. He just didn't know it.

The little curtained alcoves were open but the door to the music room was ajar, so Consuelo took the precaution of closing it before searching for her book. At least she would hear the door open and no one could come upon her unawares. Uninterrupted, she found her volume and opened the large door back to the hall. She was relieved and disappointed. Had she wanted to meet Leandro? She examined herself. No, she hadn't. The person she had hoped for was Doña Josefina. She was deeply in need of counsel.

As she walked back to the nuns' wing she opened the book, looking at the beautifully painted drawings of the native plants of New Spain. It was a valuable work and there were few in existence. They took years to produce, each copy made by printing from painstakingly engraved etchings and bearing its own coloration of the prints. *Maguey*, for healing cuts and burns, and for making *pulque*, the slippery, foul-smelling drink of the poor. *Hediondilla*, or *gobernadora*, for snakebite and the French pox. *Verbena de Luisa* for another less deadly infection of the private parts, and *yerba buena* for almost anything.

"Getting a brew ready to poison someone?"

Consuelo almost tripped over Juan Carlos coming from the direction of the nuns' quarters. "What are you doing down here?" she asked, startled. Men, except young boys and priests, could not go past the curtain that divided the nuns' wing from the rest of the castle. Sister Portress' words flashed through her head. "*He is my son.*" The son of the old Marqués's footman, and another, higher placed maidservant, perhaps, who crossed the curtain to hide a growing belly, and stayed, having little choice after her idiot child had come. She shook her head.

He steadied her with his hand on her shoulder and she did not move away. "You seem leagues away. Is your father still here?"

"No. He left earlier." Consuelo looked suspiciously at Juan Carlos. "Why are you asking?"

Juan Carlos shrugged, his pale face turning a little pink. "No reason. And Leandro?"

"What about Leandro?"

"Come, let's walk somewhere private. I must speak with you."

Consuelo hesitated. She wanted nothing more than to be with him, but the die had been cast. She was not free to speak with him privately any more. If Leandro were to see them…

"I know a place," Consuelo said. That stone room had become her own private meeting area. She led him to the room and opened the door.

"My God, Consuelo. How do you know about this cell?"

"Cell? It is a resting room for ladies." And an assignation room for her and Leandro, a meeting room for her and her father, and now Juan Carlos.

"Resting room? What a joke! It is where the old Marqués used to take women to have his way with them. My mother told me."

Consuelo felt a flush of embarrassment rise on her neck. "Maybe then. Now it is not."

Juan Carlos chuckled and threw the lock hook over. "You could scream all you wanted in here and no one would hear you."

She thought of Leandro. "I won't be needing to scream. Now, tell me what you wanted to tell me."

Juan Carlos paced the small room. Consuelo sat on the daybed, waiting, her volume of plants still in her hand. His normally confidently calm face was a theater-work of emotion. Consuelo watched him silently until her patience ran out. "I will need to bring this book to Sor Carmela soon."

"No, I told her already that I needed to speak with you. She won't be expecting you." He swallowed. "Is it true that you have come to an understanding with Leandro?"

"Is that it? Is that what all the secrecy is? Yes and no. My father has spoken with Leandro but they have not come to an agreement yet. There are issues of dowry and the like to be worked out. Why?" Consuelo realized she was holding her breath and let it out slowly.

After a moment Juan Carlos answered. "And you? Do you want to marry Leandro?"

"My father wishes it and I am his to command."

Juan Carlos let out a harsh laugh. "Right. You are his humble, obedient daughter. Are you looking for poisons in that book? For yourself, or your future husband?"

"What is it to you? I am not yours, in any event, to command or even to question!"

"What is it to me? It's true, you aren't mine. Am I nothing to you? Does everything we were to one another mean nothing to you? You would marry that shallow, self-centered, money-grubbing Spaniard?"

Consuelo stared at him. "What we were to one another? Do you mean for the two years you were at the university in Salamanca and never wrote? Or the two weeks you were back and never called on me? Or the night you came to me because my father was in debt to yours and you could use me as a whore for your pleasure? A little bit of collateral up front?"

"I used you? You were irresistible in your chemise, but I would never have lain with you without intending marriage."

"But you did not propose marriage!"

"Because I realized that you let me have my way with you because my father had lent yours some money! Sort of a down-payment!"

"I knew nothing of my father's predicament that night." She could not relive this. She rose to leave.

"No. Wait. Nor did I at the time. I only learned it from my father when we rode to the cattle market that week. I would never have thought that you would allow me as much as you did otherwise. But I am honorable and would never tell a soul."

Consuelo stiffened. "You left without a word and the next thing I knew I was being sent away to study. I thought it was to get me as far from you as possible."

"No. This was my mother's idea, to give you a chance for freedom from your home, a home that had become your prison. And to let you learn and grow in your healing skills. I had nothing to do with it, and as you see, it did not get you away from me. I never expected Leandro to go for you. I thought Maria Elena was more his prey, as he is in the market for a rich wife."

"If he is looking for a rich wife he will be sorely disappointed." *And if he needs a rich wife, I and Father will be even more distraught.*

"He doesn't need money, he needs land. And you have none. He doesn't understand the way our society is structured here. In Spain, an *alcalde* is usually a younger son, with land but no capital. Leandro's family's land was so divided in his father's generation that he has only the family home in Granada, and from what he implies, it is mortgaged to the hilt to the moneylenders."

Consuelo winced at the last part, comprehension teasing her mind. She chose only to address the financial news. "So he has capital, then."

"I assume so. He spends as if he does."

"My father's need for capital exceeds his care for my happiness."

"Your father's imprudence has put him in financial straits, but you should not live the rest of your life with a man who will care nothing for you after the first blush of desire is past, just to rescue him from a bad investment."

"You speak poorly of Leandro, but not well of yourself."

"You said there was nothing left for me to hope for and so I will not humiliate myself by begging or bragging. Be happy. Where will you live? In your father's house? Or will he buy a house in Mexico City, near the Viceroy's castle? For he fancies himself a nobleman."

Consuelo looked away. "No. We will return to Spain. Leandro has said we will live in Granada."

They were silent. Finally, Juan Carlos reached for Consuelo's hand and held it. His hand was hard from riding, warm and dry. She wanted to stay like that forever. "Consuelo," he whispered, "no one goes to Spain. People go *from* Spain. There is nothing there. Please, Consuelo. Don't go."

*   *   *

Good Friday dawned hot and breezy. It was the beginning of the summer in Central Mexico, when the dust and the dry air started to choke one, and the rains, far off in June, seemed like a lifetime away. The mellow Spring had disappeared overnight.

Inside, the sun was but an illusion. At noon all the curtains would be pulled closed and darkness would descend upon the castle, upon the earth, as a commemoration of Our Lord's suffering on the cross. From noon to three there would be silence. No one would speak, nor eat, nor drink. The nuns would spend the whole three hours on their knees in the chapel, praying. At three, when Our Lord expired, breasts would be beaten, cries to Heaven would sound, and the somber evening would follow with meager meals even at the great hall.

Consuelo came out of Mass prepared to return to her room for the rest of the afternoon. The other guests had done the same and the nuns' wing was silent and deserted. She pulled her chair near the small window, eager for a bit of air as the room warmed with the new season. She opened the plant volume. *Feverfew, santamaria,* for fevers; *calendula,* for stomach ailments; garlic, for insect bites; meadowsweet, *reina de los prados,* one of the great pain relievers, horribly toxic in excess; *granada,* pomegranate, for cancers. *Granada,* for cancers, she thought. Tears came to her eyes.

She had not slept the previous night, tormented with worry. Her father, her poor, poor mother. Leandro. Juan Carlos. It was all she

THE DUEL FOR CONSUELO 145

could do to rise for Mass and it took even more of an effort to maintain a stoic face. She closed the book and closed her eyes. Granada.

She was startled awake by a sound in her room. She whirled, disoriented by sleeping in a chair in the heat. Leandro stood by her chair looking down on her. "What are you doing here? A man can't be in here!" she said, aghast. "Sor Carmela will kill me!"

"They're all in the chapel on their knees. A fine place to be, I might add."

"You can go to the chapel, then. You will be more welcome there than here."

"I meant on your knees. That would be a fine place for you to be. And where you may soon find yourself. I am disturbed by your chilly welcome."

"It is only that you cannot be in the nuns' wing. It is off limits to men, you know that."

"Is it only that? For I sense that you are suddenly less than enthusiastic about our nuptials. Why is that, Consuelo? Have you changed your mind since you spread yourself out before me in the stone cell near the library?"

He leaned toward her and she smelled wine on his breath. She turned away.

"Don't speak of that, Leandro."

"Why not? It is my favorite thought. And now, one of great concern."

"Concern?"

"I saw you leave the little room across from the library and you were not alone. Did you raise your chemise for Juan Carlos today? Or your skirt?"

"No! We went to talk."

"Did he see what I saw? Touch what I touched? Or more?"

"Nothing at all. You should be ashamed to speak that way to me."

"You should be ashamed. And I am impatient. I have a proposal for you, since we are to be wed. Evidently your father needs money to cover a short term investment loss. True?"

"How did you hear that?"

"You asked me for a loan, remember? And he hinted as much himself. While I was pondering our proposal I sent word to my financier in Mexico City. His report to me about your father's situation,

his potential for remaining as Alcalde, is not terribly rosy. It would
be improved, I understand, by a capital infusion."

"I am glad you are so well versed in finances. That is a trait I admire."

"Are you suggesting there's Jewish blood in me?" It was a possibility.
She thought of Juan Carlos' revelation regarding Leandro's home.
Either could explain his vehemence on the subject. But now, she thought,
was hardly the time for that question, and the answer, ultimately,
didn't matter, for he would despise her taint either way. She shook her
head as he continued. "In any event, I could offer a bit of silver to your
father in anticipation of a healthy marital dowry. What do you think?"

Consuelo closed her eyes. The trap was closing. Juan Carlos' words
echoed. Did she want to spend the rest of her life in Spain, with a
man who didn't love her? But the money would save her mother.

"It will be a fair exchange, Consuelo. Some money up front and
some of my husbandly rights in advance." He leaned over her in the chair
and taking her dress by the collar, pulled it open to the waist. "Well?"

"No!" She pulled away sharply, grabbing his wrist. She used it to
pull herself up from the chair. "We will not. Not until our wedding
day!" If ever, she thought.

"Oh, my darling. I don't want your precious virginity. That we will
save for our first night, most definitely. I cannot sleep with anticipation
of driving my shaft into you, watching you arch with maidenly pain,
the flower of blood blooming beneath us, until my strokes turn agony
to ecstasy. I will not deprive us of that moment." He pulled her towards
him, wrapped his arms around her. She shivered.

"All I want right now, in exchange for a small loan, is some taste
of what's to come." He lifted her skirt as he spoke. "Take this off."

"No, we can't. And you shouldn't be here in the first place. You
know that. They could come back any moment."

"I will not be the first man to enter the nuns' wing." She thought
of the Sister Portress. He unhooked the rest of her dress, watched it
fall to the floor. She stood before him in chemise and stockings. "No
little heathen trousers today? Too hot for zaragüelles?" He lifted the
hem of her chemise. "Take the rest off yourself," he said.

"No, Leandro. I will not. Now go back to the rest of the castle. Go!"

"Don't tell me what to do!" he said quietly, grabbing her arms.
"Think of the money if you can't think of love."

"I'm not for sale!" Consuelo cried. "Let me go and go away!"

He twisted one of her arms behind her back. He lifted it and she bent forward. He used his free hand to slap her bottom. "Ah! I understand your game now! Surprising for a virgin, but then, you colonials are part savage anyway." He slapped her bottom again. "But I will insist. Use your other hand, Consuelo." He raised her twisted arm some more and she could not hold back a small cry. "Take the stockings off. I will help you with the chemise."

"Stop! I will not! And I will not marry you, Leandro. You are a beast, not a man. Let me go!"

He pulled the chemise over her head. "Won't marry me? You won't marry me? Of all people, you think you can turn me down?" He pushed her towards the floor. She scrambled up and he grabbed for her. Her height gave her a moment's advantage, and as he was bent to reach her she swung her hand hard into his jaw.

Leandro roared furiously. "I will teach you! You think you won't marry me? You, a savage, poor wench who thinks she's too good for me!" He took her by the waist with both hands and threw her on the bed. "And your precious maidenhead? That too will be mine!"

He pulled off her stockings as she kicked at him. "Help me!" she screamed.

"They're all in chapel, remember?" He grabbed at her flailing arms. "This is nice, much better sport than I thought I would have this afternoon. Be still!" he said sharply as she landed a kick in his ribs. He grunted but grabbed her leg. His other hand shot out and clutched her between her legs. "Hah!"

She wriggled away from his hand and pushed herself to sit. He pushed her back down, hard enough to strike her head on the iron bedstead. She put a hand to her head and in an instant he grabbed her tightly by wrist. He dragged the other arm up and held them against the iron rod. Then he pulled her, naked, across his lap. He sat back, breathing hard.

"Now," he said, panting slightly. "This is an unexpected pleasure."

He spanked her lightly, then harder, letting his hand rest on her between blows. After striking her several times, he lifted her and laid her back on the bed.

She closed her eyes as he looked her over. She was nude, and though he was fully dressed, she knew what he would do next. She heard his belt unbuckle. "If I don't marry you," he said, "no one else will. You will be sullied, ruined, and worthless. And if I don't go forward with the wedding, don't think you will be able to get your father to force my vows. I will be gone before your belly starts to show."

She knew that she must stop him, though the initial damage had been done months before, and pennyroyal tonight could repair the rest. Where one sin had gone unpunished the next would go unrewarded.

Keeping her eyes tightly closed she felt him mount her. He pushed her legs apart and knelt between them. His fingers parted her and plunged inside, preparing for his entry. She thought back to the night Juan Carlos had come to her. She had been scared but willing. Now she was neither. She would have taken the money, she knew, but now it would not be offered. She had one weapon left.

"If you take me you will be the one ruined," she said.

He laughed. "I told you, I will be long gone."

"You will be tainted. It is you who will never be wed after that. I am contaminated."

He pulled back from her. "You are a virgin. How can you be diseased?"

She squirmed away slightly. "I only tell you because you will otherwise shame me. I have a colonial pox. It is not the type one dies from, but men will itch and burn for months without respite. If you leave me with child my family will be shamed and I will be forced to live in the convent forever. But you will suffer too, and your member will ooze pus for months and months. Women, alas, cannot be helped, but for men the herb that cures it can be obtained. Of course it does not exist in Spain," she added.

"You lie," he said. "Shut your mouth or I will put it to better use."

But she saw doubt in his eyes. She heard a rustle outside. It must be near three and the bells would soon ring. Another sound. The door opened slowly and the figure of a man was outlined. "Get away!" she screamed. "Get away from me!" Leandro lunged at her.

"I'm sorry!" came the voice and her door slammed shut. Abelardo. Leandro froze. Consuelo screamed again. "Get Sor Carmela!"

The sounds of feet running mixed with Consuelo's screams. "Help! Help!"

"What in the devil? Shut up!" He put his hand over her mouth. "Be quiet!" He scrambled off her. "You poxy bitch!" he shouted grabbing at his clothes. The sounds of running feet returned. She pulled her dress over her, without the chemise, and buttoned it partly. Leandro had his pants up and was buckling his belt when the door flew open.

Abelardo stood there wide-eyed, with Juan Carlos behind him. "I have a message for you, Señorita," Abelardo said, holding out a rolled paper, sealed and tied in leather. His hand shook as he held it out. Consuelo stood motionless, staring at Juan Carlos's ice blue eyes.

CHAPTER 7

CONSUELO

"YOUR FATHER HAS CHOSEN TO REMAIN at his home but your mother will spend the feast of Easter with us. On Sunday you may obtain your mother's release with the payment of her fine. Or on Monday, she will learn to swim in the floating gardens of Xochimilco. Until then we will instruct her in the ways of the Lord. You may come and collect her, if you choose, by attending Easter Mass at the Church of San Bernardino, north of the market in Xochimilco. We will make ourselves known to you, and you alone."

The silence in her ears was deafening. She turned her back on the three men and buttoned her dress. She did not pull on her stockings but she slipped her feet into the shoes that she had discarded while she had been reading, and despite the warmth of the afternoon, she pulled a shawl around her shaking shoulders. Then she addressed them all.

"Abelardo, please return to Sister Portress."

"But you said I was to find you, wherever you were," he bleated.

"There is nothing to fear. You have done right and you will be rewarded. Now go, and only speak of this, if you must, to her. Gentlemen, you may withdraw. Leandro, if we had a contract, it is at an end." Her mouth was dry. "Please leave now, both of you. The sisters will be returning and our lives are already too complicated by half."

If they didn't leave immediately she was going to collapse in front of them.

"*If* you had a contract? Leandro, if you did not, Consuelo's present condition will require more than a dismissal to make it right." Juan Carlos said haughtily.

"Juan Carlos, I thank you, but not now. Please, both of you." Her voice was starting to crack and her hand had dampened the note so much that the ink was staining her fingers.

"I will answer him," Leandro said. "She is no better than a strumpet with a higher price. And a poxy one at that."

"You will answer, and more, for that." Juan Carlos grabbed Leandro's lapel.

"She is not worth shedding blood over, Juan Carlos. But if you touch my coat again I will be forced to recognize the insult."

The sounds of the returning nuns made them both turn. It was too late to get out undetected. "We will name our terms later," Juan Carlos said, walking out of the room.

Leandro turned to Consuelo, who stood, still clutching the shawl to herself. "You may speak to your father if you dare. If you do not I will tell him myself of your shameful condition." He spat on the floor, and bowed to the diminutive Sor Carmela as he passed her, standing with her eyes popping, at the door.

As soon as he was gone, Sor Carmela stepped through the doorway and shut the door. "This is scandalous. You cannot receive men in here. You know that. And what shameful condition have you brought upon yourself?"

"None, Sister," Consuelo said, her reserves drained. "None. Though not for Leandro's lack of trying."

"You are half dressed and there were two men in your room. That in itself is enough to be shameful. Why were they here? On the most holy of days? Why are you undone, like a streetwalker after a client?"

"How would you know what a streetwalker looks like after a client, Sor?" Consuelo regretted her words as they left her mouth but her nerves were raw and her self-control had vanished.

"Your education here is ended, Consuelo. I will report your loose tongue and looser morals to Doña Josefina, who had so generously funded your instruction. You may leave on Monday, after Easter."

"I will go. But there is an explanation."

"No doubt, but all that explanation would be is words. I saw, and the other sisters saw, the men emerge from your room and you standing there half dressed. You should have stayed in chapel, on your knees, praying for your soul. "

Leandro's foul words echoed. She shook them away.

"No? You disagree?" Sor Carmela asked, her voice rising with increasing outrage. "On the day of Our Savior's death, in the darkest hours, you are entertaining not one, but two men in your room, in our sacred hall which is as an extension of the convent, and you have no need to pray? The modern thoughts you have engaged in have destroyed your maidenly piety, to say nothing of your maiden condition."

"It was not thinking that destroyed me, Sor."

Sor Carmela went on, unheeding. "Some women can manage to become educated, and I thought you were one of them, but the others are too weak and are corrupted by learning. I blame myself. Your mind is strong for learning and you are a gifted healer, but I should have known when you questioned me about the need for prayer as well as careful dosage. You are the type of healer who will misuse the herbs and fail to bring our Lord into your ministrations. You are a dangerous person, Consuelo, and I will not add to the possible harm you may do by continuing your instruction."

Sor Carmela stopped and took a deep breath. The tiny older woman was wheezing with the exertion of her speech and her fury. Consuelo reached out her hand. "A bit of *yerba buena* and some chocolate, for the wheezing, Sor. I am not bad, nor am I corrupted. I was studying when Leandro entered uninvited. My father had talked of a marriage contract and Leandro wanted to take his rights before they were due. I fought him off, and Juan Carlos, hearing my screams, came to my rescue. That is all. I know that the shame is mine, but the fault is not."

"A man of Señor Almidón's refinement does not presume to take a lady of character's virtue in advance of marriage unless he believes himself to be, by her actions, so invited."

Consuelo took back her hand which had been left hanging in the air. "You do not need to forgive me, Sor. My education was to end in a fortnight anyway and I am deeply grateful for everything you taught me. But I have received distressing news from," she paused, "from home, and will doubtless leave shortly. I will not trouble you now for I must dress." She looked down at herself. She truly must appear wanton, her dress mis-buttoned, gaping over her bare skin in places.

"Go with God, then," Sor Carmela said, turning away. "I am deeply disappointed in you but I will do what I can, without lying, to minimize the tarnish to your reputation by your foolish and wanton behavior."

ISIDRO

Isidro worked at the rope that tied his hands to the bed where Leila had been sleeping when the men had entered the house. The knuckles on his right hand were swollen and he could not move his fingers, broken no doubt on the hard head of Elizonte. But there had been three of them this time. And though he had broken several noses, ribs and, he thought, a jaw, and none of them his, they had gotten Leila in the end. Against his will he wept.

The sun was coming in the bedroom window so it had to be late afternoon. He had arrived home on Thursday night, anxious and hurried, and his relief at seeing Leila asleep had given him a false sense of security that he could only regret. His wife was safe, his daughter as good as betrothed to a gentleman, the money could be gotten through him, he was sure, and now that he was home nothing could harm Leila. He had lain down beside her, wrapped his arms around her as she slept, and fallen into a deep sleep himself.

They had come at dawn, just as the world was reawakening. Isidro, still exhausted from his worries, his journey and his relief, still slept. He heard the door open as if in a dream. He had locked everything up but no home was a fortress. He shook himself awake only to find Elizonte's ugly face close to his. Father Bernardo reached for Leila while Elizonte held him down. From his disadvantaged position on the bed the fight was difficult but a surge of energy had allowed him to escape his attacker's assault.

He rolled off the bed and smashed Elizonte's ribs in. Isidro remembered without thinking that Elizonte was left handed and dodged to his own left instead of right. Isidro could fight with either hand and the advantage it had given him as a boy had not been forgotten. He was much taller than Elizonte, as well, and he followed with a jab down at his nose. It was the second time Isidro had hit him there and this time Elizonte had seen it coming. He turned his face away and Isidro felt his knuckles break on the man's jaw.

His rage spared him the pain of the breakage, as did the satisfaction of seeing the lower half of Elizonte's face go one way, the upper half the other. A roar of pain from the man brought a third through the door. The shock of seeing his own deputy rush into the room momentarily distracted Isidro, and then his vision was blurred by the men hurling themselves upon him.

He had fought to the end, but his last thought as he saw Father Bernardo carrying Leila, sleeping or unconscious herself, out the door, was that of despair. They were taking her away and he would never see her again.

Most of a day had gone by. He had regained consciousness several times but his disorientation was so complete that it was not until now that he was fully aware. The church bells were ringing, it had to be three in the afternoon. He recalled that it was Good Friday. The kitchen help and the girl who helped care for Leila would all be at Mass. No one would be coming to the house until now. They had chosen their day well.

When the timid knock came he knew that the native girl had come to check on Leila. She entered and stepped back when she saw Isidro, bloody and tied to the bedstead.

"Come here," he said softly. "Untie me."

She understood enough Spanish and the need was obvious. Then she tended to his cuts and bruises, patting gently with a warm cloth. "Thank you," he said in Nahuatl. She smiled and cast her eyes to the ground.

He dismissed her, asking for a bowl of soup. He needed to come up with a plan. He had to find Leila, get her back, get her free. He had no idea where to begin but that would not stop him. Nothing would stop him, nothing ever had. He would find her and bring her home.

CONSUELO

Juan Carlos and Josefina sat in her sitting room watching Consuelo pour herself a cup of chocolate. The cup clattered in its saucer and Josefina reached out to steady the pot before Consuelo dropped it. Juan Carlos took a sip of Madeira. Josefina's thin, lacy shawl set off her caramel colored skin and enlivened her plain yellow muslin dress. She looked composed and elegant without the least bit of pretention. *I would like to look that calm,* Consuelo thought.

After she had pulled herself together from her interview with Sor Carmela she had sent word to Juan Carlos, asking him to meet her in the music room. She had showed him the note and begged a meeting with his mother. He had read it in silence and handed it back to her. Saying only that he would see what he could arrange before dinner, he had left the room. Consuelo had sat in the library staring at a page in a book she didn't read, awaiting his return.

Men were the same, all of them. He had taken her part against Leandro but it was amply clear that he would not hold her blameless.

Now she looked from mother to son with eyes dulled by fear and worry. They waited quietly, both sharing the traits of patience and measured speech, one by nature, the other by experience and necessity. She, herself, felt possessed of none of those qualities. *If only they would ask me something it would be easier to begin.*

When it became painful to sit in silence she took the plunge. "Doña Josefina, I am desperately in need of your help, your counsel. My mother, and most likely my father as well, are in grave danger. I must do something."

She handed the note to Josefina. "This is quite a threat," Josefina said after reading it. "Do you know why?"

Consuelo nodded miserably. The time had come. "My mother is a Judaizer." Juan Carlos breathed in sharply but Josefina did not react. "Not a very great one," Consuelo temporized. "She only lights her candles on Friday and says an incomprehensible prayer. Or did, before she became ill. That is all. But this is the result."

Josefina shook her head. "I know that. She spoke to me of it over ten years ago."

ROSA, 1693

The room was hot, unbearably hot. Leila choked on the steam of the tea that Rosa offered. "Breathe, Leila. You must breathe regularly. Inhale!"

"I am, Mother. I am. I can't get any air!"

"Shhh, the midwife will be here soon. Breathe, Leila."

Leila gasped as the pain tore through her. There was no rhythm to the pains. They came and went with such speed that she could not count between them. "Hurry!" she cried out as another pain crested and crushed her.

The midwife came in with her bouquet of herbs and her birthing bowl. She knelt between Leila's thighs and pushed her hands inside her. Leila screamed.

"Get water. Hot. Get away from that tea, it's worthless!" the midwife said, knocking the cup Rosa held to the floor. She grabbed the pitcher of water from Rosa. "Get back. You are a hindrance."

Leila writhed on the pallet. Sweat poured off her face, the smell of blood filled the room. The midwife pressed on her belly and Leila groaned, a guttural sound that hung in the damp air. The midwife lit the herbs and the smoke swirled around them.

Another hour passed. Leila's sobs were almost soundless, her will to live ebbing with each pain. The sheet beneath her was soaked through with blood, and the air was thick with smoke and steam.

Suddenly Leila arched back, her face twisted, and her eyes rolled back into her head.

"Four dead boys you've pulled from this girl," Rosa cried. "Four dead boys with their cords around their necks. Get away with your bowls and your smoke and your herbs! Go!"

The midwife stood, swaying on her feet. Her hands were bloody to her elbows. "I cannot save this baby and I may not save the mother. Call for a priest, her time may be at hand."

Another pain; Leila was far too weak to scream.

Rosa fumbled with a drawer. She pulled out two silver candlesticks, two white, pure candles. Tears ran down her cheeks as she pulled a stick of smoldering herbs from the bundle. She approached the candles, started to make the sign of the cross, then stopped. She wiped her hand off, almost as if cleaning off the sign she had almost made.

She raised the stick to the wick of the candle. She shut her eyes. "Baruch ata Adonai, eloheinu melech ha olam, asher kidshanu b-mitzvotav, vitsivanu, le hadlik ner shel shabbat."

"Jew!" the midwife screamed. "Jew! No wonder the babies are born dead!" She threw her bowl on the floor, spat, and stormed from the room. The candles flickered as the draft from the opening door blew clean air into the close quarters.

Leila moaned and her legs opened. Rosa knelt between her thighs, reaching down to the black-haired head that crowned through the stretched skin. She pulled gently, repeating the prayer. Another moan and Rosa had the head in her hands, the little red body slipping out, wriggling and landing on the blood-soaked pallet.

The cord was not around her neck. Her face was not black and purple. She opened her mouth and with a gasp took her first breath, the breath of life, and with a great cry, Consuelo, our consolation, brought life back to the world.

CONSUELO

"She did it to save your life," Josefina said.

Consuelo felt her tears on her cheeks. "Yes. But now it will end hers, and horribly. My father says this in not the first threat. He has been threatened several times, and that was why—," her voice broke.

"Why he borrowed the money from Don Manuel. To pay the fines."

Consuelo nodded. Could she tell them the rest? She decided not to. This was the worst of it, anyway. "We cannot let anyone know," she said, "or the Inquisition will have us imprisoned."

Josefina nodded. "This is not the way of the true Holy Office. Their methods, cruel as they are, do not involve skullduggery." Her voice, always slow, became labored. "There are times when the Holy Office does not know what its outposts are doing. There are rogue priests and they have no scruples or boundaries."

Juan Carlos looked at his mother whose face had darkened. Her breathing was uneven. "Are you well, Mother? Can I get you some help?"

"No, Juan Carlos, my love. I am well. Sometimes memories are so powerful that one relives them with almost as much pain as the events themselves. But no, I am fine."

Juan Carlos spoke gently, putting his hand on Josefina's. "Mother, know that I am here and ready to serve you however you need me."

"You are a good son, Juan Carlos. Now, Consuelo, we must look at that note again. It says your father has remained at home but your mother has been taken to Xochimilco. To me that means they kidnapped her. Your father, as I know, would never let them take her voluntarily."

Consuelo sobbed. "It's true. He would fight to the death. Oh, God, do not let him be dead!"

"You love your father dearly, don't you," she said softly.

"Yes. Despite all. He is a strong and brave man, for all his shouting and pomposity. He loves me and only wants the best for me. Oh, let my mother be unharmed! She will not live long but she should not die in the hands of torturers!" She bit her lip to stop herself from sobbing again. This was no time for weakness.

"If your father wants the best for you why did he betroth you to Leandro?" Juan Carlos said bitterly. "For money? For status? Though Leandro can only offer an old name, not a hectare of land to his account."

"You were betrothed to Leandro?" Josefina asked. She spoke to Consuelo, but looked at Juan Carlos.

"I misjudged her and the situation," he answered his mother. They appeared to be speaking their own private language.

"Indeed. But this is past?"

Consuelo nodded. "He wanted to—he wanted some of his husbandly rights ahead of the nuptials, in exchange for giving my father a loan of the silver he needs to pay more blackmail to these thugs. Father had approached him to discuss dowry and suggested a loan. I am ashamed, as he also has borrowed from your husband, but you understand what pain he is in."

"Did Leandro succeed?" she asked.

Consuelo looked up at the bluntness of the question, feeling her face burn. "Not quite. I told him that if he did not wait I would not marry him. In his fury at my rejection he demanded his full husbandly rights. I told him I had the colonial pox, and while he would get me with child and shame me before the world, he would itch and ooze for the rest of his days."

Josefina chuckled. "I assume that isn't true?"

Juan Carlos looked pale. Consuelo smiled through her tears. "No. But I had studied the herbs for it earlier in the day and it seemed that would buy me respite. It did, and then Abelardo and Juan Carlos came in, ending the attack."

"Thank heavens for that," Josefina said. Something in her voice made Consuelo wonder at hidden meaning, but she had no mental strength to figure it out.

"So your father was willing to give his daughter to a stranger for money," Juan Carlos said, shaking his head.

"The depths of his despair have driven him to actions he never would have considered in better days," Consuelo said. "And he thought Leandro was a gentleman. I did too," she added, casting her eyes down. "I confess, I was not completely against the match, not at first. I encouraged him until I began to see his true nature."

"I warned you about him," Juan Carlos said.

"But that was for your own purposes."

"Both," he said. "For mine, and for yours. I misjudged you, Consuelo. I am deeply, deeply sorry. If I had not, you would not be in this horrible predicament. Forgive me."

Consuelo looked at his blue eyes. She hoped he was sincere but she no longer trusted her own instincts. "And I misjudged you. I thought if you knew of my mother's practices you would run from me at best, and report me at worst. To think you knew all along."

"I did not, my mother did."

"I met a Jew once, a long time ago, when I was but a young woman," Josefina said. "He read the most beautiful poetry and I learned a great lesson from him about what we must do to survive. I have never forgotten him and cannot hate his kind." Josefina's eyes clouded with the memory.

"And I find those hatreds anathema," Juan Carlos added. "They do not stand up to critical thinking. Leandro, enlightened though he claims to be, would have spurned you *and* reported you to salvage his own pride."

"I know. I could not live that lie. But now we must think of my mother. I must go to her, but I am afraid it is a trap. They will have both of us, and my father will be bankrupted. And we, we could be tortured..." She shuddered.

Juan Carlos took her hand. "We will come up with a plan. I will go and rescue your mother. I can't imagine if it were you, Mother--I would be distraught. No, I would kill them. I will go and bring Señora Leila back here."

Consuelo shook her head. "I must go. They will only give her to me, it says they will, on Sunday. I must bring money. But in case they refuse me or take me prisoner, you will know where I am."

They sat quietly, holding hands. Finally, Juan Carlos spoke. "I love you, Consuelo. I don't care if your mother Judaizes, your father dug a financial pit for himself, or Leandro violated you."

'He didn't. And none of those things would be my failings, they would be the failings of my family. Judge me for myself, Juan Carlos, as I will judge you."

"Brava!" Josefina said. "Now that is the Enlightenment made flesh. Juan Carlos, what do you say? Can you love Consuelo for herself?"

"All of her," he replied.

"And you, Consuelo, can you love Juan Carlos for himself? With all the failings he brings with him?"

"What failings, Mother?" Juan Carlos said, half laughing.

"You are quick to judge, you are slow to forgive."

"Not slow to forgive," Consuelo said, "and I do love you, Juan Carlos. This sounds like a marriage ceremony, Doña Josefina."

"Well, it cannot be, but it can be your betrothal ceremony. Now, about your parents. We cannot do this alone, we must get help."

"Whom can I trust, besides you two? I cannot risk the exposure of my mother for it is I who lit the candles for her when she fell ill. I cannot tell anyone about this."

"There are two you can tell, and you must. The first is Don Patricio."

Consuelo sat back in her chair. "The Marqués's confidential scribe? Never! He will go to the Inquisition immediately!"

"He will not. And he will help you. The second you will learn in time. There is no time to waste. It is Friday evening and you have but 'til Sunday. Your father may need help before then, as well. We will beg audience with Don Patricio for after dinner tonight. And keep your promise to one another secret until I tell you."

Josefina leaned back, exhausted from so much speech. Juan Carlos stood and kissed her brow. "Mother, I am grateful and honor you with all my heart."

Consuelo did the same. "I must lose my own mother soon, I am afraid, but I am grateful to gain you as my second mother now. Thank you, Doña Josefina. I will trust, and in that trust, regain hope."

*   *   *

"Don Patricio will see you in his office after the evening meal," Doña Josefina told Consuelo as she walked slowly to her chair at the dining table. Juan Carlos appeared and helped his mother to sit and Consuelo arranged Josefina's shawl around her shoulders. "For now, except for Don Patricio, to whom you must tell everything—everything,

Consuelo—you should keep your betrothal a secret. It is too soon since rumors of your engagement to Leandro began swirling for there to be other rumors about you."

"Too late," Consuelo said. "Elisabeta and Blanca already came around asking if it was true that I had been caught *in flagrante delicto* with Leandro in the chapel. I can imagine the source."

"Leandro?"

"No. Abelardo. He's the half-idiot page for the sister Portress."

Josefina nodded. "They do well to keep him on, sheltered from the world. It is the castle's fault he was created and he is the castle's responsibility to maintain. But he should not be speaking out of turn."

"It could be Leandro himself circulating rumors to tarnish you further," Juan Carlos said, "in which case I now have three reasons to kill him."

Josefina put her hand on her son's arm. "Do not. Do not engage in any more foolishness. You got Consuelo, let him have his pride."

Juan Carlos took his mother's hand off his arm but did not answer.

Dinner was a brief affair in keeping with the solemnity of Good Friday. Rice, beans and tortillas, with a flavorful salsa of chopped tomatoes, onions and chiles, were served to the guests, followed by a dish of nopales in lime and salt. Wine was offered and bitter drinks of chocolate as well, after dinner, but neither meats nor sweets were served. Consuelo felt the rightness of the meal, the penitence of the holy day. Leandro did not appear for the meal.

After dinner Consuelo took her leave and went back through the labyrinth of hallways to the Marqués's private quarters. She gently knocked on the office door. It swung open and she entered. Don Patricio shut the door behind her and threw the lock.

"Sit down, my dear girl," Don Patricio said, indicating a hard, armless chair in the middle of the room. Consuelo looked around, suddenly afraid. The room with the thick wall-hangings and carpets that had looked so inviting when she and her father had stood together not four days before now looked terrifying.

Instead of sun streaming in the windows to light the room, the shutters were closed and wall sconces were lit, casting their light upwards, and shadows down to the floor. Don Patricio stood in front of the small desk at which he had been seated the last time but the big desk where the Marqués had sat now had a new occupant: a white-haired, pale-faced man with a priest's cloak over his dark jacket.

Consuelo shot a look of panic to Don Patricio but he simply nodded at the chair. Consuelo sat. There was no table in front or next to her, nothing around her. Candles on Don Patricio's desk and the large desk both gave light to where she sat, but the men were in shadow, and once she was seated she could barely make out more than the stranger's outline.

"Doña Josefina advises that you wished an audience with me," Don Patricio said. "I am here. Speak your mind."

"My plight is of a private nature, Your Mercy. I cannot speak with a stranger."

"He is essential to your solution. You may speak freely in front of him."

"I must at least know who he is!" she exclaimed.

There was a rustling from behind the desk, and the man emerged. He was not more than Consuelo's height, and slim. His white hair was thin at the crown and fell to just above his collar. His collar, however, was the most disconcerting in that it was the raised collar of one high in the Church hierarchy. His eyes were light, though in the gloom she could not make out the color, and they were narrow.

"Señorita, I am a friend of Doña Josefina and godfather of her son, Juan Carlos. You may call me Your Grace, but you need not know my name at this time. Whatever you could say to Doña Josefina you can say to me."

Your Grace? Consuelo fumbled in her mind for the office that went with the appellation. She pulled her arms into herself in fear. She could not speak about her mother before an officer of the Church and most definitely not one who was addressed as Your Grace.

"It has been a mistake," she said to Don Patricio. "I am sorry to have bothered you." She turned towards the door.

"Foolish girl," Don Patricio said.

"Stay," the priest said at the same time. His voice was soft and low, but she was riveted to the sound. "She is not foolish, Don Patricio. She is merely terrified. Come, Consuelo, sit down." He put his hand on her arm and she could feel its warmth through the thin fabric of her dress. "Of course you are afraid but you must tell us everything. As I said, I am Juan Carlos' godfather. I will not let any harm come to him, or by extension, to you."

Consuelo sat. He had assessed it right: she felt a terror she had never before experienced. She could not fight her way out and if her words condemned her, they could condemn her mother and her father too, to horrible, painful deaths. Or at least to torture, imprisonment, and unaffordable fines.

Her mind veered between terrified extremes. Could Doña Josefina have betrayed her or played her false? She dared not believe that. And Doña Josefina would never betray her own son. Perhaps that was why the interview had been arranged for her alone. Or had Doña Josefina not been safe in trusting Don Patricio with Consuelo's story?

Now all was at risk. She needed to decide whether to proceed or withdraw. The fate of her family hung in her judgment. She started to shake, a sick, unstoppable trembling. She pressed her knees together and clenched her teeth to keep from chattering.

"Patricio, get her something, some Port to steady her."

"I don't need anything," she rasped, as Don Patricio went to the rear of the room. She heard glass clink against glass and Don Patricio returned and held out a small cup. She looked at the priest who nodded. She took the cup and, with great effort not to spill it, sipped.

The warmth of the wine had its effect and she felt some calm return.

"Now, we do not have all night, Consuelo. We know some of the story, but not all. Please, tell us the problem. We may have a solution for you."

Consuelo closed her eyes and took a breath. *Mother, if I am wrong, forgive me. I will do this for you.* She opened her eyes and looked straight at the priest.

"My mother, Leila Argenta de Costa, has been taken by the Inquisition for Judaizing. Her error was to light candles on the Sabbath, which is Friday, and say a prayer. She did this because I was the only living birth she was granted, after four stillborn boys, and only by this prayer did I survive. Her health has declined this year with a brain fever that all the herbs and medicines of the apothecary have been helpless to stop. Each day she became less present and less grounded in reality.

"My father, the mayor of Tulancingo, was approached by the Holy Office, but not in the way that we have been taught is the correct and honorable way the Inquisition operates. There has been no trial, only a series of fines and payments. My father stole from the City coffers to pay those fines, borrowed to repay the thefts, and then was threatened with more fines. If he did not pay them, my mother, who no longer can speak coherently, would be taken and tortured.

"My father came here and threw himself on the mercy of the Marqués, without telling him everything. The Marqués allowed that my mother could be brought here for shelter, but evidently, before my father could reach her, or somehow I do not know, she was taken. They have sent word to me that I may retrieve her on Sunday by payment of yet another fine. I don't know where my father is or why they have come to me, except that they know I am here. I do not have any money, I cannot go to get her alone, and I am afraid that if I do go they will take me as well."

"Do you Judaize as well?" asked the priest.

Her hands were like ice. "No, Your Grace."

"But under Jewish law you are Jewish too." She hung her head. "And your children will be, and your daughters' children."

"I am a Christian," she said. "I have gone to Mass since birth, as has my mother. I have worked on Saturday, eaten pork, and believe in Jesus Christ our Lord and Savior. I am not a Jew."

"But you have said the prayers with your mother," the priest said softly.

Consuelo did not answer. She had already said enough.

"Where are they holding your mother?" Don Patricio asked.

"I don't know but they said to go to the San Bernardino church, near the market in Xochimilco." No further harm could come of their knowing that. She was condemned as it was.

"If someone goes in her stead they will kill the mother," Don Patricio said to the priest.

"True," he replied as if she weren't there. "Can you say the blessing for the candles?" the priest asked Consuelo.

What is the answer? Is it yes or is it no? She stared at him.

"The truth, Consuelo. It's important." He came close to where she sat in the hard chair and put his hands on her shoulders. He brought his face close to hers. She could smell his scent, the lemon verbena that surrounded him. The top of his head had red patches where the sun had injured his fair skin and she thought immediately of offering aloe. Then she looked into his light eyes, breathing deeply. Her own eyes widened. His were as light blue as a powdered sky. He smiled and put a finger to her lips. "Now, answer me."

"Yes, Your Grace. I can say the blessing for the Friday candles, though my grandmother used to say that my accent is horrible. There are other blessings but I don't know them. Only the candles."

"Say it."

Consuelo shut her eyes tight knowing the damnation of saying a Jewish prayer to a priest. She was damned anyway she looked at it. *"Baruch ata Adonai,"* she began. Her voice grew stronger as she continued. *"Shel Shabbat."*

He looked at Don Patricio who nodded. "Let's go ahead then. Listen carefully, Consuelo. Everything will depend on your following instructions exactly."

The pale man leaned forward, again looking into her eyes. "The Holy Office finds itself in the most unlikely of financial straits. The King, facing his own budgetary crisis, has cut back the royal funding of the Inquisition. The Holy Office, having exhausted the richest veins of income by killing or driving out wealthy Jews, has vastly diminished its interest in Judaizers, seeking to conserve its funds for heretics like Lutherans.

"But in the provinces finding heretics takes more work and more intelligence than the outposts have to offer. Their finances are so straitened that they face elimination, and so they have ignored the Royal and Grand Tribunal directives."

Consuelo could not imagine caring about the finances of the Inquisition. "Why should my family suffer simply because the Inquisition needs money?"

"Thugs like the ones terrorizing your family should no longer be Holy Office agents. They are acting without instructions and must be disciplined. We have tried to eliminate rogues such as these for months. You will help us, and with the help of the Lord, we will free your mother as well. Will you obey us?"

Don Patricio, his age showing in the strain on his face, looked at her intently.

"I will do all I can. But I must save my mother, first and foremost."

"If it is God's will," the priest said, "then you will succeed. Now, can you travel tomorrow morning?"

"I can travel when you say."

Don Patricio stepped in. "You will travel to Xochimilco but stop outside the town. I will give you precise directions and instruction. There I have friends, a house. It is a place where they will understand what you need to do. You cannot go openly anywhere else, traveling to a church away from home, where questions will be asked. You must go where I tell you. You will ask the maid who answers the door, 'Is this the home of Don Juan de Leon?' And when she asks who you are, you tell her that you are a woman with a good heart. Do you understand?"

Consuelo nodded.

"And when the lady of the house asks you if you know something, you must say 'I am a servant of God and I try to be a good person.'"

Consuelo nodded again. "But why?" she asked Don Patricio.

It was the priest who answered her. "We must find a safe house for your mother when you get her, and keep her there until we are certain that she is safe, that we have caught the rogues. You must not put that house in any more danger than is necessary. When Easter morning comes, you must go to the church in Xochimilco, attend Easter Mass. When the crowd is leaving go to the rear of the church. We will have men there. I know the place all too well," the priest said.

"How will I know your men?"

"You will not. They will know you and you will ask the keeper of the door for permission to enter and rest. They cannot refuse that request. When you are inside I have no doubt our malefactors will show themselves. If you do not come out with your mother within the hour the men will storm the place."

"Why an hour, Your Grace?"

"We must let you persuade them to release your mother to you. I will give you some money," Don Patricio said. "You must offer it as payment for her care, that is important. If you have not come out in an hour we will know that they have taken you as well. We will do everything to rescue you."

They were silent. *They would do everything to rescue me, but what if they cannot? If they could they would simply storm in without her.* "Why don't you just go in, in the first place?" she asked.

"First, we do not know who these outlying agents are. They must identify themselves to you. Second, if they know we are after them they will kill your mother, that is certain, and flee if they can. If they get away you will be the next target, and then your father. We cannot go in until your mother is safe. And once she is out she will need a safe house, and that can only be done through you. These are not the only rogue Holy Office thugs."

"They will kill me too, then, if they don't release her."

"More likely use you as a bargaining pawn for their own safety."

Consuelo looked from one to the other. She must save her mother, even if it meant risking her own life. "I understand." She swallowed hard. "I will go. I leave tomorrow, you say?"

"Yes. You may be gone for several days, even a week. You may have to travel at night. I will arrange an escort. But who?" Don Patricio turned to the priest.

"Juan Carlos," Consuelo said. "He knows."

"He is too young," the priest said quickly, "too naïve."

"No. He is perfect," Don Patricio said. "Except for the problem of Consuelo's reputation."

"I will sacrifice it willingly," she said.

The priest looked down at his pale hands, turning his ring around his finger. "I have a better plan," he said finally. "Doña Josefina said something about an engagement?" Consuelo nodded.

"Oh, I am so glad!" Don Patricio said, a large, genuine smile spreading across his wizened face. "You are not going to marry that scoundrel, Leandro!"

"Come to me in the chapel, tonight, after Compline. I say a very brief one," the priest added with a chuckle. "I will send word to Doña Josefina. Wear your best dress."

Consuelo's eyes widened. "Can you do that? Without the banns?"

"I am the Bishop of Puebla. What is one more secret among many?"

Consuelo dressed alone for her wedding. Her mother did not arrange her lace *mantilla* on her head, there was no maid to dress her hair. Her father would not stand with tears in his eyes as she joined her hand to Juan Carlos. She put her green dress on even though it was too heavy for the season. It was Good Friday, an inauspicious, or maybe even blasphemous day for a wedding, but it was what she had.

Before leaving her room for Compline she packed all of her belongings into her trunk. She had only what she had come with and it wasn't much. She looked at the beautifully illustrated book of herbs she had borrowed from the Marqués's library then quickly put it in her small traveling bag.

She looked around the now bare room before blowing out the candle and shutting the door. When and if she returned to the castle she would no longer be staying in the nuns' wing. She left quietly, slipping past the curtain that separated the wing from the rest of the castle, saying goodbye to no one.

Wall sconces and candles lit the chapel almost to daylight. On one side of the chapel the nuns sat or knelt, saying their rosaries. The remainder of the chapel was almost empty. Two older women knelt in the back pew. In the front Consuelo could see Doña Josefina, and next to her, a dark, elaborately twisted chignon. The Marquesa was here? Consuelo went quietly to the row behind the Marquesa. This was an unexpected complication, she thought.

An altar boy came out swinging the censer. The sweet sickly smell of incense filled the room. She could see movement next to the apse, and the red robes, covered by a long black scarf for Lent, of the Bishop. She clutched her hands together.

The nuns stood and the few other attendees rose with them. She sensed him before she saw him. Juan Carlos slipped into the pew next to her and covered her hands with his.

"This may be only the second time I've attended Compline," he whispered to her.

That brought a smile and she whispered back, "The same. And among the secular it looks like we are two ahead of most."

The pale Bishop came out and Juan Carlos squeezed her hand. "He said he would make the Mass quick," she whispered.

Juan Carlos nodded. "It isn't the way I would have imagined our wedding." She shook her head and turned her attention to the service.

The Bishop was true to his word, saying the shortest Mass Consuelo had ever attended. The nuns left, eyes cast downwards in solemn humility, but Consuelo saw Sor Carmela shoot her a look from her lowered lids. Consuelo bowed her head in acknowledgement. Let her think she was doing penance for her sins. Though with Juan Carlos at her side she realized it would hardly seem likely.

At last, only she and Juan Carlos, Josefina and the Marquesa remained. Even the two devout old ladies in the back had finally departed, their evident curiosity remaining unsatisfied. A click made Consuelo turn to see Don Patricio enter the chapel. He had not attended the Mass. He closed and locked the door behind himself. It had never occurred to Consuelo that a chapel door could be locked. As Don Patricio passed her on his way to the altar he signaled that she should follow. She glanced at Juan Carlos who stood up and offered her his arm. His face was flushed but his arm was steady and she drew comfort from it as they made their way forward.

The Bishop re-emerged from behind the curtain that separated the vestry from the altar and he came to the couple now standing before them. He smiled at Consuelo briefly, then turned to Juan Carlos. Both men looked at one another for a long moment and there were tears in the older man's eyes when he looked away. Consuelo felt Juan Carlos' arm tighten under her hand. "In the name of the Father, the Son, and the Holy Spirit," the Bishop said, his voice soft. They knelt.

In a shaky voice she said her vows, her eyes on Juan Carlos. He spoke his quietly, directly to her. The Bishop took both their hands in his and looked to Doña Josefina. Consuelo heard her speak, "Yes."

"What God has brought together, let no man bring asunder," the Bishop said, and made the sign of the cross over them. Juan Carlos leaned forward and kissed her gently on the mouth as the tears ran down her face.

"It is a half a day's journey to Xochimilco," Don Patricio said to them as they walked out of the chapel. "Go and celebrate your marriage and let breakfast find you at the safe house. There will be a closed cart with two horses waiting for you at midnight. At dawn you will come to a village just outside of the city where Juan Carlos must leave you and the cart, and from there, you must follow my directions from memory."

Consuelo nodded. The weeks of study with Sor Carmela had sharpened her memory and she was confident that she would be able to comply.

"But bear in mind, Juan Carlos" he added, "you may not arrive with her nor can you know the location of the safe house. You cannot tell him, Consuelo, and must leave him to find his own lodgings. Understood?" he asked them.

"My mother has warned me of this, but I disagree. There must be no secrets between husband and wife. I insist that I be told where Consuelo will be and accompany her to the house. I will not show myself, nor will I remain there, but I will not have her traveling through a strange town alone."

"Already so protective and not an hour wed!"

"I would have protected her thus this morning, without a wedding. I will be discreet, but she will not go alone."

Don Patricio shook his head. "The Bishop was right. You are too young, too naïve, and headstrong in the bargain."

Juan Carlos colored. "The Bishop thinks too little of me."

"Or cares too much. But regardless of your discretion you absolutely shall not accompany Consuelo to Mass on Easter as you are well known, with your blond hair, and will alert the rogues to your presence."

"Reluctantly, I will obey. But I will not be far. Now, Don Patricio, if you would leave us, we have but a few hours to enjoy our new status before we must leave."

Consuelo felt herself blush and Don Patricio chuckled. "See, your mother emerges, as does the Marquesa. Go to them first and then the night is yours. Again, as this union must be kept from others until you have safely returned, be discreet I beg you, be careful."

Doña Josefina kissed her son, then Consuelo. "You will be the daughter I never had," she said softly. The Marquesa stood back, waiting for the moment to approach.

"Doña Consuelo," she said smiling, offering her hand.

Consuelo smiled. "*Doña* Consuelo… my! Thank you, Your Highness."

"You may call me Marquesa. May your marriage be a long and happy one. Your new family has always been an important one for me. From the time when I came to serve my mother-in-law before my betrothal to Miguel Angel, through the sustenance sent yearly by

Don Manuel, and Doña Josefina's continued company and intellectual guidance, I have loved them all well. I welcome you to their family, and by extension, into mine. I and all of my domain are always ready to help and shelter you."

Consuelo curtseyed. "If I am ever in the position to return the favor, rest assured that I shall, with joy."

Juan Carlos encircled her waist with his arm. "We have little time," he reminded her.

"The eager bridegroom," Don Patricio said. "Now, be sure to avoid being seen."

"Sir, you have said so for the third time. I have a plan," Juan Carlos said.

"Good, for you cannot take her to your room without someone, whether a gentleman or that ubiquitous page, Abelardo, seeing you. You must not let Leandro hear of this."

Consuelo tensed at the name. "Where is he? He was not at dinner."

Don Patricio smiled. "Called away to Mexico City by his financier on urgent business. Anything from his financier is urgent to Leandro and he will be dismayed to learn that the financier, alas, knows nothing of the summons."

"When? He was here this afternoon."

"Shortly before dinner. Sister Portress came to me with some nonsense and I felt it would be in everyone's interests to get him out of here for a few days."

"He owes me a fight," Juan Carlos muttered.

"Do not let the Marqués hear of that," Don Patricio warned. "Now be gone, the two of you. And God bless you. May I see you healthy and safe after Easter."

Juan Carlos spoke briefly to his mother. "Have Consuelo's traveling bag sent down to the Portress. We leave at midnight."

"Godspeed, son," Josefina whispered, and kissed him once more.

Juan Carlos led Consuelo down the long hall past the gentlemen's wing, the great hall, and the library. He took a taper from the wall sconce. "Not here!" Consuelo said as he opened the door to the stone room near the music room.

"It is safe and quiet and no sound can escape. We will be close to the door to the castle for a quick departure."

Consuelo felt the rush of shame as she looked at the daybed where Leandro had enjoyed his visual taking of her only a few days before, and a greater shame when she thought of his stripping her naked earlier this very day, his hands on her, his threats. With shame came desire and her breath came more shallowly. She looked at Juan Carlos, whose face was flushed and warm.

"I will burn away the memory of this afternoon with the memory we will make tonight," he said. He too had seen her, her dress misbuttoned and open in the nuns' wing, with Leandro standing over her. At least he had not seen the minutes that preceded his entry.

He lit the small lamps all around the room and their glow softened the harshness of the cold stone walls. He reached for the small buttons in the back of Consuelo's dress. "This time we will go slowly and I will not have to satisfy my imagination with more imagination." He gently removed her dress, letting it drop to the ground. "Take off the rest of this," he said indicating the chemise and stockings.

With shaking hands Consuelo obeyed. *What a difference a ceremony makes.* Had she complied two hours before, she would have been a harlot. Now she had the holy obligation to obey, and willingly. She stood naked before him.

Juan Carlos ran his hands over her shoulders, her breasts, touching her nipples, and down to her thighs. "Turn around," he said. She turned her back to him, shivering. "Cold?"

She shook her head. She was not cold in the least. She suppressed another shiver as his fingertips glided down the small of her back, across her buttocks and then dipped between her legs. He pulled her to him and with his left hand he cupped her breast from behind. His thumb smoothed over her nipple, with his right hand searching between her legs, making her quiver, and she opened her stance slightly. His lips touched her neck and she heard him moan with her.

"Lie down," he said, and she went to the day bed. As she lay there, her heart pounding, he undressed. His shoulders were broad and his chest was covered with golden hair. His narrow waist led her eye to a mass of red-gold curls. His desire for her was evident and she smiled a bit. When he pushed her legs open she closed her eyes. "Open your eyes," he whispered. "I want you to see me, be present with me. I have had your virgin's blood but this is our wedding night."

She opened her eyes, looked into his blue ones. He came close and kissed her mouth, then let his mouth slide to her breast. She held his head to her, stroking his fine hair. He pulled away and used his hands to ready her. Then, when she felt she would cry out with need, with a smooth, strong thrust, he made her his wife.

CHAPTER 8

JUAN CARLOS DROVE THE SMALL COVERED CARRIAGE. It was a modest vehicle with a seat for the driver and a small rear compartment for luggage and another person. Two horses were one too many for such a little conveyance but Don Patricio had insisted. They might need the power for rapid flight, and Juan Carlos would need a mount after leaving Consuelo.

Next to him Consuelo dozed. She had dressed for traveling, in a simple black cotton skirt, white blouse and black *rebozo*. Juan Carlos was similarly attired, having abandoned court finery for his usual ranch clothes. The cart was suited to an earthy *hacendado*'s transportation, not a carriage for a lady or a grandee, and so they were able to move with relative anonymity, not attracting the eyes of bandits or night watchmen. Don Patricio's *escudos* and Juan Carlos' pistol made for uneasy companions in their travelers' bags.

The countryside was quiet in the moonlight under a waning moon that rose shortly after they left the castle. Consuelo opened her eyes and marveled at the shadows cast by the silvery light. They stopped once, letting the horses drink from the stream that crossed the road and availing themselves of the lonely silence for a kiss.

"We are nearing the town of San Lorenzo. It will be dawn soon," Juan Carlos said as the mountains loomed dark against the slightly lighter sky.

"I will drive the cart the rest of the way, then," Consuelo said. "Unhitch the horse for yourself."

"I don't like this," he replied. It was Holy Saturday and soon the road would be filled with travelers, peasants and peddlers, all making their way to Mexico City for Easter.

Consuelo pulled the rebozo over her head, wrapping it around herself. "It can't be helped. I have only an hour to drive and I can drive well enough. I must get there before the world fully wakes up."

"No. I will accompany you. I will ride behind you and so can watch over you until you stop. Then I will go on ahead and find my own lodging."

"As you wish, but let us unhitch the horse for you now. We have very little time."

Juan Carlos pulled the cart to the edge of the road. It was getting dusty as the dry season wore on and the rains were at least a month away. The night had cooled the air but as the dawn wind picked up, Consuelo could smell the upcoming warmth of the day. Juan Carlos jumped down from the cart. Despite her nervousness, Consuelo took a moment to enjoy watching him as he moved quickly to the horses. He was a man of the hacienda and moved like a rancher. He was her husband.

When he had unhitched the horse he would ride he threw a blanket over the back and slipped a harness over him. The remaining horse, a good sized, mild bay, stamped his feet, waiting to be released as well. Consuelo hoped the beast wouldn't fuss when he saw his cartmate led away. Juan Carlos adjusted the reins to the bay and Consuelo moved over to the center of the seat. "We must go."

"Be safe," he said. She nodded, her voice stopped in her throat.

She drove steadily. The horse, having adjusted to bearing the full load of the cart, moved in a well-modulated pace. For a while she heard Juan Carlos behind her, the steady beat of his horse's hooves a comforting background to her heart. As the road turned up the hill to San Lorenzo, though, and it passed through the little villages that awoke as they went by, the road slowly became more populated and soon Consuelo could no longer distinguish the sounds that had reassured her. She turned back once and saw that Juan Carlos had dropped back, still well within sight but taking care not to appear too close. It was as it should be, she thought, but she still regretted his distance.

When she entered San Lorenzo the streets were full. Carts and horses, women with bundles on their heads and on their backs, men riding and walking burros, all converged on the main road. She watched carefully for her landmarks. She counted the streets, then turned the cart onto a small side street. She recited the instructions in her head, rhythmically drowning out the fear that threatened to blind her. *Pass a butcher's shop and a milliner, count four more doors, a red door, to the brown door, unpainted, unassuming, almost invisible.* She stopped the cart.

Fortunately it was still early enough that there was room on this side street for the cart to stand. She dismounted and tied the horse's reins to a wooden post. There were stairs leading up to the front door. Her empty stomach clenched. If it was the wrong house, if they did not understand the strange code she was to speak, if they turned her away... She squared her shoulders, wrapped the rebozo more tightly around her head, and mounted the steps.

The knocker was unadorned and no name was engraved upon it, but it was well affixed to the door. To the left of the door was a lamp, unlit in the early morning, and hidden behind it, only vaguely discernible to Consuelo thanks to her height, was a small, oblong box. A memory rose unbidden of a similar box, with a roll of parchment within, on the door to her Grandmother Rosa's home. *Bless this house.* What a terrible risk this family was taking, she thought, but there was no longer a doubt that she had come to the right place. She only hoped they believed her.

The sound of the knocker echoed in her head in the dawn quiet. She waited. Heart pounding, she raised the knocker once again, letting it fall from her clammy hand. Just as it fell the door opened a hand's breadth and a small girl looked up at her. Her eyes were wide and brown and her skin was the color of honey. She peered around the door and Consuelo could see her blue sleeping dress and bare feet. "*¿Qué quieres?*" What do you want?

"Marcela!" came a woman's voice from within. "Come back here!" The little girl slammed the door shut.

For several moments Consuelo waited, wondering if she should knock again, but the door opened and this time a woman only slightly older than Consuelo appeared. She had the same eyes and honey skin as the little girl. "Yes, good morning?" It was an awkward greeting, barely covering the unspoken question so simply phrased by the child.

"Good morning," Consuelo said. "Forgive me for waking the household so early." She could smell meat and chocolate, and something else, sweet and enticing. Her stomach growled and she blushed. She had not eaten since her miserable bites of Good Friday rations.

"We are awake," the woman replied, still holding the door to the width of her body.

"Is this the house of Don Juan de Leon?" The woman nodded. Consuelo swallowed. The next sentence would doom or save her. "I am a woman with a good heart and I seek his advice." She tacked on the second part as the first seemed too odd to leave hanging.

The woman's eyebrows shot up. "Indeed?"

Consuelo shifted her feet. Wasn't she supposed to be asked in? Perhaps she had gotten the words wrong. Her stomach growled again. "Are you hungry?" the woman asked. Consuelo nodded, embarrassed. "You now know the feeling of shame a mendicant must suffer at asking alms at the door. But you can turn around and go to the market, buy yourself ample food, and a beggar cannot."

Consuelo felt her brow tighten. Who was this woman to be sermonizing at her? "I am not a beggar. I try to be a good person."

The woman smiled slightly, opening the door wider. "Come in." Consuelo entered the foyer and the woman shut and locked the door behind her. "What is your name?"

"Maria del Consuelo Costa Argenta." *de Castillo.*

"Señorita Costa, welcome. Granddaughter of Rosa and Emilio Argenta?" The smile on the woman's face was genuine.

"You knew my grandparents? I never met my grandfather, he was dead long before I was born, but my Grandmother Rosa lived until I was ten."

"I am Susana Perez de Leon, and Juan de Leon is my father-in-law. You met my daughter, Marcela. I did know your grandmother, though only briefly. My father-in-law knew her well. And your mother, Leila, right?"

Consuelo nodded, surprised.

"Yes, my father-in-law knew her too. Is she still living?"

"Barely," Consuelo answered quietly. Susana nodded.

"Come, let us get you something to eat. You must have traveled through the night to arrive at this hour. Tulancingo is a full day's travel away, is it not?"

Consuelo shook her head. "I left from the Marqués's castle. Don Patricio sent me."

"It must be serious business indeed, and urgent, as he did not send warning ahead. Your servant is outside, waiting?"

"I traveled alone," Consuelo replied, "under cover of the night."

"That is foolhardy! You could have been attacked, robbed, killed or worse!" Susana cried. Consuelo did not answer for to answer she would have to compound a lie or give away a truth she could not spare. "Well, if that is your cart you must bring it around to the back of the house and tie the horse up in the courtyard. We cannot have it out front and no one in our household is available to help you."

Consuelo looked around at the fine furnishings. The room she had been led to had the long, high windows of a city home, and a rich, thick rug on the floor. The drapes, in similar red and gold tones as the rug, hung heavily next to the windows, and the seats, in gold and green leather, were amply padded. How was it that no servant had answered the door, no groom was able to stable her horse, and yet they could live in such sumptuous surroundings?

Susana watched her closely. "You don't know, do you?"

"I'm not sure whether I do or I do not."

Susana raised her eyebrows and Consuelo felt her heart skip. She had answered wrong, missing the cue. "At least you are honest," Susana said at last. "It is the Sabbath. We do not work on the Sabbath and we dismiss our servants for the day so that they cannot be held to that knowledge. They know, of course; they are all of our kind, but they must not be endangered by our practices. You do not keep the Sabbath holy, I take it?"

"I do nothing overtly and only lit the candles for my mother when she asked. But it is for her that I am here."

"It is late enough that neighbors are about and will suspect if a lady of quality is seen stabling her own horse. I will call my husband. A mission of mercy trumps the careful observance of the law."

"Thank you," she said to Susana's retreating form. *She is as outspoken as my dear Maria Elena but far more judgmental,* she thought. Living at constant risk must have hardened her.

When she returned she had a tray with cups, pastries, and an *olla* of chocolate. "I will not serve you so help yourself."

Consuelo took a cup from the tray and poured chocolate from the rustic carafe. She smelled the cinnamon and spice fragrance and sipped gratefully at the thick brown liquid. She reached for a pastry.

"Dip it in the syrup," Susana said. "It has honey and lemon, and mint to soothe your nerves."

The sweet pastry had been fried in oil and was crisp on the outside, with a meltingly creamy center. The sweet syrup made for a rich confection and Consuelo took another. Susana nodded then turned her head as two men entered the room. Then she stood up and looked meaningfully at Consuelo.

Still holding the dripping pastry, Consuelo rose. The men did not bow or acknowledge her. The older man with a grey pointed beard and short hair looked at Susana. "Is this she?"

"Yes, father," Susana said. "She is Consuelo Costa Argenta, daughter of Leila, granddaughter of Rosa. Consuelo," she added, turning to her, "this is Don Juan de Leon, and my husband, his son, Jose Luis." Jose Luis was thin and also wore a beard, his black with one or two streaks of grey beginning to show. He glanced quickly at her and Consuelo thought she saw amusement and intelligence in his grey eyes before he looked back at his father.

Neither man looked at her directly. "What does she want?"

"Shelter, it seems, and something more. We were just getting to it."

"If you please," Consuelo began.

Susana raised her hand to stop her. "They will not address a strange woman unless they are certain that she is not unclean." Consuelo blushed and shook her head. "I will see to her comfort, Father, but you and Jose Luis must inquire of her mission."

Don Juan cocked his head. "Are you in command?"

Susana shrugged. "I just think it would be more efficient if those who can help hear it from the person who needs it."

Don Juan turned to his son. "See to it that Señorita Costa is given whatever help she needs. Susana, I will go to my study now."

"Certainly, Father. You will not be disturbed." Don Juan turned and left the room without once acknowledging Consuelo.

"He is the keeper of our people's knowledge," Susana said, sitting down again. "He has received the traveling Rabbi and now must learn and remember everything he was taught so as to teach it to us all. We are apparently very ignorant in our language and customs, our prayers are wrong from so much time away from any source, and our habits shoddy and imprecise." Her voice held a trace of surprising bitterness.

"My wife is not guarded in her speech," Jose Luis said, sitting down as well. Consuelo followed suit. "But she is learned at a level that I cannot even hope to achieve and so is permitted a loose tongue."

"If I am not to be learned who will teach our daughter? And if we have no sons who will carry the words of the Rabbis forward if not she? And if she does not teach her children, who will?"

"She asks a lot of questions. Susana has the ability that I lack, for though I can read both Spanish and Latin, she can read Spanish, Latin, Greek, and even some Hebrew. She understands the words she reads and can write these foreign words in their own alphabets. My father, against his own morals, insisted that she sit at the doorway while the Rabbi instructed him, to better learn what he was taught. Now if you were not here she would again sit at the door while he studied the words the Rabbi left so that she may learn too and help him if he struggles."

"I am clearly not the one with the loose tongue," Susana said sharply. Jose Luis looked at her, hurt. "Oh, come. Have a pastry." He took one and smiled at her. She smiled back, a small, secret smile.

Consuelo thought of Juan Carlos, then of Leandro, and of the Bishop of Puebla with his blue eyes that still sparkled under the watery mask of age, and of all that had happened since yesterday's dawn, and felt the room swim.

"Let me show you where you may rest," Susana said. "We will talk of your troubles and their solutions later."

Consuelo was awakened by the afternoon sun pouring into the window of the little room where she had been given privacy to wash and rest. There was a cot with a thick coverlet, and a small table where she had placed the ewer Susana had given her to fill with water and take with a bowl and a towel to her room before sleeping. She splashed the cool water on her face and, refreshed but nervous, she emerged from her refuge.

She stood at the top of the stairs that led back down to the sitting room listening to the quiet. Outside the world thrummed with the activity of a holiday Saturday and there was a clatter as a cart went by, the sounds of voices calling out wares and prices, but inside peace reigned. She could smell meat cooking, and spices, but no sounds from a kitchen or pantry disturbed the air.

She walked down to the sitting room where she had spoken with the householders. It was empty and the curtains were drawn keeping the light from the sun from illuminating the room. It was too warm for a fire, too dark to read, and there was no one to talk to. Consuelo sat down and thought.

Her reverie was interrupted, finally, as Marcela, the child now dressed in a blue and white dress with a frilled collar, tiptoed in. "Excuse me," said the child politely this time. "My mother says it is time to eat."

The girl led Consuelo through a narrow, dark hall into another room, where the sunlight had been allowed to stream in. There was a long table with beautiful white and gold dishes, silver pitchers on either end, and a great pot of simmered meat in the center. The aroma almost made Consuelo swoon. There were candles in candlesticks reminiscent of the ones Consuelo had lit for Leila. There was no one else in the room. "Is your mother coming?"

"Yes," Marcela said solemnly, "as soon as grandpa is ready. You can sit next to me." She indicated a place next to one with a smaller plate and spoon.

"It smells good," Consuelo said.

"It is good," Marcela replied. "The food for the Sabbath bride."

Susana entered, followed by Don Juan and Jose Luis. Don Juan took his place at the head of the table with his son on his right and Susana on his left. There were two empty places next to Jose Luis after the rest took their seats. "We are much diminished by time," Don Juan said, "and so are glad of your company."

Consuelo was surprised that he addressed her after his earlier chilly behavior. Susana explained. "We have discussed it. You are now part of the household. Please put yourself at ease. If there is something you don't understand, ask and we will explain as best we can. There is no benefit in our trumpeting our knowledge over your ignorance after our own ignorance has been so clearly pointed out to us."

"Thank you," Consuelo said, unsure of the import of Susana's words.

Don Juan motioned to Susana who rose and took a pitcher in one hand and a bowl in the other. Don Juan held his hands over the bowl and she poured water over them. She did the same with Jose Luis and then came to Consuelo. "Put your hands out to wash and then you may pour for me." Consuelo obeyed and warm water scented with roses cascaded over her fingers. She inhaled and smiled. She looked up into Susana's eyes and saw that she was pleased.

"*Baruch ata Adonai,*" Don Juan began. They cast their eyes down as he started the blessing over the bread. Consuelo knew those words but not the ones that followed. She repeated them silently. He made a prayer over a glass. "The blessings of the bread and of the wine," he said, "though we have no wine, so it is Port."

"Like Communion," Consuelo said, then bit her lip.

"Yes," said Susana. "Communion is a travesty of our blessings which long antedate the Christian ceremony."

"Not everyone is so disdainful of the Christian faith," Jose Luis put in quickly, seeing the color rush to Consuelo's cheeks. "Susana feels her religion strongly."

Consuelo remained silent and watched as the men served themselves from the stew pot. Susana helped herself and put some in Marcela's plate. "Help yourself."

"How is this warm if you can do no work on the Sabbath?" she asked.

"I make it on Friday during the day and place it on the banked coals to cook overnight. The water for washing and for chocolate are kept hot the same way. The injunction against work has the unintended consequence of making more work for women on Friday, for we must also clean the house, change the linens on the beds, wash ourselves and put on fresh clothing before sunset."

It is like any other religion, Consuelo thought, where the work falls to the women to make the observances possible for the men. But she held her tongue. "You did not say any of the blessings, Susana. Is it prohibited?"

She smiled. "Yes, you have noticed. We as women only say the blessing over the candles on Shabbat. The blessing you say you know. I would like to hear you say it but the time has passed and it would not do to say it now since we are not lighting the candles and one must not say a nullity."

"Not even for practice?" Marcela asked, surprising Consuelo with her precocity.

Susana looked at her father-in-law for guidance. He shrugged. "If she wishes. It is apparently the only one she knows."

"No, I am afraid it will not sound right."

"Try," Susana said.

Consuelo shut her eyes and recited the blessing for the candles just as she had the night before, for the Bishop of Puebla. When she opened her eyes all four of them were staring at her. "What?"

"Your accent! It is hilarious!" Susana said, laughing. Consuelo looked down, angry and embarrassed. "No, don't feel bad. It proves you are who you say you are."

"How is that?"

"Your grandmother, Rosa, knew my father," Don Juan said, looking at her for the first time as a person. "They came in the sixteen thirties and were able to prosper thanks to their unparalleled abilities, Zoar's and Emilio, your grandfather's, to handle the King's financial interests here in the colonies. In sixteen forty-nine, well before I was born, there was another purge and anyone with a trace of our ancestral blood was called in for questioning. The story went that when asked to say a prayer your grandmother Rosa's accent was so atrocious that she was immediately exonerated."

The family chuckled and Consuelo felt a bit better. "Nevertheless, it is the only connection I have and it is the connection that now endangers my mother, no matter how poorly we say the words." She took a bite of the stew. It was spectacular. "What are your spices?" she asked Susana. She kept to herself the question of eating meat on Holy Saturday.

"Cloves, cinnamon, ginger and juniper," she answered. "Tell us your mission."

"It is hard to know where to begin. My mother has long been ill and as she has faded, her mind has disintegrated. There is a rogue band of inquisitors who have been blackmailing my father, the mayor of Tulancingo, to keep her practices secret." Consuelo managed to avoid saying *Judaizing*, guessing that the term would be offensive. "Now they have kidnapped her, and Don Patricio, who seems to be friendly towards you, has found a way to help her, but I must take her from the place and the people who have her as prisoner. He has sent me to you for shelter."

"He would endanger our entire household for you!" Susana exclaimed, red patches appearing on her cheeks. "A non-observant, fallen by the wayside former member of our ancestral nation! Why should we do this?"

Marcela stared at her mother with wide eyes then turned to Consuelo. "Are you making my mother angry?" The child looked almost as fearsome as the mother.

"I don't know," Consuelo said truthfully, "I am only grateful."

"Every so often one of our nation comes to us needing help," Don Juan said. "They may come by prearrangement or by surprise as you did, sent by one of our own."

Consuelo realized he was referring to Don Patricio.

"We do this because every member of our nation is sacred," Don Juan continued. "And your mother and her family were brave in the years past and sheltered our family during the purge. That is why. Though I do agree, we are being put unnecessarily at risk."

"Do others not know who you are?" Consuelo asked.

"No. We keep our identity a secret."

"Not too much of a secret if you have a scroll holder next to your front door," Consuelo remarked.

Jose Luis banged his spoon on the table. "Susana! Have you put that *mezuzah* back there again?" He had not spoken throughout the meal and Consuelo had almost forgotten his existence. "Do you want to have us killed?"

"The Rabbi said it was right to do so," Susana said truculently.

"The Rabbi also said it was right to remain secret and that survival was the most important," Don Juan replied. "Remove it as soon as the sun sets."

"Better, I will remove it for you as I am untouched by your laws," Consuelo said.

"You are untouched? You are here, you are family. You will observe the laws as long as you remain with us. Jose Luis, remove the mezuzah. And until sunset we will instruct you in our ways. Understood, Susana?"

"Yes, Father," she replied evenly. "I will endeavor to undo fifty years of lack of instruction in one evening. But he is right," she said, turning back to Consuelo, "for every one of us is sacred and every sacrifice our fathers and mothers made to continue our faith and our people must be honored. If they did so much at such risk so that our people could live, who are we to shy away from the little that is asked of us now?"

Consuelo bowed her head in acquiescence, and spooned more of the delicious stew into her mouth. If tomorrow was a failure it could well be the last meat she would eat.

Finally the meal came to an end. They rose and retired to refresh themselves and returned to the sitting room. Susana placed a tray of sweetmeats on the table and the family took what they wanted. Don Juan and Susana pored over a book in Latin and Jose Luis and Marcela practiced letters until Don Juan told them to stop. Jose Luis then left for a walk and Marcela fell asleep on the floor. It was a peaceful, quiet time and Consuelo wondered why this was such a sin.

"Your mother was named for the night," Don Juan said suddenly, looking up from his book. "She was younger than I, by maybe ten years, and I remember when she was born. I played with her brother, Sancho, and we went to classes together at the church. She grew into a beauty," he said, his voice deep in the past.

"She still is," Consuelo said softly.

"I can only hope. And then, of course, she fell for your father. That Isidro, though not one of us, so smart, tall, oh was he ever tall, you seem to have his height..." Consuelo smiled, sensing a lost love. "And all those babies lost. She nearly died, her body and her heart broken with each stillbirth. Until the blessings, until Rosa found her faith, and until you."

Consuelo watched Don Juan, his eyes drooping shut over his book. The man's face was lined and his beard brushed his chest as his chin dropped. He pulled his head up, went back to reading until his eyes drooped again. *He knew the story of my birth. He knew my mother when she was young and beautiful. He loved my mother. From that memory he gives me shelter.*

The room was still and peaceful. She tried to breathe that peace into herself, give herself the quiet power to go forth with her terrifying plan. She was married to Juan Carlos. That alone was amazing. She loved him, she always had, and now she was his, forever.

The quiet also gave her time to worry though, and as the afternoon wore on she looked forward to the setting sun which would free them to return to active work. As it was, she went over and over the details of her instructions until she feared that she was mixing them up by virtue of so much thought.

Tomorrow morning she would take the cart and go the rest of the way to Xochimilco. Don Patricio had explained the route but without Juan Carlos or anyone else she worried about losing her way. She would hear the Easter Mass and then the real ordeal would begin.

CHAPTER 9

CONSUELO

THOUGH HER SLEEP HAD BEEN FITFUL when it came, Consuelo was loath to rise from the soft sheets of her bed. The sun had just crested the horizon and the sky was yellow and pale blue. She closed her eyes against the light. It was time.

Consuelo thought of Easter Mass in Tulancingo. It was extraordinarily well attended, the cathedral packed with festively dressed worshipers. It was her favorite service, celebrating the Risen Christ. Today, though, she would attend in a foreign church with a heavy heart and even, perhaps, a treacherous soul. Don Juan de Leon's words echoed: *Your mother was named for the night.* She needed to bring her mother out of the night, the darkness of her imprisonment, into the light of freedom. She got out of bed.

In her traveling bag she had only brought a *mantilla* suitable for Easter Mass, and no other clothing but a clean blouse and pantalettes. Despite Leandro's mocking comments, calling them *zaragüelles* like she was some country lass from two hundred years before, Consuelo knew that most women of her class wore pantalettes on occasion. She usually wore them only during her monthly courses or during the coldest days of winter, knowing it was healthier to let air circulate the body. But she felt the need for more modesty and security during this ordeal. She winced at the memory of Leandro pulling them down below her knees. She had felt more exposed than protected by their presence.

The rest of her bag she had stuffed with herbs for soothing, for healing, and the vinegar tincture that seemed on occasion to revive her mother despite her father's objections to the smell. And of course, secreted in her purse were Don Patricio's *escudos*. She thought for a moment of Juan Carlos with his pistol in his bag and yearned for the comfort of his presence. He could not attend the Mass, he would be too noticeable. She wondered where he was now.

In ordinary times she would have a new dress to wear, with lace on the collar and the sleeves, and combs to hold her long white lace *mantilla* on her lustrous hair. She would dress her mother's hair, now softly laced with grey, and then Leila would help her twist her long, thick locks up into a crown. Consuelo bent to see in the small mirror on the wall of the room, placed too low for her, and combed her hair into place as best she could. She put the clean blouse on, folded the *mantilla* over her arm and pushed her little traveling bag under the cot. She would, she hoped, be back.

In the kitchen Consuelo found Jose Luis drinking a cup of dark chocolate and eating a pastry left from the day before. A young maid, her black braids hanging well past her waist, was washing plates and pots. "Good morning, Consuelo," Jose Luis said between sips. "Sleep well?" He held out the plate of pastries to her.

"Not really," she replied, taking a pastry. "Thank you." The maid wiped her hands on her skirt and reached for a cup. Consuelo took it and poured chocolate for herself. Jose Luis was like someone she would know in her regular life, she thought, watching him eat another pastry. He leaned against the table, not bothering to sit.

"So, you're off to church on your mercy mission," he said. "Need me to get your cart ready?"

"I would be grateful," Consuelo said. She had given little thought to that aspect of the day and realized that she was used to men or servants taking care of those types of details for her.

"Can you drive it all the way to Xochimilco? I can drive you, you know. The trading office is closed on Sundays and there is nothing else for me to do here."

Consuelo was tempted. What would Don Patricio want her to do? He clearly trusted this family but this mission was hers alone. The message from the Holy Office had been clear: bring no one with you. On the other hand it would be far less conspicuous to arrive escorted than to appear alone, driving a cart. Consuelo would have to make this decision, and quickly. Alone or with Jose Luis she had to leave soon, for the Mass was early and would be crowded.

"No, alas, though I wish you could. I am afraid that this is not possible. But if you would prepare the cart I would be very appreciative." Her voice sounded stilted and formal in her ears, constrained by repressed fear.

"Your choice," he said, taking a last gulp of chocolate and handing the cup to the maid. "I'll get the rig ready."

Consuelo mounted the seat of the cart and took up the reins. "Thank you. I will see you before nightfall." Jose Luis nodded, already going back into the house. She looked longingly at the door, then took a deep breath. She could not linger so it was best to be going.

The day was already warm and going to be hot. She put the *rebozo* around her shoulders lightly, preferring to be less exposed despite the heat. The horse moved at a good pace, its quality evident, and she joined a procession of carts, donkeys, burros and horses all moving toward Xochimilco.

Families of all sorts, with children hanging off sides of carts, boys jogging along side, and women walking with babies on their backs, all in the best clothing they could afford, moved almost as one along the road. Consuelo felt awkward with an entire empty cart but to her relief no one took much obvious notice of her. She kept her eyes forward except for furtive looks around, hoping to see Juan Carlos' shiny hair or some other known face to reassure her.

As she neared the city she could smell the lake, its humid aroma rising against the dry, dusty road and the odor of masses of people moving in the heat. In the distance she saw the tower of the cathedral. Almost there, she thought. While she would be happy to descend from the cart, at least in the cart she was safe and could escape. Once on foot there would be no turning back.

Another logistical problem presented itself. Where did she leave the cart during Mass and whatever else would follow? She regretted turning down Jose Luis's offer as yet another matter so simply handled by others was left to her. The closer she got the more elaborate and fancy carriages joined the procession and Consuelo chose one of the nicest. She would follow that one and wherever that groom took the carriage there she would take the cart. Like the occupants, she would not wish to be delayed when it came time to leave.

Her strategy took her around the back of the cathedral, where a large number of fancy carriages were already parked. An enormous courtyard separated the church from the Convent of San Bernardino, which in itself stretched as far as Consuelo could see. The church took up the length of one side of the courtyard, the walls of the convent the opposite. From the direction she had entered the road was flanked to her left by the cathedral, but on her right a field stretched, bordered at the back by extended, high convent walls, their tops glittering with shards of broken glass. At the far end of the courtyard stood several small sheds and a long stable.

The bright sunlight reflected off the well-polished trim of the carriages and the lovely dresses of the women who alit from them. Around the periphery, spilling over into the field, squealing children and laughing parents of lower classes congregated. Some had spent the night in the field area next to the courtyard, waiting in vigil for the Easter sunrise. There were stalls selling religious medals, beggars holding out their hands for Easter alms, and several musicians playing conflicting songs as loudly as they could, hoping to attract donations. The spirit was festive. After Mass there would be stalls of food sellers, cool drink purveyors, peddlers of every sort. The air was full and lively and the heat only seemed to increase the happily excited atmosphere of the courtyard.

The carriage she was following stopped and the groom jumped down. The door to the carriage opened and a man in black breeches with gold braid descended. He turned and handed out a lady in a deeply dyed red skirt with a frothy *mantilla* covering her hair, followed by two young girls in light blue with embroidered shawls over their heads. The gentleman followed his women to a wide path of patterned stone that rounded the corner and disappeared toward the front of the cathedral. Consuelo pulled up behind the carriage, halted the horse, and carefully, with as much grace as she could muster, descended from her seat.

Holding the reins she approached the groom. She let the *mantilla* fall back from her face and she put on her best approximation of haughty elegance. "My groom has vanished," she said. "Could you kindly accommodate my horse during the service?"

The groom stared at her. "Vanished?"

"Drink at an early hour." She held the reins out. "Thank you," she said before he could answer. She pulled a half-escudo from her purse. "I am Doña Consuelo de Castillo." After all, she thought, she *was*. "I will be delayed after the service so could you see to it that the cart is conveniently placed for me? I will arrange another driver for my return."

The groom bowed, pocketing the escudo. "Certainly, Señora." She nodded and walked over to the patterned path without looking back. It did not really matter what he did with the cart, she thought. She would either have plenty of help retrieving it or would have no use for it at all. But the power of Juan Carlos's family name and the greater power of money had a soothing effect on her, and she held her head high as she walked with the other ladies and gentlemen towards the entrance to the cathedral.

The cathedral of San Bernardino was magnificent. The seats were full, there were peasants standing in the aisles, and everyone had apparently poured their best perfumes or rubbed flowers copiously over themselves. At the altar, as best Consuelo could see, there were masses of lilies and roses in heaping bunches, and the statues had had their purple veils of mourning lifted and draped to the sides. Censers of incense added to the intense aromas and the hubbub of the crowd made almost a roar of sound. Consuelo edged in and pressed forward. A father lifted his son onto his lap and Consuelo took advantage of the minute space to squeeze into a seat.

The Mass began. Three priests officiated in the celebration of the glory of Christ rising miraculously from the dead. How could the Jews continue to deny this incredible miracle, she wondered. Then she smiled to herself. *Incredible miracle.* What a perfect juxtaposition of terms. An enlightened person would ask, *What proof is there? How can someone rise from the dead?* A faithful person would answer, *God can do anything.* It was simply a matter of which miracles one chose. The priests sang the Kyrie. She shook her head, amazed that she was blaspheming in the heart of the church, in the middle of the sacred Mass of Resurrection.

This troubling thought took her mind off the immediate problem, but not for long. She looked around, hoping to spot Don Patricio's men. Or the Bishop's men. She realized that she actually had no idea who was going to be backing her up. It was supposed to be like this so she wouldn't make a mistake and give them away but it provided no comfort to her to work so blindly. *It's a matter of faith, choosing to believe in miracles.* This miracle, she thought, had better be true, corporeally and promptly.

The main priest began the concluding antiphon and her hands began to sweat. There was no more time to worry. In minutes she would rise with everyone else, but begin her mission alone. "Jesus, have mercy on me, and keep me and Mother safe," she prayed.

She felt for the escudos in her purse, keeping it tightly against her body, and stood with the crowd. It would take a while to file out and she made her way slowly to the aisle where the surge of humanity moved forward towards the doors. She would go to the back unless she was approached before then. *They said they would make themselves known to me only.*

At last she emerged from the church but the sea of worshippers seemed only to have increased. There were families, children, men and women everywhere. Hidalgos and peasants, all in their best clothes, thronged the outside of the church. She needed to get to the back, to the courtyard. Had she seen a door in the back? She thought but could not remember. Surely it was there. The Bishop had said so. The church bells began to ring, tolling the hour. The sound was joyous and Consuelo allowed it to fill her with hope. *Did Jews have bells to ring?* She pushed those thoughts away. She didn't really care what they did or did not have. She was a Christian and she had to rescue her mother.

She had no one to greet and no one spoke to her. At long last she turned the corner of the cathedral and could see the courtyard. Carts and carriages had filled every space, and men, grooms and owners, depending on rank, jostled to bring their conveyances forward for their families to board. By the time she reached the back she could hear loud arguments over priority and right-of-way. Still, no one approached her.

To her dismay, she saw four doors along the rear wall. Don Patricio had instructed her to seek entry to rest until she could get her carriage. That would be her way to gain access. But, what if her mother's captors were not in the back, but elsewhere? In one of those outbuildings, or behind the forbidding walls of the convent? What if she wasn't approached, never found her mother? She looked around nervously. She would take the first door.

Consuelo adjusted her *mantilla* to cover her hair again and pulled the white *rebozo* over her shoulders so her hands were free. The purse was tucked into a bag that fit into the sash around her waist, she hoped inconspicuously. She knocked.

She shifted her weight from foot to foot. No one came. She knew that to anyone observing her she was a tall, well-bred woman dressed modestly and somewhat less festively than the occasion demanded, who had need of a private area for her womanly purposes. That was all to the good, she thought. No one could find fault with such necessity. But even after another knock there was no answer.

Frustration battled relief but she moved to the next door. "Señora," a voice said next to her. A woman, shabbily dressed in black, with a serape over her head and around her body, bobbed a curtsey. "There is a women's alcove over here." She motioned towards the next door deeply inset into a dark archway. Consuelo bit her lip. Was this the envoy or was she simply a church servant responding to the obvious?

"Thank you," she said. She followed the servant. At the worst she could find a chamber pot, as the morning had been long. At best, or perhaps this too was at worst, she was entering the lion's den. She took one last look around but saw no one who could be her potential ally if she didn't emerge within an hour. They entered the archway, made darker by the brilliant sunlight outside, and walked, single-file towards a heavy wooden door.

As they got further from the courtyard it was cool and quieter. The servant did not turn and said nothing but pushed open the heavy, unlocked door. It creaked as it swung open, and it was darker yet within. The woman preceded Consuelo into the blackness and Consuelo smelled candle wax and leftover incense. Her eyes were slowly adjusting and she saw the motion of a curtain. "In here, Señora," the servant said.

Consuelo nodded her thanks. She stepped into the alcove. There was no window, no candle or lamp, but she could see that it was indeed a privy chamber and she sighed. It would be much easier to face whatever came next without physical urgency.

She pushed the curtain aside but the maid was gone. She could turn back, go outside, and hope to find the doorkeeper or be found by her mother's captors. Or she could stay inside where it was dark and cool, and be found safely by the Bishop's men in an hour. She had come this far, it would be a waste to hide. She started back towards the door.

"Halt. Don't move." Consuelo froze. Faint light behind her created a shadow. She could hear her heart. "Turn around, Consuelo."

The man knew her name. On whose side he was on she wasn't sure, but the ordeal had begun. She turned slowly towards the light, keeping her eyes downcast to avoid losing the night-vision she had acquired. "Whom do I have the honor of addressing?" she said humbly.

"Follow me," he said without answering. She knew he was the enemy. "And don't try to run back. We have a man at the door. You failed to follow instructions, even the least of them. Was your bodily need so great that you couldn't wait for us to come to you?"

"A woman has needs," she replied, grateful that her voice was steady.

"Where did you stay last night?"

She followed the back, outlined only in shape and without detail. Don Patricio had prepared her with an answer. "The nuns keep a home for their aging sisters outside San Lorenzo. They allowed me to escort one of their own from the Marqués's castle to the home yesterday evening and sheltered me for the night."

"Indeed? Then why did you travel to the church by cart?"

They had certainly been watching. "You specified that I was to come alone. How else did you think I would travel?"

The man did not answer but he picked up his pace. Consuelo followed more quickly, her leather shoes making no sound behind him. He turned once to make sure she was there and she caught a glimpse of a sharp black beard beneath a broad face. At last he turned to the right and stopped. "Brazen lady, if you indeed came alone as instructed. Let's hope that you are not lying to us, Consuelo, or you'll pay hard for that lie. Now turn your back to me."

Consuelo obeyed. She pressed her knees together to keep from trembling. She felt before she saw the bag come down over her head and the gloom turned to pitch. The edges drew tight around her neck, not cutting off her breath but making the blood throb as it made its way past the stricture. She pulled her rebozo around her tight.

A hand took her arm and turned her back around. "Walk forward." He kept his hand on her upper arm and she could feel its hardness through the rebozo. She walked.

Notwithstanding the bag, she sensed the greater light in the room. She brushed against a piece of furniture and stumbled slightly. The hand gripped her tighter and pulled her up. "Watch where you lead her," a new voice, thinner and more educated, commanded. "There. Put her there."

"Nice doll." She wasn't sure if it was a third voice or the second man had moved. She turned her head to try to follow the sound. She put her free hand out to feel her location, and her hand came to rest on the arm of a chair. "Sit down, Consuelo." She felt around not daring to lift the bag, and finding the chair seat, she sat. "Take off the bag, Elizonte." She winced as the bright light of the sunny mid-day assaulted her eyes.

"Good morning, Señorita Costa," said the educated man. She looked at him, still squinting from the light. He was as tall as she was, slim and fine featured. He wore the long black robe of a priest with a great red cross embroidered in the front. His hair was not tonsured but pulled tightly back, neither dark nor light, and his eyes, lively and intelligent, shone with what could be humor or malice.

"Good morning," she answered.

"I am Father Bernardo and this is Brother Elizonte." She looked at the thick-set, strong-looking man nearest to her, the one who had guided her in. He appeared to be not quite as tall as she but powerful in his physique. His narrow eyes were set deep in his face, which was deeply bruised around the eyes, hideously swollen along his lips and jaw, and his nose was broken like a fighter's. "No doubt you have heard your father speak of us."

"I have not as he has not shared his acquaintance with me."

"Really? Interesting," said Father Bernardo.

The third man in the room, seated behind a desk with an absurdly large feather quill pen and a big book open before him, was the priest who had said Mass not a half an hour before. He nodded silently and looked away.

"Well, shall we dispense with further pleasantries?"

"I would be delighted," Consuelo said.

"You certainly are a very self-possessed young woman," Father Bernardo said. "Your father's daughter in that sense, no doubt, though you don't seem compelled to speak constantly." He smiled and her skin crawled. She did not smile back. "Do you lack humor?" he asked.

"No. But I don't find my family's situation humorous. Nor do you, I posit. You are concerned with heresy and I am concerned with my mother's safety. Your note commanded my presence and my money. What is your charge?"

"Charge? As in what is your mother accused of?"

"No, what is the charge for her release." She thought of the Bishop's explanation. If it was money they needed, money they would get.

"My goodness, Señorita, you behave as if you were buying eggplants. Do you wish to see your mother first?"

"I wish to see her freed and in good health. If you manage this I shall pay your fee." Consuelo wondered where this strength was coming from, and whether such boldness would irritate or speed the process.

"I like your practical forthrightness. It is commendable, and rare in a woman." Consuelo smiled at this and Father Bernardo appeared mollified. "Perhaps this business can be concluded more efficaciously than I had feared. I dreaded tears and entreaties."

Brother Elizonte sighed and Father Bernardo turned to him. "Yes, Elizonte, I know. You see, Señorita, Brother Elizonte actually prefers tears, and begging too. He would have you grovel and plead. I am more practical than he is. Isn't this so, Elizonte?"

The thick man glared at his superior. Consuelo wondered at the interchange and looked over at the third man. He did not meet her eye.

"Now, just a few formalities and we will be on our way," Father Bernardo said. "Your Holiness, could you read the charge?" He raised an eyebrow at Consuelo. "You see, your words were well chosen without your even knowing so."

"Consuelo Costa Argenta, you are charged with harboring a Judaizer, aiding and abetting her blasphemy, and consorting with a Jew knowingly. How do you plead?" read the priest in a monotone.

Consuelo frowned in alarm. "How do I plead? What does this mean? I have done nothing wrong!" She looked from one priest to another.

"Oh but you have, my dear. Tell us, have you ever lit Sabbath candles for your mother, the Judaizer?" She shook her head. Father

Bernardo laughed softly. "Oh, Elizonte. You may have your way after all. Señorita Costa, shall I repeat the question?"

Consuelo struggled to keep calm. How much time had passed since she had entered that darkened doorway? It had to be at least a quarter hour. If only she could be certain that Don Patricio's men had seen her go into the church she could survive anything for an hour.

"You needn't repeat it, Father. I am innocent. I am a devout Christian. I have," she paused, hoping to take the right tack, "I have listened in awe to this reverend priest's sermon today, the most holy day of our Lord's life, and you will not find fault with me."

Father Bernardo looked over at the priest behind the desk, still holding his quill. "Well, Monsignor, how do you like that?" The priest nodded but did not answer. Consuelo saw Father Bernardo's mouth tighten for an instant then revert to the previous sardonic smile. "Let us review, Señorita. Though we will soon dispense with honorifics I will still do you the courtesy of title in honor of your display of bravery. Or is it bravura?"

Consuelo did not answer.

"Cut the garbage," Elizonte snapped. "Let's get to it!"

Father Bernardo didn't even spare his colleague a glance. "Señorita, one last chance before we escalate measures. Did you light the candles for your mother, the Judaizer?"

Consuelo looked him straight in the eye. "No."

In the silence that ensued Consuelo strained to hear over her heart, to discern any sound of approaching help. At last, though, it was the scratching of the quill on the heavy page of a book that broke the stillness. All heads turned to the priest almost as in relief. The previously silent man spoke.

"Escort her to see her mother. I will not have death in my church on Easter Sunday, even of a heretic. Whether her Christian heart is moved by the sight or not remains to be seen." He underlined what he had written with a flourish and blotted the ink. He slammed the book shut and everyone twitched.

"As you wish, Monsignor. Come, my dear. We must do as we are commanded." Father Bernardo offered his arm. Consuelo pulled her rebozo close and turned away. She heard him chuckle quietly. "Lead the way, Elizonte." Consuelo heard the bells ring the quarter of the hour.

198 CLAUDIA H. LONG

Once again they entered the dark hall, darker yet from having again been in the light. Consuelo stepped carefully, unwilling to stumble before these men. Elizonte led and she followed. Behind her Father Bernardo kept a respectable distance, and last, shutting the door and the light behind him, came the Monsignor. They walked deeper into the underpinnings of the church. As her eyes adjusted she saw hallways branch off, small and cold, but they continued in the main one. At last she heard Elizonte's footsteps stop and she was very close behind him when she stopped as well. There was the sound of metal on metal, a lock sliding, a key turning. She held her breath, nausea born of fear making her perspire. The door swung open and the smell of vinegar and excrement overwhelmed her.

LEILA

I hear them unlock the door. Bastards are coming back.

I know that he is brave but he must not fight them. Though I admit I was grateful that he broke that lummox's jaw. Let them take me. I am finished.

Isidro is brave, he is strong, he is the biggest man I have ever seen, and so handsome. But even he cannot stop the inevitable.

The carriage is jolting. I know this must be painful but I cannot feel my legs, my arms, or even my eyes. Where is Isidro? He fought to save me but he isn't here.

If only I could have some water. I am thirsty. Mother, mother, light the candles again. Save me again. The pain is coming faster, I will lose this child. I can feel the birth agony and the birth blood flows. Mother! Stop this pain.

Why tie me when I cannot rise? Don't let them find Consuelo, Isidro. I am finished but don't let them find her.

I am thirsty.

The light is in the window. I am so thirsty. Consuelo, you are so curious, climbing on the table, so quick with your words, your eyes, your little hands. But you are growing so tall, like your father in so many ways. Come, Consuelo, bring me some water.

She should have worn her blue dress. She should marry Juan Carlos. He loves her. Doesn't she know? She is like her father, deaf to what a man is feeling, what a man is saying under his words. Perhaps there will be a child from that night. Perhaps she will light the candles now.

The door is opening. Please don't let them find Consuelo. Isidro, don't let them take her.

CONSUELO

"That whore of a maid didn't clean," Elizonte muttered.

An oil lamp sent its smoky light up in a corner but there was no window in the stone-walled room to add brightness. Consuelo hesitated at the doorjamb, unwilling to enter until she could see more, unwilling to see what was in front of her.

To the left of the door was a table about six paces in length, and four chairs. There was little room left on that side for anything else. To her right a small chair, child size, was overturned and a shovel appeared to have been flung to the stone floor. The sconce with the oil lamp was on the far wall. On the floor below the lamp, on a pile of straw, lay the small form of a woman on her side, curled into a ball. Her grey hair was undone and spread in part over her face. Her feet and legs were bare and Consuelo saw filth and bloody markings on them. A soiled nightdress barely covered her torso. Consuelo's ears rang with the horror and she rushed forward, her feet splashing and slipping in some spilled liquid, and knelt at the side of the form. She reached out her hand and pushed the hair away from the face. "Mother!" she said, pulling the woman to herself. She put her face next to the old woman's and heard her breathe. "May you bastards burn in eternal hell!"

They dragged her away from her mother.

"What are you howling about? She's alive, isn't she?" Elizonte said.

"Shut up," Father Bernardo said to his aide, surprisingly coarsely. Consuelo looked up at him. "He is ignorant of the finer emotions. Now, my dear. Let us go back to our earlier conversation." He righted the small chair and gently pushed her into it.

"How much do you want for her?" Consuelo said, sniffing hard.

Father Bernardo smiled again. "We will get to that. But first let me ask you again. Did you light the candles for your mother on the Jewish Sabbath?"

Why did he go back to that she wondered. Why didn't he just take her money and let her go? "No."

Father Bernardo shook his head. "Elizonte, you may proceed." Consuelo looked nervously over at the thug. He was licking his lips.

"Monsignor! What do they want?" she asked. Her courage was slipping.

The Monsignor shrugged and took a seat at the table. Elizonte stepped between her and the others and looked down at her. "Stand up." Shakily, Consuelo rose to her feet. Before she could think her head rang with pain and she was on the floor next to her mother. The room spun for a moment and red and black lights flashed. When the room stabilized she felt her face wet and put a hand to her mouth. It came away bloody at the same time she tasted the iron of her life force. "Stand up," Elizonte said again in the same tone, but this time Consuelo could not obey.

She waited, hopeless now, for Elizonte to pull her to her feet, to hit her, for her world to end. Sorrow almost, but not quite, trumped fear. One blow and she had failed.

"Now, Señorita, let us try another question. Do you eat pork?"

Perhaps there was still a chance she could convince Father Bernardo. His decision was all-important to her now. "Just this last Tuesday," she mumbled, swallowing blood.

"You ate meat during Holy Week?" Father Bernardo appeared scandalized. Consuelo's momentary hope evaporated. "And you call yourself a Christian?" Elizonte stepped toward her and she cowered in the straw. "Don't bother, Elizonte. We have the confession we need. She eats meat during the Holy Week. Her mother Judaizes openly. Monsignor, will that suffice?"

All eyes, Consuelo's included, turned towards the Monsignor, seated away from the women on the floor and the men tormenting them. He did not look at her. Consuelo knew he would not redeem her. And yet he appeared to take his time answering, his gaze steadily on Father Bernardo. Finally, he spoke. "The Holy Office has deemed the eating of meat during Holy Week to be a minor transgression, one that is as common to the faithful as to the heretic. You have convicted the mother. The daughter has yet to confess."

The words buzzed in Consuelo's head in the ensuing silence. Far from a reprieve it was condemnation to further pain. She understood, though she had no previous experience in torture, that the raising and dashing of hope was part of the malicious game they were playing. But it gave her more time. Father Bernardo's attention was solely on the Monsignor, and Elizonte stood bouncing his weight from foot to foot, waiting for his orders. The Monsignor was not yet through.

"You have commandeered my holy church on this most holy day for your prosecution. I have housed your penitent, for such is the way that the Judaizer must be called, for three days while you waited for the daughter. My patience is wearing thin."

The bells outside tolled the third quarter. The hour was almost up. She must survive another quarter. Then Leila moaned.

All four turned to the woman. Consuelo was not far from the mess of straw where her mother lay. She reached out her hand to her mother as Leila moved on the straw. Her filthy gown rose on her thighs, revealing more excrement, and stripes where she had been flogged. Consuelo's gorge rose in horror and then in fury. She crawled close and laid her rebozo over her mother's legs. She could not let this crime go unrecognized.

"You are sick men," she said from the floor. "You have beaten an old, sick woman for no reason. She is helpless and yet you tortured her. What kind of emissaries from our Lord Jesus would do that?"

"Are you questioning the Holy Office?" Father Bernardo said, his voice bearing none of the irony or amusement it had formerly.

"I am questioning *you*. I don't think the Supreme Tribune would support what you did."

Elizonte did not wait for orders this time, but grabbed her and pulled her up by her hair. With one hand he grabbed her breast and squeezed viciously. Then another blow sent her back to the floor. She heard a scream and felt the sound come from her throat. She was streaming blood from her nose and gagging on the flow. Her mouth opened and she spewed forth the angry fluid.

"Enough," Father Bernardo said. "She will reflect on her sins and we will question her anew in an hour. Fear has a way of multiplying with time and is watered and fed by the memory of pain. Reflect, Señorita, as your confession will make your sentence lighter."

Consuelo tried not to move. Father Bernardo walked to the door, followed by Elizonte. "No, Elizonte, you stay with the ladies. They may have need of your services before the hour is past." He nodded to the Monsignor, whose face remained impassive, and strode out.

"The Inquisition will ferret out any heresy, Señorita," the Monsignor said as he too passed the doorway. "It would be convenient to conclude this matter quickly."

The door shut and Consuelo and Leila were left with Elizonte. She saw his feet approach her. She tried not to move but a shudder ran involuntarily through her. He crouched down where Consuelo lay crumpled on the straw next to her mother. "Your mother came to us in her night shirt and your father dropped his pants for us after a few glasses of wine," he said, breathing his foul breath into her face. "You are the first of the family to be worth the stripping. I can't wait."

Consuelo turned her face away. The bleeding had stopped but the pain in her nose and cheek had increased to a steady throb. She had to last the hour. "What do they want from me?" she asked, her voice thick and congested. She cleared her throat and spat out the clotted phlegm.

"Save your confession for Father Bernardo. I'm only interested in softening you up." He grunted an ugly laugh and licked his swollen lip. "Softening you up," he repeated. He lifted the hem of her skirt.

"But why?" She was buying time, she knew, but how much he would give her before he gave in to his base desires was unknown.

"We catch a couple of you Jews, we get more money from the King. Or his henchmen like the Viceroy or the Archbishop. They think there's no more of you to find but they're wrong. They want to close us up but girls like you are still out there, praying to your false god of Moses, and we're going to find you." He ran his hand up her leg and Consuelo shuddered. "Like that, huh?"

"And if I confess?"

"Save it. Your ecclesiastic advisor will be back in an hour. Meanwhile, you and mama here are all mine." He grabbed the waist of her pantalettes.

"Wait."

"Why? Do you think you'll reform in the next hour?" He reached under her to take hold of the back of her underclothing. With a single pull he tore the garment off and he shoved his hand between her thighs. "Now, let's see you cry a little."

She hated herself for obliging but the tears came of their own accord as he grabbed violently at her tender flesh where Juan Carlos had loved her not two nights before. She writhed away but he held her down with no intent of letting her go.

"Please don't," she whispered as he moved back to untie his pants.

Elizonte looked down on her, his wet lips twisted in a sour smirk. "Please? Oh my. Is that the best you can do? Your father begged more prettily than that."

She struggled to think of more humble words, now only desperate to survive. She listened intently but the pounding of her pulse in her injured face drowned out any sounds from outside the room. She had not yet heard the bells toll the hour and she realized that anything that was loud enough to be salvation would be audible far above her own heart. She was on her own and she would have to provide her own rescue. There was only one tack she could take. "I will give myself willingly to you. Anything you want. But I beg you, let my mother live."

"You will give me anything I want whether willingly or not." He opened his pants and his ability to make good his threat was evident.

"Wait," she said. "I understand that they want me to confess but I am a Christian. I cannot confess to a lie. I have only come to pay my mother's fine."

"So you said. But where is the gold? I don't see any purse and we don't take letters of credit. Especially not ones backed by your father!" Elizonte repeated his gargling chuckle.

"Let me show you," she said. This had to work. Consuelo struggled to sit up.

"What are you doing?" Elizonte asked, but leaned back enough that she could sit.

"I want to show you where I am hiding the money."

His eyebrows shot up in his greasy forehead. "I bet I would find it anyway," he leered.

As she rose the pain in her head rose with her. She repressed a longing to lie back down, let the horrors of the moment proceed without her. But Elizonte's leer gave her strength. She got to her knees and reached out to steady herself on Elizonte's shoulder. The move surprised him enough that he kept still and she used him as a base to rise quavering to her feet.

Her hands were clumsy as she started to unknot her sash. "Let me help you," Elizonte said. She moved away from the straw where her mother lay and Elizonte, now standing as well, moved with her. He held his pants up with one hand, still showing his readiness to have his carnal way. She looked away, took the *mantilla* she had tucked in her sash and laid it on the table where the Monsignor had been sitting. Elizonte motioned towards it with his free hand. She nodded. He walked to the table.

Consuelo took a step back and willed her legs to stop quivering. She was between her mother and the door, with Elizonte at the table. If she ran for the door, and if it was not locked, she might be able to get out before Elizonte caught her. Too many *ifs*. If the door was locked or she was not fast enough, the consequences... she could not think about them. And she could not leave her mother.

He was watching her. "Sit down and let me show you," she said, her voice still thickened by blood covering the tremor in her throat.

Elizonte took a seat. "Make it quick. I've got a couple of things to show you and if you waste another minute you'll pay with plenty of little cries." His speech seemed to arouse him more and the glitter of evil returned to his eyes.

She thought back. She hadn't heard the door lock when the men had left. She turned her back to him and looked at the door as she started to unwind the sash. When they had arrived the sound of the key unlocking the door had been loud. There had been no such sound when the men had left. It had to be unlocked. She turned to face Elizonte again and his eyes were on her hands. Greed was warring with lust and his pleasure in causing pain, and she only hoped greed would triumph. She moved slowly, trying to appear careful, not dilatory. Just as the purse came into view the bells began to ring the hour.

She stopped, listening as the whole room vibrated lightly with the strong tones. It was Easter and no mere tolling of the noon hour would suffice. An entire musical enchantment was being rung. Even Elizonte appeared to be caught in the grandeur of the moment.

She took the purse in one hand and the sash in the other. Dropping the sash on the floor she tossed the purse to Elizonte. As he caught it she moved as if to pick up the sash. Instead, she grabbed the shovel. Elizonte's face snapped up to her but he held the purse. She swung the shovel at him and he raised his arms to shield his head. Her blow staggered him but his roar sent her back towards her mother.

The bells were still ringing. The shovel would not stop Elizonte. He still had the purse in his left hand but his right hand was enough to grab the shovel as she swung it at him once more. She held on with all her force, then using her height she pulled the shovel up and away from his hand. The suddenness of the release made the shovel twist sideways. Consuelo saw her mother move, inching her way from the straw, and with a final push she threw the shovel at the lamp above the straw.

The room plunged into momentary darkness as the lamp came crashing down. Consuelo felt her mother's hand on her ankle. She crouched and lifted the tiny, emaciated woman into her arms as the straw under the fallen lamp burst into flames.

With a shout Elizonte rushed at her. His pants, not yet reknotted, slipped down and tangled his legs. His howl curdled the air as he landed face down in the burning straw.

Consuelo was at the door, with her mother flung over her shoulder like a burden. The catch stuck on her first attempt and she screamed with relief when the door opened under her tug. She ran into the dark hall, the light from the blaze behind her making shadows bounce on the stone ahead of her. She ran straight, remembering that there had been no turns from the first room to the second.

Behind her Elizonte was shouting for Father Bernardo. The bells suddenly stopped and in the silence she heard him lurching against the walls, his hard breath nearing her. Then ahead came the sound of another. "Elizonte!" It was Father Bernardo. She was trapped between them.

The light from the burning straw was now far behind her and the halls were black as pitch. She had no choice. She could not run straight or back. A small hallway branched to the left. She took it.

Deeper and deeper into the maze she ran, the sounds now of both men behind her. Again she took a hallway, another, and ran behind a curtain to another. The halls got narrower, until they were only passages. She had no thoughts of where she could be, only to keep going until she could go no longer.

She could hear the men's boots but she had only soft leather shoes. She stopped running and strove to control her breath. Her mother, tiny and thin as she was, weighed heavily upon her. "Mother?"

"Consuelo," Leila whispered. "Leave me. I am done for. Get away."

Consuelo shivered. Her mother was lucid. "I can't."

Her mother did not answer. Consuelo heard a new noise, a harsh banging as if metal struck metal, and the footsteps moved away, getting fainter as if they had chosen a different turn. She put her mother down and breathed again. Leila moaned. She couldn't leave her but she couldn't carry her further. Consuelo strained to hear any sound of rescue but there was none. She felt the walls until she came to an opening. There was faint light in the distance. She went back to her mother.

"I am going for help. I will be back, I promise." Her mother didn't respond. Consuelo could not see her, except now that she had adjusted to the darkness, in outline. She tucked the rebozo around her mother, kissed her, and made the sign of the cross over her. She blinked back tears and tiptoed away toward the passage.

She counted her steps, hoping to remember how to get back, but she kept her footfall silent. If the light led her to her captors she would have to double back before they saw her. If they saw her she would die. There was another loud bang but she had no choice, she had to go on.

Quickly she came to the source of the light, a high window with metal crossbars, about a hand's breadth above her head. Too high to see out of and too small to escape through, she made note of it and went on. The illumination showed her that there were again choices of passages and she counted, two left, two right, to keep her bearings. She chose the wider of the halls and felt a sudden increase in the temperature.

She slowed her steps, inching forward. Another harsh noise and then she caught the sound of a woman's voice. More light came from the next hall and she turned towards it. Another turn and without warning she was in a small kitchen. The woman who had let her in and had shown her to the privy curtain was at a tiny wood stove, stirring a pot. The smell of *atole* reached her through her still blocked nose and Consuelo felt the room swim.

The woman said something in the native language and crossed herself. She came towards Consuelo and Consuelo stepped back. "No," said the woman in Spanish, "don't be afraid." She grabbed a rag and a pitcher of water and poured water onto the rag. She held it out to Consuelo. "Your face."

Consuelo took the wet cloth and patted her face. It hurt and the cloth came away with dried blood all over it. The woman motioned to the only chair and Consuelo shook her head. "I need to get out," she said.

The woman nodded. "Something is happening this way." She led her out through the other side of the little kitchen and Consuelo glanced at the *atole* pot with longing as she went past. The porridge of ground maize bubbled gently and Consuelo's stomach growled.

They went into another hall and shortly afterwards turned. Consuelo realized that they were passing the privy curtain to the door where she had first arrived. She heard men and she froze. The sounds were coming from the other side of the door. A thick bar had been dropped across the door locking it from the inside.

"There are men outside," the woman said. "The Monsignor said to keep the door locked. I can open it, but I am afraid."

Consuelo hesitated. If the men outside were Father Alonso's she was saved. If not, she was doomed. "The two men, the tall monk and the thicker one, did anyone else come with them?"

The woman shook her head. "They brought an old person. I don't know, man or woman. Looked almost dead. Did they smash your face?" Consuelo nodded. "I thought they were evil even though they wear the dress of God. Are there more outside?"

"I don't know. We will have to look."

The sounds from the other side of the door had stopped. Consuelo and the maid stood still. Then a strange roar started behind the door. Consuelo pushed the maid to the side just as a violent jolt hit the door. The metal bar jumped, but held.

From the hall she heard the clatter of boots. She whirled just as Father Bernardo rounded the far corner, a huge knife in his hand.

They ran back through the kitchen. "There is another door," the maid hissed, and taking a turn in the hall they reached a door just as another crash reverberated through the stone. Consuelo opened the little door a crack in time to see men with a battering ram storm the larger door breaking through the lock and into the under-passages of the cathedral.

"What are you doing to our church?" a man screamed from the courtyard.

A shout from within told her that the arriving forces had met up with Bernardo and Elizonte. She smelled smoke. The straw, she thought.

She needed to get her mother. "I have to go back in," she said to the maid. She turned and ran back, this time paying no heed to the noise. She could let Don Patricio's men deal with the priests. She ran back into the passage, counting desperately. She ran down one hall but she should have seen the little window, she thought. She turned back and took the next one. It turned and she tried to count back.

Something ran under her foot and she stumbled. Her hands hit the floor and she felt her sleeve tear. She shuddered. If there were rats in the passage they would be running all over her mother. She lurched back up and felt her way along the wall. The smell of smoke was stronger. *Stone won't burn,* she thought. She coughed and her eyes began to sting.

She crouched down, as the smoke was stronger higher up. She heard a faint moan. "Mother. I'm coming," she cried, and moved faster. She fell over the form on the floor before she saw it and managed only barely to break her fall before crushing Leila beneath her. Her mother moaned again.

Her hands and shoulders ached but Consuelo took up her mother in her arms once again, this time cradling her gently. She retraced her steps through the now familiar passage to the kitchen, keeping low as the smoke followed her. Her eyes were streaming when she reached the hall to the small door. She stumbled forward and pushed the door open with the last of her strength. She sank to the ground in the sunlit courtyard, Leila in her arms, as, from the larger door, a thick, muscular man emerged screaming, his hair and his clothes on fire.

Consuelo sat in the small carriage with her mother in her lap, spooning *atole* into the barely conscious woman's mouth. At the driver's bench Juan Carlos drove the horses forward along the main road towards San Lorenzo. "We can't go far with her," he said. "It is more than seven hours to the castle from here by cart." Consuelo barely heard him and did not reply. "You will have to give me directions," he said.

"I don't know if I can take you to the safe house," Consuelo said. "I may need to proceed alone again." Her voice was flat. She didn't want to be alone again.

The water brigade had arrived and the cathedral reaped the good fortune of being situated at the crossing of the Xochimilco lake and the canals that led from it. There was ample water, those canals having fed the aqueduct that brought water to Mexico City since the Aztecs' time. They had put out the fire that Consuelo had started, but only after Juan Carlos, furious at the hesitation of Don Patricio's men, had stormed the basement in search of her.

Father Bernardo and Elizonte had left in the custody of the Marqués's men, Elizonte carried, still screaming, on a plank. Consuelo had watched with disgust as Don Patricio's emissary bowed cordially to the Monsignor on the way out. He had done nothing to protect her but had stood by while Elizonte had beaten her, had left her to his lecherous torment, and yet was being thanked by Don Patricio's proxy.

"I couldn't wait for them to negotiate entry," Juan Carlos muttered. "I almost lost you."

Consuelo nodded. It was his ax on the door that had distracted Elizonte and Father Bernardo from their pursuit of her, and he who had insisted, finally, on the battering ram. It was he who had stormed the cathedral just as Father Bernardo had come round with the knife. If he had waited any longer she and her mother would have died.

"But they hurt you anyway." His voice was rough. "He had a knife. He was going to kill you."

Consuelo put her hand up. She could never tell him of Elizonte's handling of her. His love had survived Leandro's abuse of her but the disgust he would feel for her once he learned of Elizonte's gropings would likely be more than he would tolerate as a husband. And she wondered how she would lie with Juan Carlos and not let the memory of Elizonte's leer lie between them.

None of that mattered at the moment for now she needed to get Leila to the safe house. She shielded her mother's face from the brilliant sunshine, so welcome after the darkness of the cathedral basement. Leila moaned.

"We've got to get her to shelter," Consuelo said once more. Leila had stopped eating a while back and was breathing raggedly. With two horses and Juan Carlos' expert handling of the cart they had reached the outskirts of San Lorenzo in less than two hours but Consuelo was getting desperate.

"We're as far as I have gone before. You have to guide me."

Consuelo looked down at the limp body in her arms. She would risk Don Juan de Leon and his family for her mother. "Count the streets and turn at the twelfth one, then we will go until you see the well." *God help us if Don de Leon turns us away. Or more likely if Susana turns us away.*

They passed the butcher shop. "Look for a red door."

"Your secret safe house has a red door? Brilliant, hiding in plain sight."

"No, it is the drab brown one next to it." But she thought about what Juan Carlos had just said. "They will not welcome you. You could mean trouble."

"They will not turn us away."

They pulled the cart up to the house and Juan Carlos jumped down from the driver's seat. "I'll go get the groom." Consuelo smiled to herself despite her anxiety. He was so sure. She watched him climb the few stairs to the door and rap sharply. Moments later the door was opened by Jose Luis.

"Sir?"

"I am Juan Carlos Castillo and I must speak to Don Juan de Leon."

Jose Luis sketched a bow and stood aside, but as Juan Carlos was about to step in past him Jose Luis' eyes lit on the cart and Consuelo. He stepped back into the doorway. "What does this mean?"

"I have my...my neighbor, Señorita Consuelo Costa Argenta, and her mother, and they are in urgent need of shelter."

"Jose Luis," Consuelo said from the cart. He nodded to her, his eyes widening, but turned his attention back to Juan Carlos.

"I shall speak with my father," he said crisply closing the door on Juan Carlos.

Juan Carlos turned to Consuelo. "Not a very welcoming family, I must say." She did not reply as she could not speak aloud the reasons for their careful rudeness. She had been as Juan Carlos was until a week before: knowing in her mind that the secret Jews were in constant danger but never, until now, understanding the fear in their hearts.

At last the door opened again and Jose Luis nodded to Juan Carlos. "Get your women in and I will take care of the cart. Again," he added to Consuelo, with a glimmer of a smile.

Juan Carlos took the few stairs in a jump and reached in to the cart.

He lifted Leila into his arms, and holding her with one, gave his hand to Consuelo. Consuelo stood and the toll of the morning showed in the pain in every joint. She breathed hard and then, pursing her lips against any complaint of her own, alit from the bed of the cart. She walked up the stairs quickly, hoping she gave no outward sign of pain. Her face, bruised and swollen, would be sign enough.

"We only need shelter until my mother can be brought home or to the Marqués's castle in a condition that will not raise questions," Consuelo said. "We cannot have anyone spread rumors and our home is not safe from prying eyes, as I have learned."

"And you think we are safe?" Susana's sharp voice made her turn. Susana gasped. "What have you done to your face?"

"What has she done?" Juan Carlos asked, his voice rising. "She has done nothing. This is what was done to her. And worse, and worse to her mother."

"You bring us this trouble?" Susana was close to shrieking.

"Take them upstairs," an older voice said, and Don Juan de Leon appeared at the end of the hall. "My God, what have they done to Leila?"

Juan Carlos mounted the stairs to the second floor, Leila in his arms. "Left door," Consuelo said, guiding him into the room where she had spent the night. As he turned she caught sight of a dark stain on the arm of his light summer coat. "Juan Carlos! Were you hurt?"

He looked back over his shoulder. "It's only a scratch." The size of the stain now reddening again from the motion of carrying Leila told her otherwise.

He laid the woman on the bed. Consuelo took his coat lapels in her hands. "Let me look at it."

"It is the least of the wounds in this party," he said, but allowed her to take his coat off. The sleeve of his shirt was torn and a long gash ran the length of his left forearm. "That priest wielded a nasty knife," he said.

"I will need to dress it, though it looks clean enough," Consuelo said. She glanced at the bed upon which her mother lay. Leila had no color left, her skin stretched over the fine bones of her face, translucent and pearly. The bed looked inviting and Consuelo fought the urge to lie down next to her mother and close her eyes. "I must attend to my mother first," she said, turning away. She caught her own face in the mirror and gasped, shocked. "Good heavens. I traveled all the way across the city looking like this?"

Her eye was swollen and had started to color. Vestiges of dried blood coated her nose, cheek and lip, and her mouth was swollen on one side.

"You looked worse when you came out of the church," Juan Carlos said smiling. "You've improved."

"I will only need a piece of beef to bring down the swelling. And maguey for your arm. It is my mother that I am worried about. What shall I do for her? Vinegar, of course, and fennel if I can get it, but what else? I am at a loss. My studies did not give me enough to cure the horrors of what she has suffered."

"It may be in God's hands," Juan Carlos said.

"Then I hope He is merciful."

*   *   *

"*You* cannot stay here," Susana said pointedly to Juan Carlos. "We cannot have you, along with Consuelo and Leila, in the house. It will draw too much attention to us. If anyone who knows the reasons for Leila's imprisonment were to trace her here we would be doomed."

"Susana," Don Juan said, "enough. I am a respected businessman, entitled to receive any guests I choose. I accept Señorita Consuelo's word that you are to be trusted," he added to Juan Carlos, who nodded. "You shall stay tonight with us and then go on your way. The women will be safely attended to here."

"I need some herbs," Consuelo said, "and some maguey." Susana nodded distractedly. "And a slice of beef for my face."

Susana rose. "I will get what you need. You can tend to your mother." She did not look at Juan Carlos as she left.

Consuelo stood up too. "I will go now. My mother needs me."

Little Marcela hurried into the room with a small pitcher and a towel. "This is for you to wash the cuts. Mother says they have to be washed before they are dressed." Marcela smiled. "Mother says everything

has to be washed before it is dressed. Even me!" She turned to Juan
Carlos, her eyes big. "You have washed your hair too much! It's like
an angel's hair! Like the angel in the Church picture."

"Thank you, Señorita," Juan Carlos smiled back at her, then threw
Consuelo a quizzical look. She nodded back. Of course the de Leon
family attended Mass regularly. They were not suicidal.

Consuelo took the pitcher and mounted the stairs. She shut the
door and lifted the gown off her mother. It was fit only to be burned.
She washed the woman who lay unconscious again then covered her
nakedness with a blanket. "Sweet Jesus, be kind to my mother," she
prayed. "Holy Mary, pray for us."

There was a tap at the door and Consuelo rose to open it. She
stepped back in surprise at the sight of Don Juan. "Señor," she said.

"I want to see her," he said softly. He approached the motionless
woman. "Leila?" He looked at her, tears on his cheeks. Consuelo stood
back, watching in silence. "Leila, it's me."

Leila stirred slightly and Consuelo felt her heart speed up. She
watched as her mother opened her eyes a bit.

"It's me, Juanito."

She closed her eyes again and Don Juan de Leon dropped to one
knee and buried his grey head in his arms.

The night passed slowly. Leila burned with fever. Consuelo, her
body aching and her own face on fire, mopped her mother's brow with
vinegar, poured a distillation of *reina del prado* into a spoon and tried
to feed it to the twisting woman as she lay in agony on the narrow
bed. At one point Juan Carlos came in and offered to sit with Leila
while Consuelo slept, but she sent him away. Susana had insisted on
wrapping a piece of molding bread on his cut arm and the smell
made Consuelo retch. "Go away. I will stay with her."

As the sun rose Juan Carlos returned to sit with her. He had taken
off the bready bandage and the cut was serene and healing. "What is
that alchemy?" Consuelo asked. "I will have to learn it. There is so much
I have yet to understand."

Juan Carlos put his arm around her. "I love you, Consuelo. You
are brave and good." She leaned her head on him, exhausted.

When she awoke the sun was streaming in the window. She was lying on the bed, Juan Carlos was sitting by her side. "Where's my mother?" she said panicky.

"I moved her to the other room. Susana is sitting with her."

Consuelo struggled to rise. Every part of her body hurt. She moaned then bit her lip. That hurt worse than moving. "I will bring you some chocolate," Juan Carlos said.

"No. I am up. Let me clean my face again and I will tend to my mother." She poured what was left of the water in the pitcher onto a cloth and looked in the mirror. She was a fright.

Cleaner but no better she went to the little alcove where Juan Carlos had been given a bed and found Leila, motionless but still breathing. Susana dozed in a chair beside her. She put her hand to her mother's forehead and pulled it away from the burning skin. The fever was worse.

She stood helpless beside the bed. Should she call for a priest? Her mother would not last long with this fever and should not die unshriven, and yet, in this house could she provide her mother with the last rites to which she was entitled? She did not know but she was sure of one thing: no one should be made to die without the final unction. Judaizer or not, her mother had been a Christian in acts, and in bringing up her only child.

Susana opened her eyes. "Oh, I have been asleep but a moment."

Consuelo smiled a bit, the most she could with her swollen lip. "Thank you for watching over my mother. I am grateful to your entire family."

Susana rose. "Take the chair. I hope it was not improper to let Juan Carlos watch over you last night. I could not stop him in any event."

Consuelo nodded. She could not say, *I am his wife.* "I am certain there was no impropriety. But my mother. Susana, I must have a priest for her."

Susana's eyes flashed but she said nothing as she left the alcove. Consuelo took her chair. A few minutes later Marcela came in wearing a plain cotton dress, carrying a cup of chocolate and a roll. Consuelo took them gratefully. "Can you bring something, broth, perhaps, for my mother?"

"Surely, but my mother says your mother won't need anything much longer."

Consuelo frowned at the child. "You mustn't say that."

"My mother says you should say anything that's true and that saying something won't make it happen or not happen."

Impertinent child, Consuelo thought, but she had a point. She was relieved of further commentary as Leila twisted suddenly. Consuelo leaned over her. "Mother?"

"Isidro! Consuelo send in Isidro! I must see him! Isidro!" Her mother called out, loud and shrill.

"I will," she said immediately.

"Who's Isidro?" Marcela asked.

"Quiet, child. Get Señor Juan Carlos. Now."

"The angel-haired man?"

"Get him."

Consuelo stroked her mother's hair. She knew the look, the wildness in Leila's eyes. There was not much time.

Juan Carlos came in followed by Susana. "Get my father. Ride to him, bring him. My mother is going."

"You can't bring another here!" Susana said.

"I can and I will. Consuelo, your father is at the Marqués's castle. He arrived there after we left. I heard that much from Don Patricio's worthless men. I will ride to him, it is less than a half a day's journey for me on a horse. But can your father ride well?"

"Yes. Brilliantly."

"Good, then we will be back tonight."

Consuelo stepped out of the alcove and followed Juan Carlos down the stairs. "I will need a priest to give her the last rites. But I don't know how to do that here."

"I will manage that as well," he said grimly. He kissed her quickly and left.

The hours passed in silence and the midday meal was served. Consuelo was hungry but did not want to leave Leila. Marcela brought broth but Leila could not be roused so Consuelo drank it. If Juan Carlos did not return in time could she say the prayers for Leila?

Susana came in as the sun was setting. "They will be back soon. There isn't much time. We will help her die in the faith."

"You will admit a priest?" Consuelo was surprised.

Susana laughed bitterly. "We will admit him and it will be past the time where he can change matters. Your mother maintained her faith against all odds. She lit her Sabbath candles, the only element of the faith that she could recall, and look how she suffered for it. And yet, from what you and Juan Carlos have said, she never denied it, even under extreme duress. We will not make her die a Christian."

"But she was a Christian."

"Like so many of us. Our faith or belief in one God, in the God of Moses, will not die with her, will not die with me. We will suffer to preserve it and we will endure to the end of days. But I am not a fool. We will say a novena. If anyone asks, a novena was said for your mother's soul."

"Thank you."

"*Baruch ata Adonai*," Susana began. Consuelo joined in until the prayer changed from the candles one she knew. Nine times, Susana said a prayer. Nine times, Consuelo made the sign of the cross over Leila. Nine times, Susana turned away.

The sounds of horse hooves in the street rose to the open window. They could not come rushing in for that would give news to the neighbors that someone was dying. Consuelo heard voices in the hall, the sound of her father taking the stairs three at a time. She emerged in time to see him, long legged and pale, as he reached the head of the stairway. "Father!" He looked at Consuelo and pulled her into his arms.

Consuelo laid her head upon his chest. He stroked her back. She felt tears run down her face and he rocked her back and forth, for once not saying a word. Then she moved away. "This way," she said and led him into the alcove.

"Leila, my Leila." He stood above the bed looking down at his wife. Consuelo pulled the chair for him but he shook his head, then lay down on the bed next to the motionless woman. He wrapped his arms around his wife and held her as the life seeped from her body.

"Isidro," Leila whispered, "stay with me."

"I am here."

Gently, he turned her face to the wall.

A half an hour later Juan Carlos rapped on the front door. In the dark Consuelo could see his hair picking up the light of the lantern. A form stood behind him. "I have brought the priest to give Señora Costa her last rites."

Jose Luis opened the door. "Thank you, Father. Our aunt is upstairs. She has been calling for you this past hour. Her time is very near."

Juan Carlos and the priest entered and Jose Luis led the way to the alcove. Isidro stood at the head of the bed, his face impassive. Consuelo returned to Lelia's bedside and knelt, keeping her face concealed. She knew her role. But as she started to cry the weight of the week broke upon her. The tears did not have to be forced.

The priest lay his hand upon Leila's brow and turned to Jose Luis, frowning. "I am too late."

"No! That cannot be! She lived while I sent my cousin to fetch you!"

"The ways of the Lord can be swift," the priest said. "You did not delay?"

Juan Carlos shook his head. "Of course not, though you were at your dinner."

The priest nodded. "It is too late for the *viaticum* but prayer is never misplaced."

"She was confessed before Easter and we said a novena as we waited," Susana said.

"It is as well," the priest answered. "I will perform the last rites." He opened his bag and Consuelo breathed in the aromas of the spices and oil. "*In nombre patri, filis, spiritu sanctu,*" he intoned, and Isidro, Juan Carlos and Consuelo crossed themselves. Susana and Jose Luis had moved out of range of the priest. "Amen."

ISIDRO

"I am sorry, my old friend," Don Juan said to Isidro. He put his hand on the man's shoulder. Isidro did not step back, feeling the comfort of childhood friendship.

"It has been a quarter century," Isidro replied hoarsely. "I am grateful for the care you showed Leila at the end." His voice broke on his wife's name and he could not go on. He sank to the settee.

The two men sat silently. "I killed her," Isidro said finally.

Don Juan said nothing.

"I let them take her. I fought them but they were too strong. And I could not save her."

"Your daughter did," Don Juan said finally.

"She tried."

Isidro knew he should thank Consuelo for rescuing Leila but he could not bring himself to do so. She was upstairs with Susana washing Leila's body for burial. Susana had a clean shroud ready.

"Juan Carlos Castillo insisted that I ride the last part of the journey behind him on his horse, blindfolded. I did not know I was prohibited from knowing where my erstwhile rival lived."

Don Juan smiled wryly. "We live openly. There was no need. But my daughter-in-law fears for us all the time."

"You are one of the best known traders in the colony," Isidro said, allowing the momentary distraction from his grief. "You made a lot of money in the twenty five years since we saw you last."

"Yes, I have been blessed with success."

"And sons, from what I heard. Four sons."

"Two living. You met Jose Luis and his wife, my daughter-in-law Susana. They have given me but one grandchild to date, a girl. But I have hope. My other son has gone north to the mining towns to make his fortune. I hear from him only yearly and as yet he has no wife, no child."

"Sometimes a wife is harder to get than others," Isidro said with a small smile. He recalled, so long ago, the beautiful girl, her long black hair shining, her bright eyes merry with the attention of her two suitors.

"She only chose you because you were tall," Don Juan smiled back.

"And because I was *interesting*, as she said," Isidro replied. Both men sighed as one and their eyes met. "I tried to give her a good life."

"And you succeeded, Isidro," Don Juan said softly. "She called for you until the end."

CHAPTER 10

CONSUELO

"LEANDRO HAS CALLED ME OUT," Juan Carlos said to Consuelo. They sat in the kitchen of the de Leon house watching the sun rise in the window. "He met me at the castle when I went to get your father. There was no time to argue with him. He handed me a formal summons. He commands a duel. He says that I have stolen you from him with false promises, and have brought a slur upon his family name."

"He has lost his mind, then. I made no promise to him."

"Well, I can't let a challenge go unanswered. And if I did want to he has added fuel to the challenge by slandering me. He says I am a bastard and not my father's child. If I deny it, he says, I will bring forth black babies. If I do not deny it then I have besmirched my mother's name. And my father's. He leaves me no choice."

"Does my father know of this?"

"I doubt it. For one, he was only at the castle for a few hours, and he talks more than he listens so if there was any gossip he did not hear it. For another, he was with Don Patricio a large part of the time he was there and so would not have been in conversation with anyone."

"This is folly. It was I who told him there would be no marriage and he who tried to sully me."

"But see it from his view. Everyone knew there was a potential engagement between the two of you. He was supposedly called away by his financier to Mexico City, but his financier denied calling him. He knows there was a trick and he believes I was the originator of the ruse. You left, I left, in the dead of night. He returned to find us both gone. My mother has done much to quell any gossip, putting out the tale that you have been called away to your mother's bedside, true as far as it goes, and I have simply gone back to the Hacienda. But he believes he knows better and fears that someone will assert that I, a potential bastard or half-breed, which ever is worse, have stolen his prize. He cannot let that stand."

"The Marqués will forbid it. He has forbidden duels in his marquisate and will order both the victor and the loser, if he survives, to death."

"I know. It is the new way, very enlightened. And Leandro and I both profess enlightenment. But that does not stop Leandro from challenging me and he has found a way to circumvent the Marqués's orders. He will fight me here, outside of Mexico City."

"How did he know you were here?" Consuelo could not bear yet another complication.

"He didn't. This is a well-known dueling site. We are beyond the reach of the Marqués in San Lorenzo."

Consuelo was silent. She knew he would not back down and she could not dissuade him of the fight. "I am not opposed to fighting him. At the castle I would have killed Leandro on the spot when I came upon him in your room. And again when he called me a bastard, had I not such a mission to fulfill." His blue eyes flashed with anger.

She knew it wasn't a fight only because of a summons. It wasn't even just about Leandro's having taken liberties with her. It was also because Juan Carlos had caught Leandro in the act. Neither Leandro nor Juan Carlos could ever pretend that he didn't know. Despite her fear, Consuelo knew that Juan Carlos had to fight this duel for their marriage to be sound.

"I would not be a widow so young," she said.

"You will not be a widow at all. It is first blood, and I am good with a sword and great with a pistol. He is a fine swordsman himself and will not make an error. I have never heard Leandro to shoot a pistol and I knew him for two years at Salamanca. He doesn't believe a Criollo could have any fencing skills at all, provincial as we are."

"Why does he bother? Why doesn't he just go back to Granada as he said he would?"

"No doubt he will. Notwithstanding the unexpectedness of Leandro's visit his financier took the opportunity to have words with him. It appears that he has been spending profligately and his accounts have lost value as the King's needs have grown. And of course the whole castle had heard of his supposed engagement to you. He has seen both his name and his funds mocked."

"His finances had been mocked earlier. You saw the results."

Juan Carlos flushed redder. "Again, all the more reason for me to fight him."

Consuelo sighed. The whole week had been more than she could digest. "When?"

"Tomorrow night. Behind the churchyard."

"We bury my mother there that morning. Could your timing be worse?"

"It is what it must be."

Consuelo looked down at her hands twisting in her lap. "We must marry openly, Juan Carlos. We cannot go on like this."

He nodded. He took her hand. "My mind is not on a wedding, it is on a duel. And yours is on a funeral. When I have vanquished Leandro we will announce ourselves."

"What will happen to those horrible priests?"

"The thug may not survive his burns and the Bishop has promised to send Bernardo to do the Lord's work in Peru."

"I pity the poor *Peruanos.*"

"Yit'gadal, v'yit kadash sh'mei raba," Don Leon said.

"Amen."

They had returned from the church at San Lorenzo. Throughout the funeral Consuelo had kept her face veiled with a black mantilla borrowed from Susana, preventing questions from the priest. She removed it only when they entered the de Leon home, exhausted and spent. She longed to retreat to the little room above the stairs, to shut herself away from the world for bit. But at Susana's insistence they had all washed their hands and now stood in prayer in the sitting room. "It is the prayer for the dead," Susana said. Isidro and Juan Carlos stood in the doorway not entering the room. "You must come in," Susana said to Consuelo. "You are her daughter, her blood, and of us."

After the prayer they sat down to dinner. Fish and olives were served. Isidro turned to Don Juan. "You know, Juan, there is nothing to stop you from visiting us. We have a gracious home and my daughter will make you welcome. I expect, Consuelo, that you will have to return now and no longer study with the nuns as I will need you to keep house for me. But that is how it must be, of course. We will have to tell young Leandro, won't we, that you cannot be married for a year while we mourn your mother. He must learn to be patient."

An awkward silence settled over the table. "What?" Isidro asked the company. "Oh, of course, he won't want you right away, looking like that. Well, we will keep you hidden at home until your face recovers, won't we? I doubt the consequences will be permanent."

"Father, I am still in too deep a grief to talk about this," Consuelo said finally.

"You cannot put your obligations off forever," her father answered. "And those goons will have no more hold on me," he said. He looked around the table. He dropped his eyes to his plate. "I am sorry, Juan. I am also grieving and my tongue got ahead of my head."

"Still happening to you, I see," Don Juan said.

"Never stopped."

"I will return home tonight," Isidro said, taking one last bite of fish. "Consuelo, I imagine you will follow as soon as you can be seen."

"I will stay here a few more days," she answered, "as long as Don Juan will permit it."

"You are welcome for as long as you need," Susana answered shortly.

Don Juan nodded. "As usual my daughter-in-law speaks for us all."

*   *   *

"It is first blood. I will injure him the least amount possible."

"Do you know the weapon?"

"I would choose as I have been called out, though Leandro may not even possess a pistol. I have asked Jose Luis to second me."

Consuelo's eyebrows shot up. "I had not thought of that. Is he willing?"

Juan Carlos laughed shortly. "Willing? He is delighted. Delighted to get out for a night and do something his father and his wife would be horrified at. He wishes he were fighting the duel himself!"

When they had walked from the churchyard that morning he had quietly pointed out the dueling ground to her. It was less than a quarter hour walk, and beyond it was a field apparently well regarded as a popular dueling spot for those who lived where such events were forbidden. "We may have to wait our turn. We have appointed midnight as our time but if others have the field we may be later."

"You make it sound like an event at a charreada instead of an illegal, possibly lethal, and definitely stupid way to settle men's claims."

"Ah, you are healing," Juan Carlos said, smiling. "When it is over we shall announce our marriage to your father."

"No."

Juan Carlos stopped. "No?"

"I want a proper wedding. My mother is gone but I want my father there. I want Maria Elena, and your mother and father, and a charreada. And I want to be married by the priest of the church, not by the Bishop of Puebla."

Juan Carlos' face turned dark red. "He will always be a part of my story."

"I knew that night after Compline," she said. *I saw in his face the same square jaw, tears in his penetrating blue eyes, and understood at last.* "Our hearts are truly wed."

Juan Carlos reached for her hand. "I will be back before morning."

Consuelo lay awake listening to the quiet footsteps descend the stairs. Her heart pounded. They were leaving. It had to be close to midnight. She closed her eyes. At last she heard the church chime softly. It rang on the hour until midnight then not again until five in the morning. It was time. *What if he were killed? What if he were injured? Would Jose Luis know what to do?* Jose Luis would come back and get Susana. Everyone leaned on Susana. She imagined her acerbic tones. She did not want Susana involved.

I did not come this far, suffer so much, only to lose Juan Carlos to his masculine pride.

Consuelo rose and dressed quickly. Her black skirt was still stained and dirty from the terrors of the cathedral but it was the only one she had. She pulled the black shawl from the bed and wrapped it around her shoulders hoping to conceal her white blouse. At least it was clean as she had not worn it on Easter.

She took her little traveling bag and checked for the healing herbs. Her store was much depleted but there was still some maguey and some other powders. Her Easter shirt could serve as bandages and she stuffed it into the little bag. She slung the strap over her shoulder and holding her leather slippers in her hand she crept down the stairs and out the back door next to the stable.

The night was dark but the moon would rise in a few hours and would be high enough to see, or be seen, well before dawn. Consuelo moved quickly through the empty street, clutching her bag and keeping close to the houses. She had never been out at night like this, alone, and no decent woman was safe doing so. If the night watch caught her, or a brigand or worse, there would be no recourse. She pushed the thought from her mind. The church was not far.

She hurried, keeping her footfall as silent as possible. There were no shadows and she saw no movement. Finally the church loomed in front of her. Quickly she skirted the building, passing the graveyard where her mother's grave was freshly mounded. She crossed herself and repressed the sob that surprised her throat.

In the distance was a darkness that was so unimpeded that it could only be the field. She stubbed a toe on a stone and hopped a step to keep from stumbling. Her eyes had adjusted to the dark and the stars were bright enough to shed a bit of light. She thought she saw shadows up ahead. She slowed her pace.

As she neared she could see that there were indeed people at the field. Several different groups were clustered together. She inched forward, careful not to emerge from the shadow of the church. At last she discerned the glimmer of Juan Carlos' hair.

He stood hatless in the field and behind him was the thicker form of Jose Luis. She could make out Leandro, taller and thinner, and someone else behind him. Another cluster of men surrounded what was obviously a fallen fighter. She pursed her lips. Men were such fools. To her relief the fallen form stood, and leaning on his comrades, hobbled towards the church. She crouched behind a creosote bush to avoid detection but the group was headed the other way and having concluded their business would no longer be worried about discovery.

She watched as the next team stepped to the middle of the field. She was close enough to hear their voices but too far to make out the details of their faces.

"You have besmirched my name. Bastard."

"You are the one fouling my name, cuckold."

They stood facing one another and they seemed to quiver with anger or excitement. Consuelo closed her eyes. They were both fools. "Swords, my friend. First blood." Juan Carlos set the terms. "Agreed." They bowed to one another. At least with first blood there would be no death. She hoped.

They removed their jackets and took swords from their seconds, and the moon, a week past full, rose in a lopsided half behind the church. In the light Consuelo could see them clearly now. They needed to complete this quickly before the moon rose higher and the danger of detection grew too great. The seconds stepped back and for the first time Consuelo saw who had seconded Leandro: the artist, Juan Rodriguez Juarez. Rodriguez was the last person she would have expected. From the avid look on his face she had no doubt that images from the event would find a way into a painting some day.

The men bowed again and took an *en garde* stance. Consuelo held her breath. The swords clanged, the metal ringing in the silence. She was sure the entire town of San Lorenzo could hear them. The moonlight picked up the glint of the steel and the white of the men's shirts as they moved gracefully back and forth. For a minute it seemed as a dance, a game between men. Then blood began to seep through Juan Carlos's shirtsleeve.

"First blood!" Rodriguez called out, triumphant.

Juan Carlos uttered an expletive and looked down at his left arm. "It is the reopening of an earlier wound. Leandro has not touched me."

"I will not win on a lie," Leandro said, returning to opening stance. Juan Carlos sketched a bow and stood back *en garde*. They nodded and resumed. They were well matched and the parries were faster, the lunges sharper.

They both were breathing hard, circling and feinting. Juan Carlos held his bleeding left arm close to his body and blood now stained the middle of his shirt as well as the sleeve but he had a small smile on his face. He thrust again, stopping a hairsbreadth away from Leandro and leaning back. Leandro lunged and this time Juan Carlos parried it in a circular move and Leandro almost lost his grip on the sword.

Consuelo just wanted it over. Juan Carlos was showing to be the better swordsman but Leandro was no tyro and she prayed for an ending. As if in answer, Leandro broke from his pace for a surprise lunge to Juan Carlos' left. This time it looked as if he had caught Juan Carlos' arm but with the blood already showing she could not tell. Juan Carlos didn't flinch or cry out but instead turned sharply to his right. His sword came around and barely missed Leandro's shoulder.

Again they backed off. She looked at Jose Luis, holding Juan Carlos' coat. He was leaning forward, unwilling to miss a single moment of what was probably the most exciting night of his life thus far. Everyone's intent focus on the fighters made Leandro's cry all the more shocking. "Consuelo! Show yourself, woman!"

She stood still, stunned, unwilling to leave what she had thought was a secure hiding place.

"Come out!"

Juan Carlos turned towards the church, looking for her. At that moment Leandro lunged. She screamed.

Juan Carlos wheeled in time for Leandro's sword to slide by him, opening a gash in his right arm, as his own sword plunged into Leandro's left thigh. Leandro collapsed on the ground. Rodriguez ran to him.

Juan Carlos stood over Leandro, his sword pointed at his throat. "You are a cheat. You got first blood, Leandro. But you have lost your honor."

"And maybe his leg," Jose Luis said.

Leandro lay on the ground panting. Rodriguez knelt over him, trying to stanch the bleeding with his hands. "Consuelo, where are you?" Juan Carlos called.

Consuelo came out from the shadows. "Are you hurt?" She ran to Juan Carlos. He put his hand up.

"No. But Leandro is. Why are you here?"

"You were there when I needed you, I wanted to be here if you needed me."

"This is no place for you. But since you are here you could be more effective than this dunce of an artist."

Consuelo knelt next to Leandro and began tearing her Easter blouse into strips. "So it was true," Leandro said. He was breathing hard and sweat poured off his face. "You did go with him."

"I owed you nothing, Leandro. If you had left quietly no one would have thought poorly of you. I was simply not rich enough for you."

"You left me for that bastard? You will have black babies and poxy ones as well."

"Be still, Leandro, while I dress your wound. It is not too deep. You may keep the leg. Be still!" she said sharply as she put an elixir of caléndula and brandy on the cut. When she had finished she wrapped the wound with strips of the blouse. "Does he have a horse?"

Rodriguez nodded. "We have a carriage. I will take him back to Xochimilco. There is a hunter's lodge there."

Jose Luis and Rodriguez bent down and Leandro put an arm around each of their shoulders. "Be quiet going in the house," Jose Luis said to Juan Carlos. "If Susana hears you we will all sleep in the stable."

They headed off to Leandro's conveyance and Consuelo turned to Juan Carlos. "Let me look at the cuts on your arms. You are covered in blood."

Juan Carlos reached for her. "You are a brave woman, Consuelo, to come out alone at night for me. My arms will be fine. Let me show you." She waited for him to take off the shirt so she could examine the wounds but instead he reached around her and pulled her tight into his bleeding arms.

They arrived in Tulancingo on Thursday as the noonday meal approached. Juan Carlos tethered the horses outside of Consuelo's house, wincing a bit as the sleeves of the shirt Jose Luis had lent him rubbed the cuts on his arms. Consuelo dismounted and together they went into her home.

Isidro had just come home from the City offices to eat. He sat at the table, alone. The Indian woman brought in his soup, looked up and almost showed surprise when the two came in. She turned back wordlessly into the kitchen.

"Father," Consuelo said.

He startled, then stood. "What brings you home?" He reached for her hand. She gave it to him. "And Juan Carlos. My, what a surprise."

The servant came in with two more bowls of soup, put them on the table without a sound. Consuelo looked down at the sparkling consommé with bits of greens and chicken floating in it. Home.

"Señor Alcalde," Juan Carlos said. "I have come to speak of a very serious matter."

Isidro raised his eyebrows. "Indeed?"

"I have come to ask for your daughter. I wish to marry Consuelo."

"Sit down," Isidro said, doing so himself. "I am afraid that is not possible. She is promised to Leandro Almidón. I thought you knew that. *You* certainly did," he added to Consuelo.

"No, Father. I am not. Leandro and I have spoken. He did not feel our finances matched his expectations and has withdrawn his suit."

"We don't match *what?*" Isidro's voice rose in fury.

"You know we don't, Father."

"And will he be trumpeting this throughout the colony?" Isidro's face went from anger to despair.

"No. He will not. He is returning to Granada and I do not think we will hear from him again."

Isidro sat for a minute staring down at his soup. Finally he looked up. "Well then, Juan Carlos, speak your mind."

"I have, Señor," Juan Carlos said with a smile. "And Consuelo has consented, pending your permission, of course."

Isidro toyed with his spoon. "It is the match I wished for in the first place. What trouble would have been saved..." He paused, shook his head. "You have my consent. I will write to your father, Juan Carlos."

"Thank you, Señor," Juan Carlos said. He took Consuelo's hand.

"Oh, how I wish Leila were here. Your mother would have been so happy," Isidro said. He bowed his head.

"She knew," Consuelo said softly. "I told her."

Consuelo set out the trunk, her clothing neatly folded and arranged, barely filling half of it. She stared down into the empty space. The candlesticks and the plates lay on her bed wrapped and bundled in a coverlet. If she left them their story would finally end. She would be free of Toledo, the Inquisition, the secrets and the pain. From her great-great-grandfather's conversion with a knife at his throat to the stripes of the scourge on Leila's legs, the fear would be over.

She closed the trunk. Men carried the trunk to the carriage and Consuelo climbed in after it. Her father mounted the carriage driver's seat and flicked the whip at the horses. She looked back at the blue door of her home as she rode away to the Castillo hacienda once more to be wed. Next to her was a carefully wrapped bundle. *If we don't teach our daughters, who will remember?*

HISTORICAL
POST-SCRIPT

1711 WAS A TUMULTUOUS YEAR in New Spain. The new Viceroy, Duke of Linares, arrived ready to clean out corruption. Of course, that was a monumental and thankless task as those with funds, long used to a free hand, opposed him at every juncture.

Throughout Europe the Enlightenment movement was growing, but in Spain, both a cash-strapped king who had waged war with France, England, and Holland, and the weakening Inquisition used their last gasps of power to stifle any "new thinking." Those new thinkers, unflatteringly called *novaderos*, looked to the rest of Europe for inspiration in the burgeoning sciences, streamlined poetry and prose, and a new social order.

In New Spain, for the most part the Criollos (Pure Spanish descent but born in the Colony) were "more Spanish than the Spaniards", clinging to their memories of the old ways, but reality saw an intermingling of the races to an extent never seen before. As they sorted out their land's new identity, artists experimented with early attempts at genetics. In what were called "Casta" paintings, they categorized every possible combination, with results sometimes scientific, and sometimes fanciful.

The Inquisition in its waning years saw a decrease in funding, and like any other money-starved entity, strived weakly to make itself relevant. The Inquisition was not officially abolished in Mexico until 1820, but by 1700, most reports of *Conversos* were not even followed up. In 1711, there had not been an *auto-de-fé* for over twenty years, and there wouldn't be one for another ten, but its chief proponents were not ready to retire to the sidelines.

It was a year that would bring much hardship to Mexico. Earthquakes, drought and famine were waiting for the people as the year progressed, but our story begins in January, and concludes in April, before the worst of Nature's whims were visited on them. But tidings were clear, when in January of 1711, the first recorded snowfall fell upon the City of Mexico.

ACKNOWLEDGMENTS

This book could not have been written without the patient kindness of my husband Clyde Long. I also want to thank creative writing professor Thomas Parker for his ongoing guidance. Endless thanks are due to April Eberhardt, my agent, who saw this through its long journey, and to the team at Booktrope, in particular to Laura Bastian and Cathy Shaw, who brought it to publication.

This is also a love-letter to my parents. My own father provided a living example of the unwavering dedication that Isidro showed to Leila. Most of all I am deeply grateful for the lifelong inspiration of my own mother, to whom this book is dedicated. She did not live to see the publication, but she knew.

MORE GREAT READS
FROM BOOKTROPE

Paradigm Shift by **Bill Ellis** (Historical Fiction) A rich blend of social history, drama, love, passion and determination, Ellis delivers a powerful page-turner about the struggles and perseverance to overcome all odds.

Revontuli by **Andrew Eddy** (Historical Fiction) Inspired by true events, Revontuli depicts one of the last untold stories of World War II: the burning of the Finnmark. Marit, a strong-willed Sami, comes of age and shares a forbidden romance with the German soldier occupying her home.

Sweet Song by **Terry Persun** (Historical Fiction) This tale of a mixed-race man passing as white in post-Civil-War America speaks from the heart about where we've come from and who we are.

The Old Cape House by **Barbara Eppich Struna** (Historical Fiction) A Cape Cod secret is discovered after being hidden for 300 years. Two women, centuries apart, weave this historical tale of mystery, love and adventure.

The Secrets of Casanova by **Greg Michaels** (Historical Fiction) Loosely inspired by Casanova's life, this novel thrusts the reader into an adventure overflowing with intrigue, peril, and passion.

Discover more books and learn about our
new approach to publishing at **booktrope.com**.

CPSIA information can be obtained at www.ICGtesting.com
Printed in the USA
BVOW05s1933160714

359023BV00002B/16/P